"[Jaci Burton] delivers the passionate love scenes that fans expect. . . . How sex. Burton offers plenty of emotion and conflict in a memorable, relationship-driven story."
— *USA Today*

"One of the strongest sports romance series available."
— *Dear Author*

"Ms. Burton has a way of writing intense scenes that are both sensual and raw. . . . Plenty of romance, sexy men, hot steamy loving, and humor."
— *Smexy Books*

"The characters are incredible. They are human and complex and real and perfect."
— *Night Owl Reviews*

"Holy smokes! I am pretty sure I saw steam rising from every page."
— *Fresh Fiction*

"Hot, hot, hot! . . . Romance at its best! Highly recommended! Very steamy."
— *Coffee Table Reviews*

"As usual, Jaci Burton delivers flawed but endearing characters, a strong romance, and an engaging plot all wrapped up in one sexy package."
— *Romance Novel News*

"Burton knocks it out of the park . . . With snappy back-and-forth dialogue as well as hot, sweaty, and utterly engaging bedroom play, readers will not be able to race through this book fast enough!"
— *RT Book Reviews*

Titles by Jaci Burton

Wild Rider Series

RIDING WILD	RIDING ON INSTINCT
RIDING TEMPTATION	RIDING THE NIGHT

WILD, WICKED, & WANTON
BOUND, BRANDED, & BRAZEN

Play-by-Play Novels

THE PERFECT PLAY	ONE SWEET RIDE
CHANGING THE GAME	HOLIDAY GAMES
TAKING A SHOT	(An Intermix Special Novella)
PLAYING TO WIN	MELTING THE ICE
THROWN BY A CURVE	STRADDLING THE LINE

Hope Novels

HOPE FLAMES
HOPE SMOLDERS
(A Berkley Special Novella)
HOPE IGNITES

Anthologies

UNLACED
(with Jasmine Haynes, Joey W. Hill, and Denise Rossetti)

EXCLUSIVE
(with Eden Bradley and Lisa Renee Jones)

LACED WITH DESIRE
(with Jasmine Haynes, Joey W. Hill, and Denise Rossetti)

NAUTI AND WILD
(with Lora Leigh)

NAUTIER AND WILDER
(with Lora Leigh)

Specials

THE TIES THAT BIND
NO STRINGS ATTACHED
WILD NIGHTS

STRADDLING
the
LINE

JACI BURTON

BERKLEY BOOKS, NEW YORK

THE BERKLEY PUBLISHING GROUP
Published by the Penguin Group
Penguin Group (USA) LLC
375 Hudson Street, New York, New York 10014

USA • Canada • UK • Ireland • Australia • New Zealand • India • South Africa • China

penguin.com

A Penguin Random House Company

This book is an original publication of The Berkley Publishing Group.

STRADDLING THE LINE

Berkley trade paperback ISBN: 978-0-425-26299-3

An application to register this book for cataloging has been submitted to the Library of Congress.

PUBLISHING HISTORY
Berkley trade paperback edition / July 2014

PRINTED IN THE UNITED STATES OF AMERICA

10 9 8 7 6 5 4 3 2 1

Cover photo by Claudio Marinesco.
Cover design by Rita Frangie.
Interior text design by Kristin del Rosario.

For my dad, who taught me a love of sports at a very early age, and for my mom, who was always there when I needed her, and taught me what unconditional love was all about.

I miss you both.

STRADDLING
the
LINE

ONE

"HAVEN'S IN TROUBLE."

Those were words Trevor Shay never wanted to hear, especially not less than a year after the death of Haven's dad, Bill.

Bill Briscoe had been more than just a dorm parent back in Trevor's college days. He and his wife, Ginger, had been like substitute parents, especially to Trevor, who'd needed guidance more than the rest of them.

And now he sat in Ginger's living room, in a house he'd once thought of as his second home.

Trevor had always counted on Ginger's confidence, that smile and optimism that had assured him everything was going to be all right.

Now she just looked worried.

He picked up her hand. "What's wrong?"

"She hasn't been herself since Bill died. You know Haven. She's always been upbeat, and she'd come to grips with the eventuality of Bill's death." Ginger took a deep breath. "As we all did."

Trevor squeezed her hand.

"It wasn't like we didn't know it was coming. Bill prepared us all for it, made sure we were ready. Never thinking of himself."

He saw the tears welling in her eyes and wished he could take them away.

"I know, Miss Ginger. I know. I miss him, too."

She grabbed a tissue. "He'd kick my butt if he saw me cryin' over him. But Haven, she has a great life and an amazing future. She got a job with the network as a sports journalist."

Trevor smiled. "I heard about that."

"It's an amazing opportunity for her. One she should be seizing. I told her that her father would be so proud of her."

"He would."

"Instead, what is she doing? She's thinking about quitting the job and coming back here to live with me."

Trevor leaned back and frowned. "Coming back here? Why?"

"I don't know. She said something about getting a job at the local TV station instead."

"Is that what she really wants?"

"I don't think so." Ginger leaned forward. "Trevor, I don't know what to do. She hasn't even given this new job a shot. I think she's scared, and without her dad, she feels alone for the first time in her life."

"She's not alone, Miss Ginger. She has you."

"I know that. And believe me, I don't feel slighted in the least. I know Haven loves me. I also know she's worried about me being here all alone. I don't want her to make a mistake and screw up the best job she might ever have because of me, and because of her fear."

She paused, took a breath. "I was hoping you could offer me

some advice, tell me what I could say to her to make her stay in her job."

Trevor thought about it a minute. "Let me see what I can do about that."

"Thank you. I know you're big in the sports world, and I don't know if there's anything you can do for her, but gosh, I'd sure appreciate anything. Anything at all."

An idea formed in his head. He had the pull. He could get this done. And he'd do anything for Ginger, and to honor Bill's memory. Haven needed help, and he sure as hell was in a position to help her.

He spent the day with Ginger, and honestly, it was great to see her again, to while away the hours talking about Bill, reminiscing about college life. Besides, she fixed him lunch, and he loved her home-cooked meals. Hours later as he sat on the plane on his way back to St. Louis for a game, Trevor already had the plan formulated. The media were constantly hounding him for a feature story on his life and career. After all, it wasn't too many athletes who played multiple sports. At least not too many who played them well. He'd been closed off to the idea of it for a lot of reasons.

He leaned back in his seat and smiled.

Now it was Haven's turn to shine. And he was just the person to make it happen.

HAVEN TRIED TO MUSTER UP ENOUGH SALIVA TO SWALlow as she pressed the button to return the phone call she'd missed from her boss.

She knew what was on the other end of that phone call.

Her ass was going to be fired, less than six weeks after she'd gotten the job of a lifetime.

It would have been much better if she could have resigned. It would have looked better on her résumé, but then again, what did she care? Her career in journalism was over anyway, right?

Never quit. Whatever you do, Haven, never give up on anything until you're sure you've given it everything you have.

Her father's words rang in her ears, guilt squeezing her stomach until nausea caused her fingers to pause on the call button of her phone.

It was too late to beg to keep her job. She'd already passed up multiple travel assignments, content to do the local ones, then sit in her apartment in New York, dwelling on how much she missed home, her mom.

Her dad.

This wasn't the right career for her. She'd made a mistake accepting this job. She wasn't cut out for the rigors of sports news— the travel, the insane schedule, the arrogant athletes.

What was she thinking? Her father hadn't even been gone a year yet.

She couldn't do it.

Be brave, Haven. You can do anything, be anything you want to be. Just be happy.

Tears pricked her eyes and she swiped them away as every conversation they'd had those last few weeks replayed in a reel over and over in her head.

Be happy.

She didn't know how to be happy without hearing her father's laugh, seeing his smiling face, being able to pick up the phone and talk to him every day.

Who was she going to go to when she needed advice?

She loved her mother, and in the ways of relationships and men and things like that, she had always gone to her mom.

But her dad—he'd been her buddy. She'd learned about sports from her father, had sat next to him and watched football, baseball, hockey, and every sport imaginable. He'd taught her balls and strikes in baseball and the difference between a post pattern and a shovel pass in football. They'd driven up to St. Louis together and taken in all the professional sports. She'd never been more content than to sit next to her dad and watch games with him.

She'd learned to love sports because of her dad.

She'd gone after this job because of him.

And now she was going to be fired because she hadn't had the energy after his death to do this job she'd wanted for years. For that, she only had herself to blame.

"I'm sorry, Dad," she said, then pushed the call button on her phone. It rang. She was hoping for voice mail.

"Haven. I've been waiting for you to call."

She cringed as the loud and very no-nonsense voice of her boss, Chandler Adams, came on the line.

"Hi, Chandler. Sorry. I got tied up."

"Well, untie yourself. I have a job for you."

"A . . . job?" He wasn't firing her?

"Yeah. You know Trevor Shay, right?"

"Trevor . . . yes, I know him."

"Great. We're going to do his bio. A whole feature on the life of Trevor Shay. Personal and professional. We've been after him for years to do this, and he kept putting us off, until now. He's finally agreed to let us do the feature, and he's asked for you."

"For me?"

"Yeah. Says you two go way back to college."

"Uh . . . yes. I knew him in college."

"Then it's a damn good thing we hired you, Haven. Pack a bag. You'll meet him at his place in St. Louis to get everything set up. Narrative and background first, and then we'll get camera work involved later."

Was she in some alternate universe? She hadn't been fired. In fact, she'd just been assigned to interview one of the biggest stars in the sports world right now.

"Okay. Sure. Thanks, Chandler."

"No, problem. I'll e-mail you the specs on what we're looking for from you on this, Haven. This assignment's going to take a while, so clear your calendar."

"Consider it done."

When she hung up, she sat back and stared out the window of her very tiny apartment, stunned that she hadn't been kicked out the door. She'd been mentally prepared, and as she stared at the boxes in her apartment, already half packed, she realized she'd been set in her mind that she was going to head back to Oklahoma to be near her mother, her roots.

Where memories of her dad were.

Now she had to change her focus.

Why had she agreed to do this interview? This job wasn't what she wanted to do anymore.

Was it?

She sat on the bed.

Follow your dreams, Haven.

She still heard her dad's voice so clearly in her head. Maybe he was trying to tell her something. She didn't know if this was her dream anymore, but she'd agreed to take this job.

With Trevor Shay, of all people. She hadn't seen Trevor since her dad's funeral. She wondered how he'd react knowing it was her doing this assignment.

He'd probably ignore her, just like he had in college.

No, wait. He'd specifically asked for *her*. He'd agreed to the interviews, so this time, she wouldn't allow him to pretend she didn't exist.

She got up and went to her closet to grab her suitcase.

Her and Trevor Shay. God, she'd had such a crush on him in

college, back when she was tutoring him. All those nights they spent shoulder to shoulder, when she'd done her best to try to persuade him to focus on his books, when all she'd really wanted was for him to notice her as a woman.

He'd been more interested in trying to finagle a way to get her to do his homework.

Now she was going to be in the driver's seat.

She stared out over the boxes, debating whether to unpack them.

She'd leave them, see how this assignment went. If it didn't work out, if it didn't light the fire under her after a few days, she'd call Chandler and tell him she was out.

But she'd give it a try. For her dad.

TWO

AFTER HER FLIGHT, HAVEN SAT IN THE BACK OF A TAXI bound for Trevor's place outside St. Louis, equal parts nervous and excited. The rules Trevor had set down for this exposé were a little unorthodox, but whatever. If the network had agreed to it, she could live with it. For any other athlete, she'd have said hell no. But she'd known Trevor a long time. She knew how he felt about his privacy, and she knew he liked to call the shots.

She'd be staying on the grounds of his house here in St. Louis, at least while they were here. But when the camera crews showed up, they'd have to stay in a hotel. Trevor had to approve the filming segments, and he wanted some one-on-one time with Haven to discuss the parameters, especially as it related to his background.

She smiled as she took in the view of the St. Louis Gateway Arch as the car breezed along the highway. She'd seen the view of the stadium from the plane, and it reminded her of her dad bringing her up to see a Rivers baseball game. She and her mom had been so excited that summer they'd come up for a weekend of sightseeing and baseball. She'd been twelve, and they'd gone to Forest Park to visit the zoo, and then that night had gone to see the Rivers play baseball. They'd stayed in a hotel downtown near the stadium and had even gone out to dinner.

For a twelve-year-old, it had been an exciting time. The city had been lit up, and they'd even walked down along the riverfront before the game. It had been a perfect summer weekend, her first of many here. Haven had loved St. Louis. She was happy to be back here again, and surprised at how excited she was to get started on this assignment.

Now the car took them out of the city, away from the stadium and toward the county.

Not at all what she expected. For some reason she thought Trevor would live in a condo in the city near the stadium, not in a gated community with tall, tree-lined streets.

Her jaw dropped when the car pulled up the long drive to what had to be Trevor's house.

This had to be wrong. It was like a freakin' mansion, not at all where she expected him to live. The entire drive was thick with trees, the house a massive, gorgeous, two-story Colonial. The car stopped out front and the driver opened the door for her.

Trevor came out the front door wearing casual sweats and a sleeveless shirt, a big smile on his face.

"Hey, you're here," he said to Haven before turning toward the driver. "You can put those inside the front door. I'll take it from there."

"Yes, sir," the driver said, taking Haven's bags through the double white front doors.

Haven found herself unable to move. Instead, she gaped at the house, taking it all in, trying to reconcile this reality with her expectations.

"I thought you'd live in a condo."

He laughed and laid his hand at the small of her back, propelling her inside. "Nah. I need my space. Besides, I don't want to hear my neighbors arguing all night long. I like my privacy. Come on, I'll show you around."

Blinking to clear the fog away, she let him lead her. Inside, she was greeted by amazing Italian marble on the floor, and an expansive staircase leading to the second floor.

"Want the tour first, or would you rather I take your stuff to your room? There's a separate wing to this place, so you'll have plenty of privacy. You don't need to worry about me infringing on your space."

"Oh, a tour, definitely." She couldn't wait to see all this property had to offer.

"Sure."

He took her into a formal living room. "I don't spend a lot of time in here. It's too stuffy. There's a more relaxed, informal space I like better on the other side of the house."

Next was a beautiful dining room.

"Where did you get all this furniture?" she asked, because there were beautiful antique tables and sideboards in the dining room.

"I don't know. I have a person who helped furnish some of the rooms. I think she buys some of this stuff at auctions. I don't use this room, either," he said.

Haven reluctantly left the dining room, gawking at some of the artwork on the walls.

"I do spend time in here."

She stopped and stared at the amazing kitchen with its dark wood cabinetry and stunning granite countertops. The island itself was a cook's dream come true, and the six-burner chef's stove made her want to drop everything and cook for about a week.

"This is amazing."

He grinned. "Yeah, I like a good kitchen, too." He turned to her. "While we're in here, are you thirsty? Would you like something to drink?"

"I'm good for now. How about we finish the tour first?"

"Sure. There's an eat-in area in the next room, a lot more informal than the dining room."

"Oh, yes. I see what you mean." There was a big table and a fireplace, and white-framed windows with shutters in this room. Haven felt instantly relaxed in this room, much less like she'd have to dress up to eat in there. "It feels comfortable here."

"Exactly. And the sunroom is next to this room."

"Oh, wow." The sunroom was huge, with screened floor-to-ceiling windows and white wood floors. The light was incredible in this room, and the furnishings were casual and bright, with lots of pillows for comfort. "I love this room." She could write in here, or just relax with a cup of coffee in the morning. She walked to the edge of the sunroom, which overlooked one amazing backyard and pool. She looked past the pool and all she could see were thick, tall trees. The wooded area was amazing.

"How much acreage do you have?"

"Four acres. Like I said, I don't like having neighbors I can hear."

"I'd say you're good to go, then."

He directed her toward the back of the house. "There's an exercise room back here, along with a spa and a sauna. And then this door leads out to the pool deck."

Haven was amazed by all the equipment. "You have an entire gym in here."

"Yeah. It's handy, especially during the off-season, if I need to have my trainer over for workouts."

She turned to face him. "You have an off-season?"

He laughed. "A few weeks here and there. Come on, we'll head on over to the other wing."

As they passed the staircase, she stopped him. "What's upstairs?"

"My bedroom." He gave her a grin. "Want to see it?"

"Actually, I do."

He seemed to hesitate. "I think housekeeping staff is in there right now cleaning. So maybe another time?"

"Oh. Sure."

"Come on."

He walked her across a long hallway to another section of the house.

"This is your wing. Like I said, you'll have plenty of privacy here. There are four bedrooms here, and an office. You can use the office whenever you need to, and choose whatever bedroom you want. Each one has its own bathroom."

She wandered into each of the bedrooms, all of them bigger than her apartment in New York City. She chose one with mocha walls and a beautiful bed, plus an oversized bathroom that just felt perfect to her. Plus, her bedroom had a view of the pool and the acreage out back.

"This one will definitely do."

"Great. I'll go get your bags and bring them up."

"I'll help you."

They did it all in one trip. "I'll just unpack and change clothes," she said after Trevor set down her bags.

"Okay. Are you hungry? I'll get us some dinner ordered."

"Ordered?"

"I have someone on staff here who cooks. Salmon or steak tonight? Unless you're vegetarian. Hammond makes kickass tofu stir-fry, too."

"I'm not vegetarian, and either sounds great to me."

"Okay. See you downstairs."

After he shut the door, she shook her head. Not only was she living in a huge house, he had people to help him take care of it.

Did he even live alone, or were there other people here?

A girlfriend, maybe? She hadn't even asked.

He'd been so polite, too. Not at all like his typical teasing ways. He hadn't seemed like himself, which was . . . odd.

Haven shrugged it off and chalked it up to maybe Trevor treating her differently because he was doing an interview with her. It wasn't like before, when she was just Bill Briscoe's daughter, and he could laugh and tease with her. Though she certainly wouldn't care either way. She knew when to get into professional mode, and right now she was just . . . Haven. She hoped he wouldn't feel uncomfortable around her. That was the last thing she needed. She felt uncomfortable enough in her own skin these days.

She took a look around, pretty damned impressed with what she saw. The house was huge, the furnishings expensive but tasteful. He'd obviously put some care and effort into this place, unlike a lot of guys who might just buy a condo and get a couch and a TV and not care. It was clear that he cared, that this place meant something to him.

Trevor had certainly come a long way. Much further than she'd expected. He had a chef, and people to clean his house. He'd certainly surprised the hell out of her. She had no idea he was doing so well for himself. He'd always seemed so laid back. A blue-jeans-and-T-shirt kind of guy. She'd just never given much thought to his salary, though she knew he made a lot of money playing both baseball and football. And he had all those endorsement deals, too. He was a popular athlete, both on the field and off.

She went over to the bed where Trevor had laid her suitcases and pulled out her notebook to jot down some notes. She'd known Trevor since his freshman year of college, just like all the guys who'd passed through the university and stayed in the dorm managed by her mom and dad. She'd like to think she knew more about him than anyone else she'd ever interviewed.

But she still had questions, and needed to develop an interesting angle to approach the interviews. There were very few athletes who played dual sports, at least few who did it successfully. Trevor had managed to be lightning quick at tight end for Tampa, and also put up some impressive statistics for the St. Louis Rivers baseball team. How did he do that? And how did the teams feel about a player who couldn't really give his all to either team? Did his agent negotiate his ability to move between the two? How did his teammates feel about a hotshot player like Trevor dividing his time between the two sports? She was eager to ask those questions.

She had a lot of questions about his personal life, too. Like this house, and his lifestyle.

Would he answer those?

For the first time since her father died, she felt stirrings of excitement about her job.

She unpacked and changed into capris and a short-sleeved shirt. Even though it was late September, it was a very warm day. Maybe Trevor would give her a tour of the grounds.

She took her time walking down the long hallway that connected her wing with the main section of the house. Wide windows gave an expansive view of the wooded area she'd seen while coming up to the house.

It was a beautiful view, and there were so many windows in this place, she understood the appeal.

She wound her way through the myriad of rooms, finding a tall, thin, gray-haired man in the kitchen.

"You must be Hammond."

He smiled at her. "And you must be Haven." He wiped his hand on his apron. "Very nice to meet you."

They shook hands. "You, too. I didn't mean to intrude."

"You're not intruding. I was just cooking up some steaks for dinner. And now that you're here, you can tell me how you like yours, since Trevor didn't know."

"Medium well, please."

"Okay, then, Haven. I'll just get back to dinner."

"You wouldn't happen to know where Trevor is, would you?"

"I saw him heading toward the sunroom a little while ago."

"Okay, thanks, Hammond."

She made her way toward the sunroom. At least every room led into another via the hallway, so she couldn't get lost.

Trevor was on the phone, so she hung back, watching him. Sunlight glinted off his dark hair. His long legs were stretched out and he looked . . . completely relaxed, at ease, so casual, incongruous with this behemoth of a house.

He was living in Wayne Manor. Was he Batman? She smiled at the thought of Trevor as some superhero. On the field, definitely. But off the field? Not really. He wasn't the type of athlete who made a spectacle of himself. He was very low profile, easygoing, just an everyman kind of guy, not a superstar. Whenever he'd been around her, he'd always seemed so at ease with everyone. Whereas Haven . . . well, she'd never been comfortable around him, had she?

Her thoughts drifted back to the tutoring sessions she'd given Trevor in college. Her father had suggested them, and she'd balked. She'd loved the idea of gaining experience in one of her chosen fields, since back then she hadn't yet decided between a career in journalism or teaching. So she'd done a lot of tutoring. But spending one-on-one time with Trevor had made her freeze up.

He'd intimidated her, likely because she'd been crazy in love with him—at least the kind of crazy in love a nondescript girl could have been with the unattainable type of athlete Trevor was. He'd only half paid attention to her because she'd been Bill Briscoe's daughter, and all the guys had worshiped her dad. And when her father had offered her up as a tutor, Trevor had known better than to say no. Besides, he had to pass his classes, or risk losing his scholarship, so he'd agreed.

She remembered her heart pounding incessantly, her palms sweating as she'd sat next to him in her room at the house while she'd worked with him. She'd been so preoccupied with his muscles, his clean, crisp scent, how big his hands were, and the way he always laughed with her and teased her.

That had been Trevor, even back then. Always at ease, able to laugh. While she'd been a giant ball of tension.

She'd been such a mess around him, not her usual cool, confident self. In academia she'd been a rock star. He'd even teased her about being brainy, the worst possible thing he could have said to a young woman with a monster-sized crush on a sexy athlete. She'd wanted to be sexy and beautiful, not smart, back then. At least around him. And all he'd noticed about her was that she had the smarts to help him pass his classes. He hadn't made it easy on her, either. God, he'd been lazy. At least academically. Sportswise, he'd been a goddamned superstar.

Which intrigued her, because he'd carried that perseverance into his professional career.

And look at his success now.

He'd finished his phone call, so she stepped into the sunroom. When he spotted her, he stood.

"Oh, hey, did you get unpacked?"

"Yes."

"Is your room okay?"

"My room is fantastic, thanks."

"Great. Have a seat."

She took a seat across from him in one of the cushioned chairs.

"There's some iced tea and water in the pitchers," he said,

motioning to two glass pitchers on the nearby table. "Would you like something?"

"Tea would be wonderful." She started to get up, but he stopped her.

"I'll take care of it."

"What? No servants hovering nearby to do that for you?"

"Uh, no. I'm pretty sure I can take care of this part by myself."

"But you have a chef."

"Yeah." He took a drink out of his glass, then set it down. "Hammond used to work for the Rivers organization in concessions. He'd always been a big fan, and all the players liked him a lot. A couple of years ago he reached retirement age, but he and his wife Lyla still have a mortgage to pay off. Plus they're raising two of their grandkids because . . . well, because of some private circumstances. When I heard about that, I hired him on to help here at the house. He's a hell of a cook. Wait till you taste the steaks."

What a story, and what a surprise. "You're quite the humanitarian, Trevor."

Trevor gave her an enigmatic smile. "I like good food, and like I said, Hammond can cook the daylights out of anything. I think I got the better end of the deal."

He was modest as well. He didn't want to appear the hero. She didn't know what to make of that. "That was very nice of you."

Trevor just shrugged, and she felt awful for thinking him living the rich and privileged life, when he'd just given an old man and his family a decent break.

She had a lot to learn about Trevor. And she needed to stop prejudging him and start using her investigative skills in the way she'd been taught.

She wished she'd brought her laptop down with her so she could make some notes.

It was time to put her game face on and get to work.

THREE

"SO TELL ME, TREVOR . . . WHY THIS HOUSE?"

Trevor could tell Haven wanted to make this an interview, that she wanted to get down to business right away. Maybe that was a good thing—at least for her. She seemed at ease, which he was happy to see.

"Why that question? And is it a professional question, or a personal one?" Trevor asked.

Her lips tilted. "Maybe a little of both."

"Fair enough." He leaned back in the chair. "I liked all the trees. And all the space. Plus the pool. There was plenty of space to do everything I wanted. I didn't grow up with a lot of room, so just having that freedom to wander makes me happy."

She stood, went to the window, and looked out over the back of the property, before turning back to face him with a smile. "I can see that."

How had he not noticed her in college? She was beautiful. She'd always seemed pissed off at him when they were in school together. Then again, she'd been forced to tutor him, and he knew damn well he hadn't been an easy student.

He'd been too preoccupied with football, and with trying to pass his classes by the skin of his teeth so he wouldn't lose his scholarship. Haven had been nothing but a means to an end for him. He hadn't thought of her as a desirable young woman. She'd been his salvation, and he'd used her in that way. Besides, she was Bill's daughter, and that had made her strictly off-limits.

But now? Now . . . ah, hell. She was still off-limits. He owed Ginger—and Bill—and it was his duty to get Haven fired up. And not in a sexual way.

But damn, as she stood there, her posture perfect, her legs outlined in those tight pants she wore, he realized how much time he'd let get away without really getting to know her better.

And now—now they were working together, which meant he couldn't cross that line.

Or he shouldn't, anyway. That wasn't what she was here for, and she sure as hell wasn't interested in him that way. She'd made that clear in college, and the two of them had butted heads ever since. He was surprised she'd agreed to this assignment, but he saw that as a good sign. So had Ginger, when he'd told her.

But when had his body ever cooperated with his mind? He found her attractive, especially now. She'd grown her raven hair out some. She always used to wear it very short. Now it framed her face, the breeze coming in through the open windows blowing strands of it against her cheek. She'd taken off her sunglasses, giving him a look at her beautiful blue eyes. But they weren't normal blue. They were . . . what was that color again? He couldn't remember.

"You're staring at me, Trevor."

"Was I? Sorry. Want to take a walk outside before dinner?"

"Sure."

No hesitation. He liked that. He stood and led her out the side door and down the steps toward the pool. "It's heated, in case you want to take a swim."

"Okay, thanks. It's still plenty warm outside. It might feel good."

"Yeah. Especially after a hot game."

She stopped, turned to him. "Your next one is tomorrow? A home series this weekend?"

"Yeah. Against Chicago. You'll be there?"

"I will."

They walked along the path between the backyard and the woods. He liked the quiet, the sounds of the breeze rustling the leaves of the trees. It gave him time to think.

"So you had a day off today," she said as they walked side by side.

"Yeah."

"What do you do on your rare days off?"

"I spent some time on the phone with my lawyers, hashing out some business deals. Talked to my football team in Tampa."

"They're under way now," she said.

"I know."

"Does it pull at you, knowing you're missing the start of the season?"

He shrugged. "Not much I can do about it. There's only one of me and I can't be two places at one time."

She paused and tilted her head up to look at him. "Are you sure? I mean, you are a superstar and all."

He laughed. "Yeah, that's me." He liked that her sense of humor seemed intact.

When they made the turnaround on the path, he said, "Come on, let's go see if Hammond has those steaks ready."

"Okay."

"Oh, I have one more phone call to make. Meet you in the kitchen?"

"Sure. I'll just take our drinks in there." She stopped at the sunroom, picked up the tray, and left the room.

Trevor took a minute to grab his phone and give her mom a quick call.

"Why, hello, Trevor."

"Hi, Miss Ginger. I don't have much time, but wanted to let you know Haven's here."

"How is she?"

"She seems okay. She hasn't been here long, but we had a short talk. She seems in good spirits and doesn't appear to be down or anything."

"Oh, that's a good sign."

"I'll keep you posted, but I intend to keep her busy."

"Good. She needs that. And thank you again."

"I'll do what I can, Miss Ginger."

"I know you will, honey. I'll talk to you soon."

He hung up, then went into the kitchen to find Haven in deep conversation with Hammond about how to season the perfect steak.

"Now, Miss Haven, if I gave up all my secrets to Mr. Trevor's guests, what would he need me for?"

Haven laughed. "In other words, you aren't going to tell me what that amazing smell is? If I had to guess, I'd say garlic."

Hammond smiled. "Not saying a word. Taking that recipe to my grave." When Hammond spotted him, he asked, "Where would you like to eat tonight, Mr. Trevor?"

"In the eating area is just fine, Hammond."

"You two go ahead and take a seat. I'll be serving up the meal in just a few minutes."

They went into the next room. Trevor held her chair out for

her. She slid into it and lifted her gaze to his, and she didn't look happy. "This isn't a date, you know."

"No, but you are a guest." He sensed her being defensive, though he didn't know why. "Is there any reason I shouldn't be respectful?"

"I guess not. Thank you."

"You're welcome."

He was about to ask her if she was upset about something, but Hammond came out bearing a tray with their salads.

"Miss Haven already told me her preferred dressing," he said, laying dressing to the side. "When you finish these, I'll bring your steaks."

"Thanks, Hammond. I assume you made some extras to take home to you, Lyla, and the grandkids?"

Hammond grinned. "You know I did."

"Why don't you go ahead and take off before those steaks get cold? I can serve them up."

"Are you sure you don't mind? I'm happy to serve you dinner and clean up after."

"Go ahead and have dinner with your family. I'm pretty sure Haven and I can take it from here."

Haven nodded. "We can. And thank you for fixing dinner. I already know it's going to be fantastic."

"I expect a full report tomorrow on how you liked your steak," he said as he made his way toward the kitchen. "You two have a great night."

"Good night, Hammond," Trevor said, then dug into his salad. "I don't know about you, but I'm starving."

"What you did was very nice," Haven said.

Trevor looked up at her and frowned. "What? Oh . . . Hammond? He likes to spend time with Lyla and the kids."

"How old are the children?"

"Four and six."

"Off the record? What happened to their mom?"

He hesitated.

"Seriously, Trevor. This is off the record."

He nodded. "Hammond's daughter Jasmine has a drug problem. A big one she's been struggling with off and on for years. She was in and out of jail a few times for possession. But it went from bad to worse, and two years ago she started dealing, got caught, and now she has a long-term prison problem."

Haven laid her fork down. "Oh, no."

"Yeah. So Hammond and Lyla got full custody of Amelia and Jacob."

"What about the kids' father?"

"Two different fathers, neither responsible enough to be in the picture. They were even worse than Jasmine. One's in jail for armed robbery."

Haven sighed. "Those poor children. Thank God they have grandparents like Hammond and his wife to care for them."

"Yeah. Hammond made a lot of sacrifices to try to get his daughter clean, but then finally washed his hands of her and bent over backward for the grandkids."

"Some people you can't help."

"Not if they don't want the help, no."

She laid her hand on his. "Thank you for helping Hammond and his family."

"Hammond's doing all the work. I'm just paying his salary."

"You're right. He is. But he has you in his corner, and that's great."

"I like him. And I get a benefit out of this, too, you know. You haven't tasted those steaks yet."

She laughed. "Well, let's get to it."

Trevor was glad the topic was off him and onto the food, which of course tasted damn good.

"Oh, my God," Haven said after she'd eaten a couple of pieces of her steak. "No wonder you hired Hammond. This steak is fantastic."

Trevor swallowed and took a drink of iced tea. "I told you I got the better end of this deal."

"So what you're saying is, you can't cook."

"Sure I can. But I'm on the road a lot, and while I'm here in St. Louis, I have a fantastic cook."

"And when you move to Tampa to play football? What happens to Hammond then?"

"He comes here every day to see to the house for me."

She leaned back in her chair. "In other words, you continue to pay him annually."

"Yeah."

"Because you can afford to do that and because you're a nice guy."

"Aw, come on, don't go telling people that, Haven. I have a bad-ass reputation to maintain. And besides, we're still off the record."

She laughed. "Your secret is safe with me."

After they finished eating, they cleared the table and took the dishes into the kitchen. Haven turned on the water and started rinsing them.

Trevor laid his hand over hers. "Hammond will have your ass if you start washing those dishes."

"I can't just leave these dirty dishes in the sink."

"And if you take away his job, you'll take away his pride."

Now that, she understood. She turned off the water. "Fine."

She grabbed a towel to dry her hands.

He led her back to the sunroom. But first, he grabbed a beer from the refrigerator. He held one up for her, but she shook her head.

When they settled in, she realized it had gotten dark while they were eating. And cooler outside.

"Cold?" he asked.

"I'm fine."

He reached for the blanket that was lying over one of the chairs and handed it to her.

"Thank you."

"So, about your new job at the network?" he asked after she'd settled in.

"My job? Nothing much to tell."

"Are you excited about being a sportscaster?"

"It's . . . new. So I'm still getting my feet wet."

"Who have you interviewed?"

Trevor would ask her that. In essence, he was giving her a job interview. And she was about to fail miserably. "Oh, uh. No one big yet. Like I said, this is all new to me."

He leaned back in his chair and took a sip of his beer, then grinned at her. "Yeah, but now you've got me."

"So I do. And why is that?"

"Why is what?"

"Why me? You could have gotten one of the more seasoned sportscasters to do this feature story on your career. You had to know I was just getting started with the network."

"Because you know me. And because I trust you not to fuck this up."

She laughed. "Are you sure about that? You heard the part about me saying this was new, right?"

"Yeah. But aren't you good at your job? Isn't this what you've been training for, putting in time at that Dallas news station, hoping for your big break?" He flashed a grin at her. "Baby, I'm your big break."

And there was a glimpse of that giant ego he'd carried, even in college. "You're just full of self-confidence, aren't you, Trevor?"

"I wouldn't be where I am today without a healthy ego."

She couldn't fault him for that. Self-confidence was key in

professional sports. You couldn't be a shrinking wallflower, think-ing you were second rate, and succeed, especially at dual sports. "Good point. And I suppose, what brings me here."

"True. So what's on tap for you and me, besides us eating great meals together?"

"I'll talk about your family history, you coming up as a kid, and then through high school and college. We'll talk about your life as you lead it today—" She looked around. "People love to know about a player's lifestyle. Then we'll get into your professional career and how you manage to juggle playing both baseball and football. We'll interview your family—"

"No."

Haven paused. "No? To which part?"

"My family."

"Why not?"

"I don't want my parents interviewed."

"Again. Why not?"

"Because I don't. They're not part of my career."

"I disagree. They were a big part of getting you here, of form-ing the person you are now."

"No, Haven."

There was something he wasn't telling her. She'd never met his parents. She was certain they'd visited him in college, but she'd never been around for that. Maybe he didn't get along with them. Or maybe they were media shy. She'd have to respect that. Or at least put it aside for later, when she'd push again. "Okay. Parents off-limits. But I'm still going to ask you about your background."

"You can ask any question you want. It doesn't mean I'm gonna answer it."

"Duly noted." As was typical for Trevor, he presented a chal-lenge. When hadn't he? Even in college, he hadn't made it easy for her to do her job.

But that hadn't stopped her then. And it wouldn't stop her now.

"How's your mom?" he asked.

"She's doing . . . well. I talked to her yesterday, as a matter of fact. I was originally going to—well, never mind."

"Originally going to what?"

It wouldn't do for him to know that she'd been about to abandon her dream job and hightail it out of New York to run back to Oklahoma. "I was going to visit her, but this job came up so I had to let her know I'd have to put that on hold."

"Maybe we'll both get a chance to visit her while we're doing the interview. I assume you'll want do part of the coverage at the college."

"I'd love to if you have the time."

"I'll make the time."

He sure was being accommodating. "Then yes, we probably will."

She really had to organize her thoughts—and her notes.

"So, we'll get started in the morning?" she asked.

"Why not now?"

"I'm not . . . ready yet."

"Okay. What do you want to do tonight? Do you want to see St. Louis?"

Just the thought of going out made her nauseated. "No, I think I'll head up to my room and review my notes so we can get started tomorrow."

"Are you sure? You might want to kick back and have some fun tonight. Let me show you the city. We'll go out."

"First, I've been here before."

"You have? When?"

"With my . . . with my dad. But it's been a long time. I was a kid."

He gave her a look that told her he understood. "St. Louis has changed a lot since you were a kid. There's a lot I can show you about the city."

"I'm not here to have fun, Trevor. I'm here to work."

He leaned in, giving her a view of his incredible eyes. "You can't work all the time, Haven. Life is meant to be lived. One of my teammates has a birthday today. He's invited a bunch of people to a club to celebrate."

She wasn't in the mood to celebrate. "You go. I'll stay here and work."

"Seriously?"

"Seriously. I need to get prepped for us to start tomorrow."

"If you're sure."

"I'm sure."

"Okay. But if you change your mind . . ."

"I won't. I'll see you in the morning."

She went to her room, stripped into underwear and a tank top, and climbed into bed, surrounding herself with her notes and her laptop. She spent a few hours making notes and organizing her plan of attack, then grabbed the remote to watch some television.

She startled awake sometime later, disoriented, her notes lying on top of her.

She took her laptop and plugged it in to recharge it, then grabbed her phone to look at the time, realizing it was after two in the morning.

Wow. She'd worked longer than she'd thought. Though she had no idea how long she'd been asleep. She scanned over her notes and felt good about her approach. She put on a pair of shorts and went downstairs and over to the main wing to grab a glass of ice water.

It was dark down there. She wondered if Trevor had come home already. She wouldn't know if he had, since her wing was far away from his.

Not her business, anyway. She went to the cupboard and found a glass, filled it with ice and water, and headed outside onto the pool deck to enjoy the light breeze and to look at the sky. It was nice out now. She could sit out here the rest of the night and enjoy the soft breeze and stare at the stars.

She heard a car and saw the headlights in the driveway. She stood, figuring it was Trevor. She went back inside and took her glass to the sink, intending to greet him, then head back to bed. But Trevor came into the kitchen and flipped on the lights.

He wasn't alone, either. There was a guy with him. And two very attractive women, both blondes. One of them was draped all over Trevor.

"Oh," Trevor said, his lips curving into a smile. "I thought you'd gone to bed a few hours ago."

"I did. I was working, and I got thirsty. Then I went to sit outside for a while. I wasn't really tired, so I watched the stars. It's really nice outside tonight."

And he doesn't need a blow-by-blow of your every move, idiot.

"Yeah, it is. Haven, this is my teammate, Tennessee. We call him Ten-Spot. And this is Audrey and Petra."

She nodded. "Nice to meet all of you."

"Who's *she*?" Petra, the one clinging to Trevor, asked.

"Haven's a friend of mine. She'll be staying here for a while, traveling with me. We go way back. I knew her dad a long time ago—back in college."

Petra gave her the once-over. "So . . . like a charity thing, huh?"

Haven sucked in a breath, but didn't take the bait.

"No, not like that. Why don't you all go out on the deck? We'll get in the pool."

"Come on," Ten-Spot said to the women. "Nice to meet you, Haven."

"You too, Ten-Spot," she said. "Is today your birthday?"

"Well, technically yesterday. But yeah."

"Happy birthday."

Ten-Spot grinned. "Thanks."

"I want to stay here with you, Trevor," Petra said, mimicking a very obvious pout so her glossy full lips looked even fuller.

Trevor squeezed her hand. "Just go on outside, Petra. I'll be right there."

"Okay." Petra pouted some more, then grabbed his face and kissed him. Rather sloppily. Trevor was the one who broke the kiss.

Ick. Whatever.

After they closed the door to the back deck, Trevor turned to her. "Sorry. I thought you'd be in bed."

"There's nothing to be sorry about. This is your house. And I *was* in bed."

He didn't say anything else, so she did. "Look, I don't want to cramp your . . . recreational time, Trevor. So maybe we need to talk about the whole living arrangement thing. I can stay at a hotel. The network will pay for it."

"Nothing to talk about. I want you here with me. There's plenty of space here."

But she wasn't sure it was going to work for her. "We'll talk about it tomorrow. You have fun with your friends. I'm going upstairs to bed now."

"You're welcome to join us, you know."

The sounds of squeals and laughter drew her attention to the pool. She caught a flash of naked breasts, then shook her head.

"No, that's okay. I'm tired. Besides, we have a business arrangement, remember?"

He gave her a look. "Sure. Whatever you say, Haven." He went to the fridge and grabbed several beers. "I'll see you in the morning then, right?"

"Right."

Her stomach tightened, though she had no idea why she cared where he went and who he went with. She shouldn't care. She didn't care.

She walked up the stairs and went to her room, shutting the door behind her. She couldn't shut out the sounds of laughter from below, though. And the memories came flooding back of every girl Trevor had been with in college. All the beautiful cheerleaders he'd dated, and how she'd longed for him to notice her as something other than his tutor.

He never had because he'd only been interested in how she could help him pass his classes.

She grabbed her iPod and shoved her earbuds in her ears to drown out the sounds from outside.

TREVOR SAT AT THE EDGE OF THE POOL WHILE TEN-Spot frolicked with the girls.

This had been a mistake. He'd known it, but Ten had hooked up with Audrey at the club, and Petra had come along for the ride.

Petra wasn't even his type. He didn't go for stacked blondes, especially the ones who were only interested in sleeping with a jock. The girl was obvious. She'd been grinding against him all night long, practically giving him a blowjob in the VIP section of the club. Trevor liked sex as much as the next guy, but he'd like to think he'd grown up a little and enjoyed being the aggressor. Plus, some of these women were a little too aggressive.

What the hell had happened to subtlety and seduction and letting things happen in their own time?

Maybe he was getting old, or just damn tired of the game.

Or maybe he was tired of women like Petra who were only interested in the exposure.

He didn't want a girlfriend, anyway. He only wanted to focus on his career. And he was supposed to be concentrating on Haven, on making her feel better.

This wasn't cutting it. He had to work harder, should have tried to persuade her to go out with him tonight.

Instead, he'd ended up with the drunk blonde in his pool who couldn't care less which athlete she was with, as long as she got to say she slept with someone from the team.

Looked like Ten-Spot was going to get lucky with both of them, because after Trevor made it clear to Petra that he wasn't interested, she'd pouted for about three seconds before joining Audrey in making Ten's night.

Which suited Trevor just fine. He was tired, and he needed to figure out how to better help Haven.

He'd do better tomorrow.

FOUR

WHEN TREVOR GOT UP THE NEXT MORNING, HE FOUND Haven in the sunroom, the smell of coffee drawing him there. He grabbed the pot and poured himself a cup.

"Hey, you're up already."

"Yes." She sat at the table, her laptop and notepad sitting next to her. "Hammond was here early, cleaning up in the kitchen. He makes great coffee, too." She looked around. "Where are your . . . friends?"

"They left not long after you went up to bed."

"All of them?"

He crooked a smile. "Yeah. All of them. Petra isn't my girl-friend. Or even a one-night stand, Haven."

She diverted her attention to her laptop. "It's not any of my business who you sleep with."

Yeah, right. Except she'd looked irritated last night. And he had to admit that made him curious. Was she jealous? Why would she be? Was she interested in him? He looked over at her, so focused on whatever it was she was doing on her laptop.

"Ready to work so soon?"

"Whenever you are."

"Coffee first. And then breakfast. Have you eaten yet?"

"I had some yogurt."

He poured a cup of coffee. "Yogurt? That's it?"

"It's enough for me."

He laughed. "No, it's not. How about some bacon and eggs and pancakes? Maybe some biscuits and gravy?"

She finally drew her attention away from her laptop and looked at him. "Hammond's not here. He said he had errands to run."

"I told you I know how to cook."

She gave him the once-over. "Maybe I should cook."

He laughed. "I think you'll just have to trust me."

"Really. I'm good. The yogurt was fine."

"It's not fine. And I need to eat anyway. I need fuel for the day, and breakfast should be your biggest meal."

"Uh, no thanks, really. I'm good."

"Come with me. You can sit with me and drink your coffee while I'm cooking."

She seemed to agree with that, following him into the kitchen and taking a seat at the island.

He pulled out several skillets. "I'll make extra, just in case you change your mind." She looked like she could use some calories, like she'd lost some weight since the last time he'd seen her.

"What are you working on over there?" he asked as he put bacon in the pan, then cracked eggs in a bowl.

"Just the outline for our program together."

Deciding against pancakes, he took out bread and popped some in the toaster. "Okay. So what's the plan?"

"It can wait until after breakfast."

"Do you like orange juice?"

"What?"

"Orange juice. Do you like it?"

"Oh. Yes, I do. Why?"

He opened the refrigerator and scanned the contents. "I also have carrot juice, apple juice, and cranberry juice. What would you prefer?"

"Um . . . orange juice is fine."

He poured two glasses, then flipped the bacon over and got out two plates.

"Really, Trevor, I'm not hungry."

He slid a smile her way. "No one said you had to eat."

He finished the bacon, then put the eggs in the pan. In a couple of minutes, they were scrambled perfectly. He split them onto two plates and slid one in her direction. Not paying attention to her, he pulled up a chair at the breakfast bar and started eating.

It didn't take her long to push her laptop to the side, grab the fork he'd laid on the plate, and dive into the food.

Never underestimate the power of the smell of bacon. She ate at least half of what he'd put on her plate, which he'd call a success.

When she finished, she pushed the plate to the side. "That was really good. Thank you."

"You're welcome."

"You're a good cook, Trevor."

He leaned back in his chair. "This surprises you?"

"I don't know why it should. You're good at so many things."

He shot her a grin. "Darlin', you don't know the half of it."

She rolled her eyes and slid off the bar stool. "I'll do the dishes."

"You don't have to do that. You're a guest." He got up and took her plate, and his, to the sink, rinsed them, and loaded them in the dishwasher. Then he washed the skillet.

"You're just on your best behavior because I'm here, right?" she asked as she once again took her seat at the breakfast bar.

"I don't know what you mean."

"First you cook, then you do dishes, too?"

He stacked the skillet on the dish rack, then grabbed the towel to dry his hands. "Well, yeah. Why wouldn't I?"

"This isn't the Trevor I know."

"Maybe you don't know me as well as you think you do."

She studied him. "Maybe I don't."

"Good. Then you'll have a lot of questions to ask for your super feature story on me, won't you?"

She laughed. "I guess I will. Which, now that breakfast is over, we should get started on."

"Sure. Let's spread out a little. The breakfast bar isn't comfortable. Where would you like to go?"

Haven looked around, trying to decide where to set up. "Uh, living room." Trevor would likely be more at ease, more at home there, and more amenable to answering her initial questions. Plus it seemed a little more formal than the sunroom.

"That'll work."

He took a seat in one of the leather chairs, while Haven spread out on the sofa, her notes and laptop in front of her.

"So how's this going to work?" he asked.

"I'm going to start by asking some background questions, just a few things we'll fill in on the narrative side of the equation. After we're through with all the background story, we'll start filming."

"Which will consist of?"

"You at work. And at home. Where you grew up, where you went to high school and college, plus some of you at leisure activities. People want to know about you—who Trevor Shay the person is, as well as the athlete. I've looked into some of the charities you sponsor. I'd like to showcase those."

"I'd like that, too."

"Then we're set."

"Do I get to interview you, too?" he asked.

"Ha-ha. And no. You already know all there is to know about me."

"Do I?"

"Sure. We've known each other since college."

"We've been around each other, Haven. But do we know each other all that well?"

She frowned. "I don't understand the question."

"Look. If you knew everything there was to know about me, you could write the background without needing to interview me, right? But you can't, because while we went to college together, we didn't really hang out, did we?"

"No, we definitely didn't."

"And it's not like we've spent a lot of time around each other. We know each other because of your mom and dad. We've hung out some, but you don't really know me all that well. And I don't know you, either."

"Do you know everyone who interviews you?"

"No. But you're the daughter of someone I greatly admired. Someone I thought of as a mentor. You're not just a random interviewer. You're someone I'd like to get to know better."

She didn't understand why he was interested. Or why it even mattered. "You're certainly playing a different tune now than you did in college. You couldn't wait to get away from me then."

He dipped his head, then gave her a very sexy smile. "In college it was different. I wasn't much for learning back then. The only thing I was interested in was the ball—either football or baseball. I wanted to be out on the field playing. Academics got in my way. And you represented academics."

"I see." Not exactly the same way she'd seen it back then. "So you saw me as a way to help you pass your classes so you could stay in school."

"Something like that. Why? Was I mean to you?"

"No. Not at all. You just did everything in your power to avoid studying."

He laughed. "Yeah. That really wasn't my thing."

"So I noticed. Unfortunately, charm could only take you so far, Trevor. At some point you had to get a passing grade."

"And you helped with that. So thanks again."

"You're welcome. Though I don't know that I really helped, since you managed to elude most of our study sessions, or rarely paid attention to what I was trying to say."

"Hey, I passed, so it sank in. Trust me, you helped."

The earnest way he looked at her, the easy smile on his face, and, oh, God, she could get so lost in the sea green of his eyes, how dark and long his lashes were, and his mouth—

"So . . . where do we start?"

Haven blinked, and realized she'd been staring at him. He'd done this to her in college, too, making her lose her focus.

Damn the man anyway. And now he was smiling at her, as if he knew exactly the kind of effect he had on her.

"Let's start with your childhood." At his wary look, she said, "We'll walk gently through here, and if anything makes you uncomfortable, we'll stop."

She turned on her recorder. Trevor looked down at it.

"No."

She switched it off. "No?"

"Not for this part."

She didn't know why, but she wouldn't ask, at least not yet. "Okay. I'll just make notes on my laptop. Anything you're uncomfortable with, we'll discuss."

"Fine."

She might be new at this, but she was still a journalist. Her job was to dig and dig deep, even into uncomfortable territory, to make the subject at ease enough with her that he'd divulge secrets he might not otherwise want to delve into.

She'd do it with Trevor if she had to, but she hoped he'd feel comfortable enough with her that he wouldn't even notice the probing questions.

"What was the first organized sport you remember playing, and how old were you?"

"That's easy. Soccer. I was five. Though I don't know if you could call it organized."

She laughed. "Yes, I remember. I played, too. My parents referred to it as bunch ball, because we gathered around the ball in a bunch and chased after it."

"Yeah, T-ball was a little better. I played that, too. Then Pee Wee league football."

She'd started typing in notes. "You liked sports a lot as a kid."

"I was a hellion with excess energy. My mom had to keep me busy, so I played sports year round."

"Is that what you wanted to do?"

"I loved playing. And my mom was right. I didn't like to sit and be quiet. I wasn't much for quiet time, watching a movie or reading a book. I wanted to be outside running around and doing things."

"Do you have any brothers or sisters?"

"I have a brother. He's younger than me." When she didn't say anything, he added, "His name is Zane. He's still in college."

"So quite a bit younger than you."

"Yeah. He's my half brother, actually. My parents divorced when I was seven years old. My mom remarried and had Zane."

She hadn't known his parents divorced. So much she didn't know. She was making copious notes.

"Are you and Zane close?"

Trevor grinned. "Yeah. He's great. So smart. He's premed, so he's going to be a doctor. He graduates next spring and then he'll start medical school. My mom and stepdad are so proud of him. Hell, we all are."

"I'm sure she is. Just like she's very proud of you."

"Oh, yeah, sure she is. But you know, sports isn't medicine. I'm not gonna save someone's life catching a football or hitting a home run."

"I don't think it's very fair to compare yourself to your brother's career choice, though. You're doing what you love, following where your talents lie. So is your brother."

He shrugged. "True enough. Next question."

And he glossed over the fact that it obviously bothered him that his brother had chosen an important career path and he for some reason felt his wasn't.

"How often do you see your brother?"

"As often as we can get together."

"Where does he go to school?"

"He's getting his premed degree at Washington University here in St. Louis, where he'd also like to go to med school. I think, given his grades, it's a given he'll stay there."

Haven smiled. "How wonderful for him."

"Yeah. Like I said, he's really smart."

"I'd like to meet him and interview him."

"I'll see what his schedule looks like and maybe arrange that."

"Thanks."

She looked over her notes. "Tell me about your dad. What happened after the divorce?"

"No."

"No, what?"

"I don't want to talk about my dad."

"You and your father aren't close?"

"I love my mom. My stepdad is an awesome guy and stepped in when my father wasn't around, which was most of my childhood. He's the real dad in my life. Let's just leave my father out of this whole process."

She put the laptop to the side. "Okay. Off the record, tell me about your dad."

He stood. "Not now. Let's take a break. How about a swim before it gets too hot and before I have to leave for the ballpark?"

She looked up at him. "Trevor, we've just started and there's a lot of material to go over."

He came over to her and grabbed her hand and tugged her up. "And plenty of time to get there. Come on, a quick swim and we'll get back to work. Life is meant to be lived, Haven. Let's have some fun."

She hesitated, then finally nodded, figuring if she kept him happy, he'd be more amenable to answering her questions—even the tough ones. "Okay, but only a short break."

AN HOUR LATER, TREVOR TREADED WATER IN THE DEEP end while he watched Haven sitting on the pool steps in the shallows. Her elbows rested on the edge of the pool and her face was tilted up toward the sun. She looked . . . relaxed, which was exactly how he wanted her.

This morning was going well. She'd dived into the questions, seemingly into her work, which had been the goal. Unfortunately, it had been him who'd put a stop to everything when she'd brought up his dad.

He couldn't go there. Not right now, and never on the record. This break was just what he'd needed to get Haven's mind on a different track. Plus, she seemed to be having a good time. Or at least, she didn't seem down.

"How can you ever go to work when you have a backyard like this?" she asked, tilting her face up to meet the sun. "If I lived here, I think I'd live in the pool. Plus, it's heated, so you can swim in here until at least the end of October, depending on the weather."

"Yeah, it's really nice. That's why I bought the place. It'll see me through to the championship, provided we make it that far."

"And what do you think of the Rivers' chances this year?" she asked.

"Pretty damn good. After all, they have me."

She laughed. He swam toward her and pulled up a spot on the ledge next to her. "So you think you could get used to a decadent lifestyle, huh?"

She slid her sunglasses on top of her head. "What can I say? I'm easily swayed."

"I don't believe that. You were always so driven in college. You of the dual degrees and all."

The look of surprise on her face made him smile.

"How did you know that? You barely paid attention to me."

"Maybe I do know more about you than you know about me."

"Seriously. How did you know that?"

"Your dad and I had some conversations. He was very proud of you. He said you could have done anything with your life that you wanted—you got your degree in special education and in journalism."

"And I chose journalism." She looked out over the water. "I don't know if that's very noble."

"It's what you wanted to do, isn't it?"

She shrugged. "I don't know. I suppose at the time. It seemed more exciting to me. I had the opportunity to travel and I so wanted to get out of Oklahoma. Plus, I love sports. That's why I chose journalism over teaching."

"Sports is exciting to me. I couldn't dream of ever doing anything else. You think what I do is noble?"

She opened her mouth, then closed it.

"Okay, then. So neither of us is noble. Get over yourself, Haven."

She shook her head. "You don't understand. At first I wanted to teach. I loved tutoring, loved the classes, but the lure of journalism was there, too. Hence the dual degrees. I couldn't decide what I wanted more. And that's why it took me longer to graduate, too."

"So you're beating yourself up because you're doing what makes you happy?"

"Who says I'm beating myself up?"

And he wondered if she was really happy. "I do. Journalism is an exciting career."

"Teaching can be, too."

"Teaching is a grueling, thankless career and you know it. I'm sure it was a tough career choice to make."

"But I loved it. I loved the classes, loved my students when I was tutoring, and student teaching. Why didn't I choose that instead?"

"Because you didn't love it enough?"

She sighed. "Maybe. I don't know. It's not that I don't like this—" She looked at him. "This used to fuel me. And the opportunity I had to do sportscasting for a network. God, a year ago I would have killed for a spot like that."

"But?"

"But then, you know, the stuff with my dad happened."

"And it threw you off. It banked the fire some."

"I guess so. Lately I've been in some kind of funk and I can't seem to drag myself out of it."

"Because you miss your dad, and that's okay."

"It's been long enough. I shouldn't still feel this way."

"I don't think you can put a timeline on grief. You feel it and it consumes you until it doesn't anymore."

She looked over at him. "You speak like you know about it."

"I've lost some people I care about, so yeah. I do know how it feels. And I cared about your dad, too. Losing him was hard on me. I still feel like there's a hole, like something's missing in my life."

She laid her hand on his arm. "I know you cared deeply for my dad. He loved you, too. He loved all you guys like you were his kids."

"Not as much as he loved you. He talked about you all the time. He was so damn proud of you, Haven. And no matter what choices you make, he'd still be proud of you."

She nodded, and he saw the tears fill her eyes.

"Yeah."

She stood and started up the steps. "I think that's enough play-time. How about we get back to work?"

He'd started this with his conversation about her dad. She'd been relaxed and having fun, and now she was hurting again. Time to change the mood.

"I don't know. You look like you might need to get dunked."

Before she could object, he stood, swooped her up into his arms, and dunked them both underwater.

She came up sputtering, parting her hair that had fallen in front of her face.

"Goddammit, Trevor. Talk about a blindside."

He laughed and shook his head back and forth to clear the water from his eyes and his hair from his face.

Haven pushed away, shoving her palm over the surface of the water to splash at him. She swam to the stairs and climbed out.

"Oh, come on, Haven."

"Whatever. You need to find my sunglasses, which are no doubt at the bottom of the pool somewhere, thanks to you dunking me."

"Yes, ma'am." He dove down and searched, finding her glasses resting on the bottom of the pool. When he came up, he only had a second to blink before Haven cannonballed into the pool next to him. Water catapulted over his head like a tsunami. Now it was his turn to sputter.

He swiped his face and turned to see her grinning at him. She took her sunglasses from him and slid them on. "Just a little payback," she said, before swimming away.

"Oh, I don't think so." He took off after her.

She laughed, then shrieked when he grasped her ankle and pulled her back. He tugged her against him, cradling her in his arms so she couldn't escape, though she tried.

"Hey, you started it," she said.

"And you volleyed back. That means we're at war."

Her body felt good against his. He liked holding her, liked seeing her breasts up close. And okay, so he was a little voyeuristic. Who could blame him, since Haven was beautiful, had a great body, and he liked to hear her laugh.

"War, huh? I do like a challenge."

"Not much you can do about it in your current position."

"You wouldn't think so, would you?" Until she tugged at a few of his chest hairs, causing him to yelp and let go of her. Then she dove under the water and did the unthinkable. She jerked his board shorts down, then swam away in a hurry. By the time he'd tugged them back up, she was already out of the pool, offering up a smug smile as she reached for her towel.

"Oh, now it's on," he said, climbing out of the pool and coming out after her with deliberate intent.

She backed away. "Hey. It was a means to an end, Trevor. I was trying to get free."

He came closer, and she ran.

But he was a lot faster, and caught up to her, pulling her against him and flinging them both into the deep end. He heard her shriek of laughter as they both went under, and this time, he untied the top of her bikini, keeping hold of her as they came up. Treading water, he caught the back of her strapless top and pulled it away, holding it above the water like a trophy.

"Trevor," she said, her eyes widening as she looked at her top in his hands. "I'll take that back."

"Hey, I told you it was on. And I always win." He couldn't see anything because she was under the water, but at least she wasn't mad.

In fact, she shrugged. "Have it your way." She swam to the shallow end and calmly walked up the steps, her lush, ample bare breasts visible. She went to the chaise and grabbed her towel. "Enjoy your trophy. I'm going to take a shower, then it's back to work for both of us."

He couldn't help but admire the sleek line of her back as she walked away.

She had amazing breasts, too. Her dark nipples had puckered from the chill in the air, making him want to put his mouth on them and warm them. She made him hard watching the way her hips swayed as she walked away.

Haven was a revelation, a really nice surprise he hadn't been expecting.

She wasn't here so he could seduce her, though. Too bad, because he'd like to put his hands on her again, this time to do more than play in the pool.

But he'd made a promise, and he intended to stick to it.

And as he climbed out of the pool, he looked down at her bikini top clutched in his hand and smiled.

Nothing said there couldn't be some fun in it for both of them, though, right?

FIVE

AFTER HER SHOWER, HAVEN GOT DRESSED AND WENT back downstairs. Trevor wasn't there. She looked out on the pool deck for him, but he wasn't there, either. He was probably still upstairs, so she went into the kitchen and fixed herself a glass of water, needing something to cool her down after their interlude.

She found her bikini top lying over the kitchen faucet. She shook her head, and ran her top upstairs, tossing it into the bathroom sink before returning downstairs. The last thing she needed was for Hammond to find various parts of her clothing in the kitchen. She was supposed to be here for professional reasons, not fun and games.

Damn Trevor for finding new ways to turn her on. Then again, he'd been right—she had started it. She just hadn't known how hard a player he was, how much of a competitive nature he had. Now she knew, and she'd keep her distance.

She heard him coming down the stairs, so she turned around

and leaned against the counter, wishing she could put something—anything—between them. She felt like she needed a shield to ward off all the testosterone that seemed to roll off him.

Or maybe that was just her imagination.

"There you are," he said, grinning as he walked by and looking at the sink, where her bikini top used to be. "Swimming was fun. We should do that again."

"No, we definitely should not. I'd like to not bare my breasts to anyone who happens to be watching."

He laughed and leaned against the counter next to her. "I don't have any neighbors within viewing distance of my backyard. That's why I bought this property. It's plenty private."

"There's Hammond."

"His errands will take him away from the house for the rest of the day. So no one saw your boobs but me."

"Great."

"Yeah, they were."

She rolled her eyes at him and pushed off the counter, heading toward the living room. "Ready to continue?"

"No. I have to head to the stadium and prep for the game. But you can come along."

She stopped and turned. "All right." Now she could watch him in action. She was eager to see him work, and getting to see it at field level excited her.

She gathered up her things and stuffed them into her bag. By then, he'd grabbed his team bag and car keys.

"Ready?" he asked.

"Sure."

He led her to the car. It only took about a half hour to get to the stadium, but she enjoyed the view nonetheless.

Trevor was right. It had been a long time since she'd been to St.

Louis, and she'd had a child's-eye view back then. Now everything looked different.

The city had grown so much, but she was still in awe of the Arch and the Mississippi River as they wound their way downtown and toward the stadium.

"So you'll continue to play baseball until the end of the season, then you'll head to Tampa and join the football team there?"

"Yeah. At least this season, since the Rivers have a shot of making the playoffs. It works easier that way for both teams, rather than me trying to jump back and forth."

"Easier on you, too, I imagine."

He nodded. "I travel enough with the Rivers. I don't need to go back and forth with the baseball and football teams. When baseball is done, I'll join Tampa and play out the football season with them."

She shook her head. "I don't know how you do it, Trevor. Trying to juggle two professional sports seems crazy."

He pulled into a parking spot and turned off the engine, then turned to her. "That's me, Haven. Just fucking crazy."

She laughed and got out of the car with him.

"I'll set you up inside the boxes where it's more comfortable," he said as they headed into the stadium.

"If you don't mind, I'd like to sit as close to the field as possible, unless there are no seats available."

"Are you sure? The club box seats are much more comfortable. Plus, there's liquor and great catering."

"I'm pretty sure I can handle it."

"Suit yourself." He led her inside and stopped at security, where she was given a pass. She picked it up and looked at it. "This isn't a press pass," she said as she hurried to keep up with his long strides.

"Yeah, I know. A press pass limits you. This one won't. It'll give you access to anywhere in the stadium you want to go."

"Really. Why would you do that?"

He stopped and turned to face her, and as they stood in the sun, she was struck again by how utterly gorgeous he was. "So you have all access. But don't go anywhere you shouldn't."

She laughed. "Where am I not supposed to go?"

"The locker room would be a bad idea. You don't know who you might find naked down there."

"Okay. I'll avoid the locker room. Anywhere else?"

"Management offices might be a bad idea. You don't want to get thrown out on your ass before you get a chance to interview anyone."

She sighed. "Just tell me where I should go."

"You should be safe at field level or in the club boxes."

"Thanks."

"I'll meet up with you at the exit when the game's over. If you get hot, just head upstairs to the club boxes. They're air-conditioned."

He directed her to the field—and pointed out the boxes.

"Okay."

"Do you need me to walk with you?"

"Thanks, but no. I'll find my way around. You go get your game face on, and kick some ass."

He grinned. "Thanks. I'll see you later."

He disappeared down the tunnel, and Haven made her way out to the field. There were press on the benches higher up. Since she had the all-access pass, she walked out to the field entrance where security waved her on.

Awesome.

She stood out on the field, and her first thought was of her dad, of how much this would have thrilled him, to be standing here at field level with her, surveying the players as they took the field for warm-ups.

She'd have brought him along, too, just so he could have the chance to meet and greet all the players.

He'd been such a fan of the Rivers. Through the years when the team had played like shit and ended the season in the basement, he'd always remained a devoted fan.

So had she, because of her dad.

She turned around, surveying the stadium. The Rivers had built a new one a few years ago, so this one wasn't the same as the one she'd been to with her dad all those years ago.

But still, it was Rivers baseball, and she'd give anything to be sharing this with him right now.

God, she missed her dad so much right now it physically hurt. She laid her hand over her stomach, massaging the ache of loss that seemed to swell and grow inside her. Part of her wanted to turn tail and run like hell, to leave the stadium and all the memories that swirled around her like a thick cloud.

Part of her was still that little girl, eating popcorn and a hot dog and cheering on the Rivers with her dad.

The other part of her was a grown woman, scared to death that she couldn't handle the responsibilities of her new job.

And nowhere in that scenario was the pep talk she so desperately needed from her dad right now.

But her love of baseball—of sports—was because of her father. She owed it to him to stay and give this a shot. He'd be mad at her if she didn't, so she blinked back the tears pricking her eyes, forced back the ache of loss and the fear of failure that welled inside her, then took a deep breath to center herself. She climbed up to the field-level seats and one of the staff directed her to an empty chair where she could watch the game.

She took out her laptop and started making some notes. People started filing in. A lot of women, too. Wives and maybe girlfriends of the players, no doubt. She wanted to talk to them, as well, but not tonight. She'd do that some other time.

When Trevor took the field, her heart skipped a beat. She'd seen him play on TV, of course, but never in person. He was so tall, and God, he looked mouthwateringly good in uniform as he trotted out to the field to warm up. She'd thought she was over the crush she'd had on him in college.

As she watched him run, she realized what she felt was nothing more than the rush of close proximity, the fact that she had one-on-one time with him. He was paying attention to her, giving her his time. If there was one thing Trevor had, it was charm, and he knew how to use it. He'd always had a reputation with women, and for all his talk about focusing on nothing but sports in college, that hadn't been the case at all. He'd had plenty of girlfriends—or at least he'd gone through a lot of women.

From the initial research she'd done about his adult life, it appeared he was still going through them. Approaching thirty, he remained unattached and hadn't had a serious girlfriend. She wondered why. She made a note to ask him, then focused on the practice.

They got into positions while the pitcher warmed up. Trevor was in left field. She knew a lot of these players, though the team had made a few changes in recent years. Gavin Riley was still at first base, anchored by Dedrick Coleman at third, the veterans who were still the glue that held this team together. They'd traded for a hotshot shortstop, Chase Henderson, who looked to be an up-and-comer.

She had high hopes for the team this year. The Rivers were currently in second place with two weeks to go until the end of the regular season. They were three games out of first and in the hunt for at least a wild card spot.

She loved sports, and always had. Maybe it had been a product of her growing up around sports players, being around them all the time because of her parents. The sports dorms had housed players of so many different sports—football, baseball, lacrosse, tennis—any sport imaginable. And her parents had treated every boy who'd gone to college there as one of their own. They'd often gone to the games, and if there was one thing her father had been good at, it was spotting a boy in trouble—someone who needed a little extra TLC.

Haven remembered her dad spending a lot of time with Trevor, though she hadn't known why, by that point not paying so much attention to Trevor because she'd been in college herself, focusing on her own studies, her own social life. Whatever pitiful social life she'd had, anyway. One would think she would have been incredibly popular since she'd known all the jocks.

Not so much. None of the guys had wanted anything to do with her. She might as well have had *Off-Limits* tattooed across her forehead. Being the daughter of the dorm parents was just as bad as being the daughter of one of the coaches. No one had touched her. Not that she had wanted any of them.

Except for Trevor, who continued to wow her with the distance on his throws. He had one hell of an arm.

He was simply too good at this. Which, she supposed, accounted for his popularity, and the reason the teams made allowances for him playing two sports.

Seats were filling in all around her, but she barely paid attention because the teams were taking the field. She focused on Trevor in the outfield as the Rivers were on defense first and Chicago came up to bat.

Garrett Scott was pitching today. Her mom said Garrett had come by a few weeks ago to visit, along with his fiancée, Alicia, who also worked for the Rivers as a physical therapist.

Mom had loved that visit. It had brightened her spirits.

Haven saw Alicia out on the field working with one of the players. Very pretty woman, and, as it turned out, she was Gavin Riley's cousin. Alicia and Garrett were getting married at the conclusion of the baseball season. She couldn't wait to go to the wedding.

Closing her laptop, she focused on Garrett. His shoulder looked completely healed because he was throwing a combination of pitches out there, all of them hitting the mark. The first batter grounded out to second base. Garrett struck out the second batter, and the third batter hit a pop fly that Trevor ran down and caught.

Easy top of the first. Now the Rivers were up. Trevor batted fifth in the lineup, so she wasn't sure she'd get to see him in action this inning.

The first batter grounded out. But when the second batter singled and reached first base, and the next doubled, unless Gavin Riley hit into a double play, she'd get to see Trevor hit.

Gavin took two pitches low and away for balls, the next right in the strike zone. He hit the next one into left field, which scored the two runners and sent Gavin to first base.

The stadium erupted into wild cheers. The Rivers were up by two runs, Trevor was up to bat, and there was only one out.

She could see how serious he was as he stepped into the batter's box. Her stomach twisted in knots as she waited for Chicago's pitcher to throw the ball.

Trevor took a strike on the first pitch, then two balls. He fouled off the next pitch.

Two balls, two strikes. She clasped her hands together and leaned forward.

The pitcher's next throw resulted in ball three.

Full count now; she waited for the next pitch. It was right on the money, and Trevor slammed the ball. Unfortunately, it went foul.

So did the next ball, and the one after that. He was hanging in there, though, and she hoped he'd get a piece of one of these pitches.

He did, on the next pitch, sending it sailing into the left-field corner. She launched out of her seat, screaming along with the rest of the stadium as Gavin rounded the bases and headed for home. Trevor stopped at second base.

Excellent.

The next batter was out on a high pop fly, and the batter after that struck out, stranding Trevor, but he'd gotten an RBI and the Rivers were up three to nothing after the first inning.

The rest of the game was just as chock-full of excitement, with Chicago scoring two runs in the fifth, and the Rivers coming back to score four more before it was all over.

What an exciting game, and one the Rivers needed to stay in contention. Every player had given it his all. Haven had been tense the entire time.

She headed to the locker room after the game.

"Hi, Haven."

She turned and saw Alicia standing there. They hadn't had a lot of interaction, but they'd spent some time together at the hospital and getting to know each other after the funeral.

"Hello, Alicia. How are you?"

"I'm good. How are you doing?"

"Great. It was a good game today. Garrett pitched so well."

"He did. Those three runs kind of sucked, though. He'll be pissed about that." Alicia paused. "Oh, I probably shouldn't have said that. Are you covering today's game for your news station?"

"No. I'm actually doing a feature interview on Trevor Shay."

"That's interesting. And should be fun. We love Trevor around here. He's great and has been an incredible asset to the team. All the guys love working with him."

Haven wasn't sure if that was the truth or just the company line. "I'm glad to hear that. And you work for the team as well. That must have been so complicated for your relationship."

"Are we on the record here?"

Haven laughed. "Not at all. I'm not writing about you and Garrett."

"Then, yes. It was complicated as hell for a while. But we worked it all out. And the team has been great about it. I just don't work with Garrett in any official capacity."

"You do sports medicine, right?"

"Yes. So if he's injured or needs any kind of physical therapy, one of the other therapists works with him. The only interaction we have together now is at home."

"I guess that makes sense. No conflict of interest that way."

"Exactly."

"Have you worked with Trevor before in therapy?"

"I have, though mostly for general conditioning. He's like . . . bionic or something. The guy has never been hurt. He knows his body well and knows how to take care of it. And considering that he plays two sports, I'm surprised he hasn't had any issues. Doing as much as he does is hard on a body. But not on his."

Yeah, he had a hell of a body, for sure. "I guess that's a good thing, though, right? For both of his teams."

"That's what the coach says, though Manny—that's the Rivers' coach—grumbles a lot about Trevor playing football for Tampa. He wants him dedicated to baseball."

Haven's lips curved. "I would imagine Trevor hears much the same thing from the Tampa coach."

Alicia laughed. "You're probably right."

The doors opened and the players started appearing. Garrett walked over and put his arms around Alicia, giving her a kiss that made Haven's cheeks heat up.

"Good game, babe," Alicia said.

"Eh. Gave up three earned runs. But I recovered and shut them down after that."

"You did."

Garrett turned and smiled when he saw Haven, then came over and folded her into a hug. "Haven. I didn't know you were here today."

She wrapped her arms around Garrett and hugged him back. "I'm here on assignment. It's so great to see you. You pitched an amazing game."

"Gave up a few runs, but at least we won. So it's all good. And what kind of assignment?"

"With Trevor. I'm doing a feature story on him for the network."

Garrett's brows shot up. "No shit. Are you sure the rest of us will be able to handle the ego burst from him getting all that media attention?"

"Oh, suck it up, Scott. It's about time someone besides you pretty-boy pitchers got some focus around here."

Trevor came up to stand next to Haven.

"Please. I'm not the one with all those endorsement deals like you, Shay," Garrett said. "Every time I turn on one of the sports channels, I see your ugly face."

"If I was ugly, you wouldn't see my face so often, now would you?"

"Aww, he thinks he's pretty. Are you sure you can handle spending so much time with this guy?"

Haven nearly swallowed her tongue as Gavin Riley joined the crowd. He kissed his cousin on the cheek and nudged Garrett in the ribs.

"Haven, this is Gavin Riley. Who's just jealous because he thinks he's prettier than anyone else on the team. This is Haven Briscoe. She works for the network and will be doing a feature story on me."

She laughed. "Nice to meet you, Gavin."

"You, too, Haven. Sorry you have to spend so much time with Trevor."

"The network's paying me to do it. Otherwise, no way."

Gavin laughed and looked at Trevor. "I like her."

"Haven and I have known each other since college. That's why I chose her to do this whole The-Life-and-Career-of-Trevor-Shay thing. She'll do justice to it and portray me in a fair light."

"So you think," Haven said with a wink to the others. "How do you know I won't spill all your deep, dark secrets?"

"Mainly because you don't know any of them."

Gavin laughed. "Okay, I gotta go. Liz and my little princess are waiting at home for me."

"I read about the birth of your baby girl, Genevieve, Gavin. Congratulations."

"Thank you. I'm pretty stoked to be a dad. And surprisingly, even my work-obsessed wife is super excited about being a mom. Her maternity leave is about to end and she's dreading having to go back to work."

"I can imagine."

"Hey, before you go, we're doing a couples wedding shower thing after the game on Sunday," Alicia said. "Will you and Liz be there?"

"Wouldn't miss it," Gavin said. "I'll have Liz call to confirm."

"Okay. See you then."

After Gavin left, Alicia turned to Trevor and Haven. "Several people from the team are coming. It's very informal. Just a get-together celebrating our impending wedding. Trevor's invited. Will you come, Haven?"

Haven looked at Trevor.

"We'll be there. It'll give Haven a chance to meet everyone." Trevor turned to Haven. "Don't you think?"

Haven just nodded. "Sure. I'd love to. Thank you for the invite, Alicia."

"You're welcome. Do you have the address, Trevor?"

"Of course I . . . probably don't."

Alicia rolled her eyes. "This is what happens when I leave it to Garrett to invite people." Alicia pulled out her phone. "Are you ready?"

"Why don't you put all that in your phone?" Trevor said to Haven. "I think mine's in the bottom of my gym bag somewhere."

"Oh, sure." She dug her phone out of her bag and typed in the date, time, and information. "Got it."

"Great. See you all later."

Trevor led her outside to his car. There were several people hanging outside near the fences.

"Do you mind waiting?" he asked.

"Not at all."

He went over and spent fifteen minutes signing autographs and taking pictures. She liked that he took the time. Many athletes didn't. A lot of the rookies did, because they wanted to establish themselves. But once fame hit, many felt they didn't need their fans any longer.

Garrett and Gavin had lingered, too.

She liked this about these athletes. It showed class that they cared about their fans.

When Trevor was done, he picked up his bag and led her back to his car.

"Are you hungry?"

"Actually, yes. I thought I'd grab a hot dog and beer at the ballpark, but the game was so intense I never took the time."

He smiled as he pulled out of the parking lot. "It was a pretty intense game, wasn't it?"

"Yes. A good game, too. You played very well."

"I did, didn't I?"

She stared at him, and then he winked at her. She laughed.

"I never know when you're giving me a hard time."

"Good to know."

He took a turn and headed onto the highway. It was dark. A lot of the restaurants had to be closed by now since it was almost eleven.

"Where will we eat? At home?"

"Probably. I don't feel like crowds tonight. But I thought we'd pick up a pizza."

"Oh, pizza sounds good."

What kind of pizza do you like?" he asked.

"Any kind. My favorite is sausage, though."

"Sausage it is."

He pressed a button on his car. The center display called a place named Imo's. He ordered the pizza and hung up.

"It'll be ready when we get there."

"Convenient."

In twenty minutes, they'd swung by and picked up the pizza and headed back to Trevor's house. Haven was starving by the time they got inside, especially after smelling the pizza.

"You're going to love this," he said as he laid the box on the counter and grabbed plates.

"What would you like to drink?" she asked.

"Water's good for me."

"For me, too." She fixed two glasses of ice water, then they grabbed seats at the breakfast bar. He had opened the box and the pizza looked glorious. He helped her scoop hers onto the plate.

"Best pizza around. Trust me on this," he said.

"Right now I'm so hungry I'd eat the cardboard box. But the pizza smells great." She took her first bite, and had to admit Trevor was right. It was excellent pizza. She ate a lot of it, too, until she couldn't stuff another bite in her mouth. She pushed back from the counter with a grunt.

"I ate too much."

He laughed. "I ate way more than you."

"You're bigger than me. You burn a lot more calories than I do, too. I'm so going to regret this."

"You were hungry."

"I was, but that's no excuse to eat that much this late. Now I'll be awake all night."

"Come on," he said, grabbing the now-empty pizza box to take to the trash. "Let's go walk it off."

"Great idea."

She put on her tennis shoes and they headed outside. The night was clear, a little cool, but she didn't mind that at all. The brisk weather would help clear her head—and maybe help her digest. They strolled down the long driveway and outside the gate.

She understood the privacy, the allure of this neighborhood. There were only six houses on his side of the street, all as big and as sheltered as Trevor's. No one was out and about this late at night, so it was like the two of them were entirely alone as they walked. She wasn't sure she'd go out on her own, but then again the neighborhood was secured by a guard and a gate.

"Do you get out and walk along here much?"

"Not really. I have the gym inside the house for exercise. But the weather's nicer now, so it's good to get some fresh air."

They took a long walk, too, as there were more houses in the neighborhood than what she'd originally seen when they'd come in. The area wound around beyond just the circular block. She wished now that it wasn't dark, that she could see beyond the thick trees that guarded the entrances to all the million-dollar estates nestled beyond the privacy fences and gates.

"This area is amazing. So private, and each property has so much space."

"Yeah. It's what drew me here, and it's not stuffy or pretentious. During the day you can see people out with their kids. It's a neighborhood to grow into."

"So you plan to stay here in St. Louis?"

"I like it here. And it's not too far from where I grew up in Springfield, Missouri, so it's close enough I can still visit home. Plus, Zane will be going to school here. And he likes it here, too, so I could see him staying on after he finishes medical school."

She liked that he thought about his family—or at least, his brother—and wanted to stay in close proximity.

"What if you got traded to another team?"

He laughed. "That's not likely to happen."

"You just signed with St. Louis a few years ago."

"Yeah. That was a move my agent and I made at my request. The Rivers are a good fit for me. I like their organization, their coaching staff, and their philosophy. Plus, like I said, Zane's here. I'll stay here until I decide to quit playing baseball."

She turned her head toward him as they walked. "And when will that be?"

He offered up an enigmatic smile. "When I'm done playing baseball."

"A very vague answer, Shay."

"It's the only one I have right now, Briscoe."

She laughed. "Spoken by someone used to dealing with media questions."

They had walked all the way to the main security gate. Trevor waved to the guard on duty, then they turned around.

"Tired?" he asked.

"Not at all. Invigorated."

They started the walk back. She was thankful they'd picked up the pace by then, because the wind had picked up, making it colder, and she could smell rain in the air.

And when she heard thunder and felt a few drops hit her skin, she looked up at Trevor; he looked at her and said, "We might get wet."

The words had no sooner left his lips than it started raining. Hard. He took her hand and they made a run for it. She knew he could run a lot faster than her. His legs were longer, but he held back, keeping a tight hold on her hand as they dashed back to the house. By the time they reached the side entry and he keyed in the security code to the raise the garage door, Haven was completely drenched.

She toed off her soaked tennis shoes in the garage, happy to be out of the rain.

Trevor kicked off his shoes, then used his fingers to comb back his hair. "Let me go grab some towels for us. I'll be right back."

"Sure."

She really wanted to strip right now, but no way was she going to walk on his expensive wood flooring in sopping wet clothes. She'd wait for the towel.

TREVOR DUCKED INSIDE AND GRABBED TWO TOWELS from the cabinet in the laundry room in the hall, then came back out to the garage, slowing his walk long enough to get a good, long look at Haven standing there all wet.

Her hair was plastered against her face, ringlets of dark curls against her cheek. Her white T-shirt was pressed against her skin, outlining a pink bra that was nearly see-through. And since he'd flipped on the garage light, he could see plenty, including the fact that she was cold.

He wasn't a teenager anymore. He'd seen breasts and nipples—plenty of them. But he had to admit, he liked the peek at Haven's, and would like to see even more.

"I should strip out of these wet clothes before I head over to my wing. I don't want to drip all over your floor."

Frankly, he couldn't care less about the floor. But how could he pass up the opportunity to see an impromptu striptease? He wasn't dumb. "Yeah, probably a good idea."

He figured she was going to do some kind of secret wrap-the-towel-around-herself thing while trying to be modest.

Nope. She drew her top off, then undid her pants and let those drop, too, leaving her in just her underwear. She dried off as best she could, then wrapped the towel around her and picked up her wet clothes. He had only a brief view of her in her wet underwear, but it was enough to make him want to see a lot more of her skin.

She had a great body. Nice curves, long legs, and a great ass.

"Are you going to stand there dripping and ogling me, or are you going to get out of your wet clothes?" she finally asked.

"Sorry. My brain cells sank right to my dick when you started stripping."

She laughed. "I'll take that as a compliment. In the meantime, I'm going to go to my room and take a hot shower."

"You don't want to wait while I undress?"

She actually paused to look him over, then said, "Probably not a good idea. See you later, Trevor."

He liked that she'd pondered the idea. "Yeah. Later, Haven."

SIX

"I TALKED TO ZANE," TREVOR SAID BEFORE SATUR-day's game. "He's coming out to the game today, then we'll visit after."

"Really? That's awesome. I can't wait to meet him. Does he need someone to sit with?"

Trevor laughed. "I got tickets for him and a few of his buddies from school. I think he'll be fine."

"Okay. I just didn't want him to sit alone."

"Trust me, my brother is very rarely alone. He's plenty social."

She leaned back in the chair and sipped her coffee, studying Trevor. "In other words, he's a lot like you."

"In some ways, yeah. In other ways, we're different."

"How so?"

"You'll see."

Now Haven was very curious about Zane. "I'm looking forward to it. But first, the game, right?"

He gave her a confident smile. "Yeah."

She waved at Alicia, who was in team uniform colors near the dugout. Haven snapped a few photos of the team in warm-ups, then made her way to her seat.

Chicago started out with two runs in the first, and the Rivers didn't answer with any offense for the first three innings.

Haven was worried, because it seemed like the Rivers' bats were cold tonight. But in the sixth, Henderson singled, and Sanchez doubled him home, getting one run in the sixth. The Rivers tied the game in the seventh on a single home run by Coleman.

But Chicago homered in the eighth, and the Rivers put up no more runs, so they lost a close game. She felt bad for Trevor, who went one for four on the day. The loss wasn't entirely his fault, though, since it seemed as if all the players had mediocre offense.

"Tough loss," she said after the game.

"It was a close one. If any of us had managed to get just one run, we could have tied the game up. I think we could have won this one."

She wanted to lean into him, to offer him comfort. But that would be too personal, and she'd already crossed that boundary. "I'm sorry. You all gave it your best."

A lousy platitude, but it was all she could offer without outright hugging him.

They got into Trevor's car.

"Where's your brother?"

"He has to drop the other guys off back at their places. He's meeting us at a bar."

"Sounds good."

They ended up at a vodka bar in what Trevor referred to as the Central West End. It was a great area, perfect for the younger crowd, especially the university set. Trevor found a parking spot and they walked the short distance to the bar.

Inside, the bar was loaded with atmosphere—and people. The

place had a wide expanse of windows, so those seated nearby could watch people walking by. Closer in was an incredible bar that touted it served more than five hundred different types of vodka. There was also an attached restaurant that served burgers, chicken, and fish.

Trevor took her hand, then said, "It's crowded in here. I don't want anyone to carry you off."

She smiled at that, and didn't mind him holding her hand as he zigzagged his way through the throngs of people milling about. He waved at a guy sitting at a table, a very handsome young man in his early twenties, who looked like a younger version of Trevor. Tall, with dark hair cut shorter than Trevor's, he stood when they approached.

Definitely no mistaking this was Trevor's brother. And they hugged each other. For some reason, Haven liked the sign of affection between the two of them. It showed they were close. It also made her wish she'd had a brother. Or a sister. That would have been nice.

Especially now, when she needed someone to lean on.

"If you're going to invite me to a game, you could at least win."

Trevor cracked a smile. "Smartass. Maybe you were bad luck."

"Not me. I'm always good luck. You just sucked tonight."

"That we did." He turned to Haven. "Haven, this is Zane Mellon, my brother. Zane, this is Haven Briscoe."

With a wide smile, Zane shook her hand. "Nice to meet you, Haven."

"You too, Zane."

They pulled up chairs, and Zane signaled for a waitress who looked to be buzzing the place at a thousand miles an hour.

"What's up, Zane?"

Zane held up his beer. "Hey, Rachel. I need a refill." He looked at Trevor and Haven.

"I'll have something fun and vodka oriented," Haven said to Rachel. "What do you recommend?"

"How about a vodka martini?" Rachel suggested. "Pick a country and we'll bring you a fantastic drink."

Haven looked at the menu, aghast at the selections. She closed her eyes and landed on Iceland.

Rachel grinned. "Perfect." She looked to Trevor.

"I'll have what my brother's having," Trevor said.

"Two beers and a vodka martini, coming up."

"Thanks, Rach," Zane said.

"I suppose you've dated her," Trevor said.

Zane took a swallow of his beer. "Nah, she's a friend. She takes classes at Wash U."

"I don't know. You two seemed awfully friendly."

"She has a boyfriend, and unlike you, I don't sleep with every female I meet." Zane looked at Haven. "No insult intended."

"None taken. And we're not sleeping together."

Zane looked at Haven like he didn't believe her. "So you're doing an interview, huh?"

"Yes. And you're premed? I had thought about premed, but oh, all the science and math classes."

Zane laughed. "Yeah, they're pretty brutal. But I've gotten through it and there's almost a light at the end of the tunnel. At least until medical school starts."

"You're going to make a great doctor," Trevor said.

"Spoken like a true brother. But thanks for the vote of confidence. And hey, have you spoken to Mom lately?"

"Last week. Why?"

"She got a new job at that salon she always wanted to work at."

Trevor turned to Haven. "My mom is a hairstylist."

"And a damn good one," Zane added. "She's always wanted to

work at this trendy salon in Springfield, but according to her, none of the stylists ever leave. They had an opening, and they asked her to come in and interview."

"Really," Haven said.

Zane nodded. "Anyway, they hired her and she starts next week."

Trevor grinned. "She must really be excited. I'll give her a call to congratulate her."

"Dad bought her flowers and candy and took her out to dinner to celebrate," Zane added.

Rachel brought the drinks, and Haven sipped what had to be the best martini she'd ever had. She sat back and listened to the brothers catch up for the next couple of hours.

Trevor was good about letting Zane lead. It was clear he was interested in what was going on in Zane's life, both academically and socially. How could she have not known about this part of Trevor's life before? Of course, she hadn't been involved in his personal life when they'd been in college. Her attraction to him had been all physical. She'd never taken the time to get to know him, to ask him whether he had brothers or sisters, or to find out about his family situation.

They hadn't been close then.

They weren't now, either, but she liked spending time with him, liked seeing how funny he was with his brother, how they teased each other. It was obvious Zane adored Trevor, which spoke a lot to Trevor's character.

"So are you going to grill him hard, Haven, and ask him why he thinks he has to work all the time and thinks he has to be the best at everything he does?" Zane asked.

"I intend to."

"Good." Zane finished his beer. "He thinks he's a superstar."

"No. I *am* a superstar. In sports. Just like you're going to be a superstar in medicine. And shouldn't you be back at your apartment studying?"

Zane rolled his eyes, then shifted his attention to Haven. "It's like having another parent around. Always checking up on me. He wouldn't even buy me beer before I turned twenty-one. What kind of big brother wouldn't hook you up like that?"

"I'm shocked," Haven said.

"At what? Me being law abiding and making sure my little brother didn't get into trouble?"

"Yes. It definitely doesn't fit in with your exploits in college."

Zane leaned back in his chair. "Now these I want to hear about. He told us all he studied hard and went to bed early."

Haven laughed. "He told you that?"

Trevor stood. "Time to go."

Zane leaned back and crossed his arms. "I don't need to leave."

"Then we do." Trevor took some money out and laid it on the table. "And you definitely do. Get back home and hit those books."

Zane rolled his eyes. "Whatever, Dad." But he grinned, then stood and clasped his brother close for a hug.

"Thanks for coming, Zane," Haven said. "It was a pleasure to meet you."

"Great to meet you, too."

"Take care, little brother. And hit those books."

"Yeah, yeah. Love you."

"Love you, too."

Haven felt wrapped up in all the affection between Trevor and Zane. As they walked to the car, she looked over at him. He had a small smile on his face.

They got in the car and drove off, and she made several mental observations.

"So, what did you think?" he asked as he pulled onto the highway.

"I think you really love your brother."

He cocked a brow. "And that surprises you?"

"I don't know. It shouldn't, I suppose, but I never pictured you with family before. And then you were so adamant about them not being mentioned, so I didn't expect this open affection between you and Zane."

"My issue isn't with Zane. Or with my mother."

He was in such a good mood, she didn't want to delve into his father—a topic that would obviously ruin that mood. "Zane's a great guy. Very smart."

Trevor visibly relaxed. "Yeah, he is. Much smarter than me."

"Why do you say that? Just because he chose medical school and you chose sports? That doesn't make someone smarter. That's just a different career choice."

"Trust me, he's a lot smarter."

She decided not to debate the issue with him.

"But I can kick his ass in sports."

She laughed. "Ever the competitor, aren't you?"

He slid a smile in her direction. "Always and forever."

SEVEN

AFTER SUNDAY'S GAME—WHICH THE RIVERS WON, thankfully, after losing that tough, close game on Saturday—Haven and Trevor went back to the house to change and get ready for the party at Alicia's.

"Do we need to bring a gift?" she asked after she'd showered and found Trevor waiting for her downstairs in the living area. She'd decided on a dress, something casual, along with heels, since it was going to be an evening event.

He didn't answer right away, and she took a moment to admire him. So far he'd dressed pretty casually at the house, wearing either workout pants or shorts, depending on the weather. Tonight he had on dark jeans and a Henley. His dark hair was getting a little long, and the ends brushed the collar. Her fingers itched to wind their way into the thickness of his hair, to brush his hair back from his forehead.

She intensely avoided that urge and brought her focus back to his face, noticing he was staring at her.

"What? Is there something wrong with what I'm wearing? Too casual?"

"Uh, no. That dress is perfect. And, damn, Haven, you have spectacular legs."

She smiled at the compliment. It wasn't like she'd never heard that before. She'd dated—casually—since college. Had a few boyfriends, one serious relationship that she and the guy had ended mutually when he'd gone off in one direction and she in another, and she hadn't been broken up about it.

That had been a while ago—before things with her dad had gotten bad and she'd put all her energy and time into seeing to his welfare. She hadn't thought about men a lot in the past year and a half.

Now?

Well, now there was Trevor, and she sure as hell wasn't going to have a relationship with him, but she definitely enjoyed the way he looked at her. Probably because he'd never even noticed her in college.

He was noticing her now, and she liked it. There was nothing wrong with that, right?

"Thank you."

"And, no. Alicia said no gifts. It's just a party, a little get-together for each of them and their friends. They have a new house that they bought and they want to show it off, just relax a little before the big day. At least that's the way Alicia described it."

Haven nodded. "Sounds fun."

"Great. Let's go."

They got in the car and Trevor drove to another beautiful neighborhood, located only about twenty minutes from his place.

Alicia and Garrett's house was a gorgeous brown-and-white two-story in a new subdivision, with a large front yard containing incredible landscaping. They stepped up onto the wide, welcoming front porch and rang the bell.

Alicia was right there to open the door. She looked so pretty wearing a sleeveless white dress that clung to her curves. She smiled when she saw them.

"I'm so glad you're here. Come on in and make yourselves at home."

They stepped in, and Haven marveled at the expansive foyer, the high ceilings, and the amazing décor. It had a modern, contemporary feel to it, yet very warm and comfortable.

"Your house is beautiful."

Alicia grinned as she walked them through. "Thank you. We spent some time building the place. I have to admit, I had a lot of fun choosing everything. It's like every woman's dream come true to pick out flooring and wall colors and furnishings."

"I can imagine what fun that was," Haven said.

She led them into the living area. "Drinks are in the kitchen. Help yourself. There's also plenty of food in there as well as in the dining room. Feel free to wander and check out the house. Garrett's . . . somewhere around here. I have no idea where."

"We'll find him," Trevor said. "Don't worry about us. And thanks for the invite."

"You're welcome. And if you need anything at all, come find me."

"We will," Haven said.

After Alicia wandered away to see to her other guests—and there were a lot of them—Haven turned to Trevor. "Beautiful house."

"Yeah. The Rileys always have to have a big place."

"Really. Why's that?"

"Big family. There's Alicia and her brother Cole, and then the cousins—Gavin, his brother Mick, and his sister Jenna—and all their spouses and the parents and the kids."

"Really. That does sound like a big family."

"All the guys play sports, too," he said as he led her into the kitchen. Someone was bartending, so Trevor turned to Haven. "What would you like?"

"I'll just have a club soda with lime."

"Beer for me," Trevor said to the guy at the bar, who fixed their drinks and handed them over.

"All the guys in the Riley family play sports?"

"Yeah. Gavin and Garrett, of course, play baseball. Mick and Cole are football. Jenna's husband, Tyler, plays hockey."

Haven tried to take that all in. "Um, wow. That's a big, sports-minded family."

"It is. And the Riley family has a sports bar, too."

She laughed. "Of course they do."

"Jenna used to manage the sports bar, but she's a singer and has a club catering to musicians."

"Oh, really? I'd love to hear her sing sometime."

He led her to an open spot in the living room where they could take a seat. "Maybe I'll take you sometime."

She sat, pondering a family like the Rileys. "Now there's a family in dire need of having a feature story. An entire family of jocks. What a story that could be."

"And you're just the person to do it."

"I could. It would be an amazing piece. All those sports? What it must have been like growing up in that family, and to have all the guys end up playing professionally. Even Jenna ends up marrying a professional hockey player. And Alicia is engaged to a baseball player. What are the odds of that happening?"

Trevor took a long pull of his beer, then shook his head. "No idea. But hey, you have to work on me first."

She patted his knee. "Believe me, you're going to take up enough of my time. But I'm filing the Rileys away for later. I'm definitely going to revisit the topic."

"The Rileys are an interesting topic for any day. We're never dull, that's for sure."

Gavin took a seat next to them.

"Hey, Gavin," Trevor said.

"Hi, Gavin. Trevor was just telling me about your family—everyone who plays sports. It's pretty amazing to have a family like yours."

Gavin sprouted a grin. "On most days it is. But there's a lot of ego, too."

"You are not talking about me, are you?"

A beautiful redhead sat beside Gavin.

"This is my wife, Elizabeth. Liz, this is Haven Briscoe. She's with Trevor tonight."

Liz held out her hand. "Nice to meet you, Haven."

"You, too, Liz."

"Liz is in the business, too," Gavin said. "She's a sports agent."

And the wheels in Haven's head continued to turn. "Seriously?"

Liz smiled. "Seriously. Why?"

"I was telling her about the ties all the Rileys have to sports," Trevor explained.

Liz nodded. "Ah. Mind-boggling, isn't it?"

"Just a little."

"I used to represent both Mick and Gavin. But of course, I don't now that Gavin and I are married. I still represent Tyler and Cole, though. And I'd like to get Trevor to come over as well."

Gavin put an arm around her. "You are still on maternity leave. No shop talk."

Haven smiled. "I heard you had a baby. Congratulations."

Liz grinned. "Thank you, yes, in August. A little girl named

Genevieve. She's upstairs sleeping right now. I'm not at the point yet where I'm ready to leave her with a sitter. Plus, I'm still breast-feeding."

"Yeah, on that note, I'm off to get another beer," Trevor said, making a hasty exit.

"I'll go with you."

"For some reason a lot of men can't handle the breastfeeding conversation," Liz said with a wry smile.

Haven laughed. "I'd love to see Genevieve when she wakes. I've kind of got a thing for babies."

"The funny thing is, I never did. I was totally career focused. I had planned to be single, to devote my life to my career. Then Gavin happened, and my whole world went to shit. I fell in love, we got married, and suddenly I'm a mom. And the baby cries con-stantly, seems to barf incessantly, and hasn't slept a full night yet. I'm an absolute wreck and, God, I love her madly. I must be insane."

Haven laughed. "The whole love, marriage, and motherhood thing must suit you, though, because you look absolutely gor-geous."

"Well, thank you. I have to admit I've never been happier doing something I never thought I'd be happy doing."

Haven admired Liz's honesty about motherhood. Many women tried to portray themselves as perfect mothers, while Liz spelled out the awful reality of those first few months of sleeplessness and crying babies. "I've known a few friends who've had babies. It's that all-consuming kind of love, isn't it?"

"Like nothing I've ever felt before. And Gavin is the same way. Even when Genevieve is up all night, he'll get up with me to change her and he'll hold her and walk with her when she's crying. We've both learned a new kind of patience we never thought we'd have."

Haven smiled. "I'm very happy for both of you."

"Thanks. Now tell me what you do."

"I'm working for the network, doing an extensive interview and bio on Trevor."

"He's a fine one," Liz said, picking up her glass of water. "Oh, so talented. Not many athletes have been able to do what he's done."

Haven spotted Trevor in a group of his teammates, laughing at something one of them said. She felt a little tingle when he looked her way and smiled. "I know. He definitely has that 'it' factor."

"He's also very sexy, and no woman has managed to pin him down yet. Will you be delving into his personal life at all during your piece?"

"Mmmm, somewhat. At least as far as he lets me. I know a little about him because we went to college together. My parents were his dorm parents."

"Oh, I like that connection. Gives you a bit of an up on the personal side."

"I don't know about that. But he said he only agreed to do this if I was the one to interview him."

Liz studied her, her blue-eyed gaze intent on her. "Hmm. Maybe he likes you."

"I don't think so. I think he trusts me not to screw him over and make him look bad."

Liz looked across the room at Trevor, then back at her. "Oh, I don't know about that, Haven. I've seen him casting looks your way. It's more than just him trusting you. There's some kind of chemistry thing going on between you."

The room suddenly felt warmer. "You think so?"

"Believe me, a woman knows these things. I'm surprised you haven't caught on to those heated glances he's throwing your way."

"Who's throwing heated glances whose way?"

Alicia, who'd asked the question, took a seat next to them.

"Trevor. At Haven. She seems oblivious," Liz said.

"Really."

Haven was mortified and wanted to go hide in the bathroom. "He's not looking at me in any kind of way. We've never had . . . that kind of relationship."

"Well, maybe it's time you did. After all, the two of you have known each other forever. Maybe he's had a crush on you for years. Like, since college."

Haven shot Liz a look. "I can assure you he never even noticed me in college. I tutored him back then, and he was way more interested in getting away from me so he could go party or play football than he was in getting in my pants."

"Considering how hot and gorgeous you are, I'd wager he wants in your pants now," Alicia said with a knowing smile.

Haven couldn't help but let out a laugh at that comment. "Well, thanks. I think. But that ship has sailed. We have a professional working relationship, so that simply can't happen."

Liz looked at Alicia, and the two of them laughed.

"Gavin and I very much had a professional working relationship," Liz said. "And now our daughter is sleeping peacefully upstairs."

"So did Garrett and I," Alicia added. "And we're getting married in a few months."

"That's great for you two. But I have no intention of marrying Trevor."

"No one says you have to," Liz said. "But for God's sake, don't let work get in the way of having some fun with a hot man."

She'd never thought of it that way, had purposely avoided trying to feel anything for the past—God, for the past year. Her emotions, her feelings—everything—had been shut down after her dad's death.

Now, though, it seemed as if she was slowly awakening again. Feeling again.

Wanting again.

At the worst possible time.

"It's not a good time for me. My dad passed away last year, and I'm just now getting my feet wet in this new job. I have to focus."

Alicia grasped her hand.

"I'm sorry," Liz said. "That had to have been so hard for you."

"It was. It's kept me in a funk. He and I were really close. I'm glad to have this new assignment, because I just started working for the network and it's a great opportunity. I don't want to do anything to screw it up."

"And you think messing around with Trevor would jeopardize your job?" Alicia asked.

"I can't see how it couldn't."

Liz leaned back on the sofa. "Well, I thought much the same thing about my job when I was representing Gavin as his agent, and he and I got involved. Talk about a major conflict of interest. But when chemistry is involved, there's not much that'll hold two people back who really want to be with each other, you know?"

She could see how Gavin and Liz would fit together. Liz was definitely a dynamo who said what was on her mind. And Gavin— he was hot. "Yes, I can see that."

"So how do you really feel about Trevor? Any . . . feelings there for him?" Alicia asked.

She took a deep breath and chanced a look at him across the room. It was as if he could sense her, because his gaze pulled away from his friends and landed on her, and again, there was that wickedly sexy smile of his that never failed to get her motor running.

She smiled back, just a little one, and returned her attention to Alicia and Liz.

"There's something. I just don't know how to categorize it. He kind of ignored me in college, so I never thought he was interested."

"But you were interested in him?" Liz asked.

"Yeah. I had an epic crush on him, but nothing ever came of it since he pretty much ignored me."

"College guys can be dumb and oblivious sometimes," Alicia said. "All the guys I was interested in in college never knew I existed."

Liz nodded. "But it seems as if he's interested now. The question is, what should you do about it?"

She enjoyed having these women to talk to. Her friends back home had all scattered after college, and while they e-mailed back and forth, she didn't have a lot of women to talk to, especially after her dad died. Her emotions had been in flux, and she'd been a ball of confusion. "I don't know. I'm not sure I trust my feelings right now."

"Maybe you should just do what feels right—what makes you happy," Liz said.

She glanced over at Trevor again. "Maybe I should."

EIGHT

TREVOR KEPT AN EYE ON HAVEN WHILE HE WAS TALK-ing with the guys. She seemed engrossed in conversation with Alicia and Liz, and eventually disappeared upstairs with Liz after a while.

He knew why, when Liz came downstairs a little while later with Genevieve. Many of the women surrounded her and the baby. And really, Genevieve was kind of hard to resist. At almost two months old, the infant was cute as hell with a full head of red hair just like her mom's, and her cute chubby cheeks.

She sure was loud, though, crying when anyone but Gavin or Liz tried to hold her. Liz apologized, but shrugged and took the baby and held her. The baby eventually quieted, and they left early.

It must suck having a kid. Something he never intended to do, anyway, so he'd never have to worry about those sleepless nights Gavin was always telling him about.

Haven came over. "Did you get a chance to see the baby?"

"Yeah. She's cute."

"She's adorable. Liz said she's going to hate when she has to go back to work soon."

"Yeah, I'll bet. Though maybe she'll get some rest then," he teased.

Haven laughed. "I doubt she'll rest. She'll probably worry about the baby the whole time. And I can't imagine with all the travel she has to do how she's going to deal with leaving Genevieve. Though she said her mother-in-law has offered to watch her, so I'm sure that's going to give her some peace of mind."

"That's good."

"Are you having a good time?"

"I am. How about you? I saw you spending a lot of time with Alicia and Liz."

Her lips curved into a smile. "I did. We had a nice conversation."

"About?"

"Work. And . . . stuff."

He arched a brow. "What kind of stuff?"

"Oh, just some stuff about you. And me. And you and me."

"Really. Care to share?"

"Maybe later. I'm a little hungry right now. How about we grab some food?"

"Sounds like a good idea." He led her into the dining room, where food was spread out across the table. They grabbed plates and filled up, then found a spot outside. It was a cool night, but there was a fire pit and heaters set up.

They took seats next to Garrett, who was seated with Alicia and a couple of other guys from the team.

"How's it going, Haven?" Garrett asked.

"Good. You and Alicia have a beautiful home. Thank you for inviting us here tonight."

"We're so glad you came," Alicia said. "Liz and I had fun talking with you. We hope you heed our advice."

Haven tilted her head and smiled. "I'll definitely give it some thought."

"What advice is that?" Trevor asked.

"I'll tell you later."

"Girl talk," Garrett said. "It's always a mystery. Whenever Alicia gets together with the Riley women, it's like an hours-long chat fest. They spend a whole day together, doing the lunch or dinner thing. It's like I've lost my woman."

Alicia patted the side of his face. "Awww, poor baby. You know I like my girl time. Besides, we all have to get together to complain about you guys. It's like free therapy."

"Come on. We're not that bad," Garrett said.

"Of course you're not." Alicia grinned at Haven.

Trevor laughed. "I'm glad I'm not a Riley. This sounds like torture."

"Oh, but didn't Haven tell you? We've officially adopted her into the women clan. She's going shopping with all of us next week. And then out to dinner. So we can indoctrinate her into our cult."

Trevor cast a glance at Haven. "You are?"

Haven looked just as surprised. "I am?"

"You are. I just decided. You're saying yes, aren't you?"

"I . . . yes."

"Good," Alicia said. "I'll call you with details."

Trevor liked the smile on Haven's face. It'd be good for her to make some friends out here, rather than hanging out with him all the time. And he liked Alicia and Liz.

After they visited a while longer, they said their thanks and left.

"Do you have a game tomorrow?" Haven asked when they got in the car.

"No. It's an off day."

"I see."

"Why?"

"Just asking."

"Did you want to spend some time on the interview?"

"Yes."

He got the idea there was something else on her mind besides just scheduling interview time tomorrow. "What else, Haven?"

She half turned to face him. "There's nothing else. Just work."

Somehow, he knew there'd been more. She'd gone quiet, as if she were thinking hard about something.

They were both silent for the rest of the drive. Once they were inside, Haven started toward her wing of the house.

"I'm heading up to bed," she said, hardly looking at him. "See you in the morning, Trevor."

"Haven."

She stopped. Looked up at him. "Yes?"

"Is there something you want to talk about?"

She paused for a few seconds before answering. "Not tonight. See you in the morning, Trevor."

He stood at the entryway, watching her. "Okay."

He could have pressed it with her, could have poured her a drink and they could have gone outside. Maybe he could have drawn out of her what she was so pensive about.

But he didn't want to push, and they had time. So he'd let it go.

But he sure as hell wanted to know what was on her mind.

NINE

HAVEN WENT UPSTAIRS AND CLOSED HER DOOR, THEN got ready for bed.

Though she didn't know why. She was restless and not at all tired, still keyed up after the party—after the conversation she'd had with Alicia and Liz about Trevor.

She sat in bed and turned on the television, then immediately turned it back off.

She wandered to the window, staring out over the sky. Her gaze was drawn to the pool area. She could take a swim. The pool was heated. There was a hot tub down there, too. Maybe she'd pour a glass of wine and sit in the hot tub. That would relax her a little and then she might be able to sleep.

But then she caught sight of Trevor, beer in hand, coming outside to take a seat on one of the chaises. He sat away from the deck, near the pool house storage area. She could barely see him, so she shifted to the far window to get a better view.

She should mind her own damn business and quit peeping out the window like a damn stalker. He probably just wanted some alone time to think.

But for some reason, she couldn't walk away from the window. She could go down there and have a drink with him, but being near him was disconcerting, and her thoughts about him were confusing enough at the moment. It was best to just—

Just what? Hang out here and observe from the window?

She was a moron. A moron who wasn't moving away from the window.

For the longest time, he didn't move at all. He'd set his beer down on the table next to him.

Maybe he was sleeping. And she shouldn't be watching him.

She started to turn away, except right then he moved his hand between his legs. Frozen in place, she couldn't seem to move when he grabbed what had to be his cock. Even though he touched himself over his shorts, her body instantly tightened. Her nipples beaded against her thin tank top and she reached up to cup her breast, using her fingers to strum across her nipples.

When Trevor slid his hand inside his shorts, her breathing quickened.

Was he really going to do that outside? Where anyone could see him? Where she could see him? Though she supposed no one else could watch. He was secluded, the chaise in the shadows against the wall of the deck. The only one watching was her, and nothing could tear her away from the glorious sight of his hand moving inside his shorts.

She pulled her tank top down, exposing her breasts, rubbing over her nipples with abandon, wishing she could feel Trevor's large, rough hands on her skin. Her pussy quivered, and she slid her hands over her sex, massaging the ache, feeling the wetness that had seeped through.

She needed sex. It had been too long, and the sight of a hot, supermasculine man like Trevor getting himself off turned her on in the worst way. Or maybe the best way, because she quivered everywhere.

She tucked her hand inside her panties, reveling in the dampness of her sex. She felt swollen, achy, and so ready for a mind-blowing orgasm that she hovered on the brink of marching downstairs and climbing on top of Trevor's cock, demanding he be the one to give it to her.

But that would be reckless, and if there was one thing Haven wasn't, it was reckless. Which was too bad, because Trevor had pulled his shorts down, taking out what looked to be one magnificent cock. If she were brave enough—which she wasn't—she'd sneak downstairs and spy on him through the back door, where she could get a better look. As it was, she'd have to make do from up here, where the light from the moon gave her only glimpses of the way he masterfully stroked his cock with rhythmic up-and-down motions, causing her to rub her pussy back and forth, tuck two fingers inside and use the heel of her hand against her clit until she was so ready to burst she had to pull back.

She'd come when he came. And she'd try not to scream when she did, because she could already feel her vaginal wall tightening around her fingers.

When his strokes turned faster, so did hers. And when he tilted his head back, she could swear he was looking right up at her room. She almost ducked back into the shadows, but she was too far gone, and by now she didn't care. Let him see. Let him come up here and finish the job by plunging his cock inside her.

But then she noticed his eyes were closed, his hips pumping up as his hand worked his cock in a beautiful, twisting motion at the same time her fingers dove into her pussy.

"Take me there, Trevor," she whispered, perspiring as she feverishly worked her clit and pussy. "Make me come—hard."

He lifted his shirt—oh, God, those abs were a work of art. He directed his cock toward his lower belly, and white ropes of come spurted across his stomach as he jerked his hips forward.

"Ohhh, yes," she whispered, trembling as she released while watching Trevor's orgasm. It was the most erotic thing she'd ever seen, and she came hard while imagining his hips pumping hard into her while both of them climaxed together.

Spent, her legs still shaking, she lay her head against the cool windowpane. Trevor lay still for a few minutes, then grabbed a nearby towel, wiped his abs, and pulled up his shorts, then finished off his beer and got up. He grabbed the towel and his beer and disappeared into the house.

Taking a deep breath, Haven went into the bathroom to clean up, then climbed into bed.

She had planned on doing some work, but she lay in the dark staring up at the ceiling, her mind replaying visuals of Trevor's cock, of his rock-hard abs, and wishing she'd had the courage to go out there and interrupt him.

She knew he would have been receptive. He didn't strike her as the shy type at all. Whereas she didn't have a ballsy bone in her body. Which was why she'd been thinking about sex with Trevor all night, yet hadn't done anything about it.

Someday, maybe, she'd change that. For now, she lay in her bed, strangely unsatisfied despite that amazing orgasm.

And she still felt as alone as ever.

TEN

TREVOR HAD COFFEE OUT IN THE SUNROOM. HE'D told Hammond to hold breakfast until after Haven got up, which she did about an hour after he did. With cup in hand, she joined him.

"Morning," she said, taking a seat on one of the chairs as far away from him as she possibly could.

"Mornin'. Sleep good?"

"Yes. Just . . . fine." She sipped her coffee and looked out the windows.

She looked pretty this morning in her capri pants and button-down long-sleeved shirt.

"So what's on the interview agenda today?"

"Mmm, I don't know for sure yet. I made some notes, but I need a full cup of coffee in me before I can think coherently."

"Gotcha." He decided to stay quiet until she decided to talk to him. He got up and told Hammond to go ahead and start breakfast, visiting with his friend about a couple of the baseball games that had been played the day before. By the time he came back into the sunroom, Haven was pouring another cup of coffee. He came up beside her, touching the small of her back as he eased around her for the sugar.

"Hammond's making breakfast."

She shifted out of the way in a hurry. "Great. Thanks." Trevor felt Haven's body stiffen as he laid his hand on her. He didn't know what to make of that. Did he make her uncomfortable? Or was it something else?

He'd thought about her last night when he'd been sitting in the chaise drinking his beer. He hadn't meant to, but visions of her had popped into his head, and suddenly his dick had gotten hard. Since he'd been alone out there, and it had been a while since he'd gotten off, he'd started rubbing his dick through his pants, thinking about Haven's soft body, the sweet way she smelled, and the way she looked at him, especially last night.

A man knew deliberate sexual intent in a look, and Haven had it when she looked at him. He'd wanted to explore it with her, but she'd put a quick halt to any conversation when they'd gotten back home last night.

All he'd wanted to do was go knock on her door and pull her against him, put his mouth on hers and taste her. It hadn't taken much for him to take out his cock and jack off thinking about getting her naked, putting his mouth on her nipples and sucking them until she was writhing and begging him to fuck her.

His cock twitched and he had to refocus his attention on the here and now. It wouldn't do to get a hard-on in front of her. She was skittish enough around him as it was. He didn't want to scare her away.

"So today we're going to start with the basics," she said, pulling him out of his fantasies about her. "We'll start with high school sports and work our way up."

"Sure. We can do about an hour after breakfast, then I'd like to take a break to work out, if that's okay."

"That works fine for me."

"You can make use of the workout facility yourself, if you'd like. I can show you all my equipment."

Her gaze shot up from where she'd been examining her coffee cup. "Uh . . . maybe."

"Come on. You can't just sit around here all the time. Your muscles will scream for a workout. Besides, I hate working out alone."

She shot him a look. "And yet there's a gym in your house instead of you going to the gym."

"Sometimes that's by necessity rather than choice. Work out with me today."

"I don't think I'll be able to keep up with you. You're a lot more in shape than I am."

"I don't care if you just walk the treadmill. It'll be nice to have your company."

She looked like she was making the painful decision to have root canal surgery, but finally she nodded. "I do need to get some exercise. I'll work out with you."

Geez, was it that awful to be in the same room with him? He didn't know what was up with Haven today. They had breakfast, then Haven grabbed her laptop and they settled in the office.

"Let's talk about high school. Did you play multiple sports then as well?" she asked.

"Yeah. By then I'd settled into football and baseball. The coaches wanted me to choose one or the other, so I'd be looked at more seriously by the college scouts."

"And you, of course, declined."

"Yes. I was playing well for both teams. Why would I want to quit either?"

She shook her head. "You were always stubborn."

"I prefer to think of it as determined. I had goals."

"Really. Tell me."

"I knew from early on that I wanted to play professional sports. Back in high school, I hadn't yet decided which one, because I loved playing both football and baseball."

"Yet you went to Oklahoma on a football scholarship."

"I did, but I played baseball in college, too."

"So you've been doing this juggling thing a long time."

"Seems like my whole life sometimes."

She typed notes into her computer. "And you got drafted by Tampa for football and Detroit for baseball, all in the same year."

"Yeah." He grinned. "That was a really good year."

"It didn't scare you, or make you feel any pressure to be drafted by both a professional football and baseball team?"

"No. It was like a dream come true."

"So, you'd say you thrive on pressure?"

He liked the way she altered his words. "You could say that."

She lifted her gaze from the laptop. "Can I say that?"

"Sure."

"How was it in high school?"

"In what way?"

"With your friends—your athletic peers. Any jealousy?"

He laughed. "Nah. I had good friends. We all worked hard, and we were after the same thing—winning. There was nothing to be jealous about."

She tapped the laptop. "I did a little research on your high school career. It says here you had some run-ins with a guy named Jerome Kayman."

"That was more of a misunderstanding. And over a girl. It had nothing to do with sports."

She arched a brow. "Fighting over the same girl?"

"Uh, no. It was more like Heather Whitfield pitting Jerome and me against each other. Neither one of us knew we were both dating her."

"Oh. Oops."

"Yeah. Heather was a hell of a flirt. She was head cheerleader, very competitive. She told Jerome she liked him, and they started going out. They dated for a few weeks, though she didn't tell anyone she was going out with him. This was all around the time of homecoming, our senior year. Heather really wanted to be homecoming queen, and Jerome was a popular guy—the quarterback of the football team. It looked like Jerome had a good shot of being king of the court."

"Which upped her chances if she was his girlfriend," Haven said.

"Exactly. Except then I caught a bunch of passes, got written up in the papers, and suddenly my popularity soared."

"So she hedged her bet by pulling you into her web as well."

"Yup. I'm not sure what she was thinking. Jerome and I were friends. And it wasn't like she could go to the homecoming dance with both of us."

Nothing Haven hadn't seen before, especially in high school. "She was thinking she could string both of you along until right before homecoming, and then as soon as she figured out which of you was the most popular, she'd dump the other."

"That's exactly what she tried to do. Except Jerome went to her house one Saturday night and found out from Heather's mom that she was out with me."

"And that's when the two of you got into it," Haven said.

Trevor nodded. "Right. He thought I was moving in on his girl, so he drove to the movie theater and waited for us outside. We had words after. Maybe a couple of punches were thrown."

"I'll bet Heather was thrilled to have two guys fighting over her."

"She thought it would increase her stock in the voting, which occurred the following week. It didn't work, though, because after I took Heather home, I went over to Jerome's house. We talked, and figured out Heather's game. I dumped her, and so did he."

Haven laughed. "So she ended up with no date for home-coming?"

"There was no way in hell that Heather was going to sit out the homecoming dance. She sweet-talked some guy from the basket-ball team into taking her. But she didn't win homecoming queen. And she was pissed."

"So who won?"

"Jerome did. I was on the court, and one of Heather's rivals on the cheerleading squad won queen."

Haven grinned. "You have to love karma."

"And high school."

"And you and Jerome stayed friends."

"Hell, yeah. Never let a girl get in between you and a friend. Or a teammate."

"I don't suppose you'll let me put any of this in your bio."

"Uh, no. Not unless you get Jerome or Heather to agree to it. Though Jerome probably wouldn't care. Heather, though . . ."

Haven laughed. "Right. Not a chance."

"I don't think she's the type of woman to mellow about some-thing like that over the years. Last I heard, she was married to Owen Lange and they have three kids and run an insurance agency in town. I remember him as a very quiet kid. He ran track and was pretty popular. Smart guy, president of student council, but kind of shy. She probably rules him with an iron fist. Poor guy."

"They'd be a fascinating story, too."

He laughed. "Look how your well is filling with ideas."

"I think my well is pretty full with you at the moment."

He stood. "I'm not nearly as exciting as you might think. Let's go work out."

"Just when things were getting interesting."

"Right. I'll meet you in the gym."

Trevor went into the gym to warm up while Haven went to her room to change clothes. He got on the treadmill and started slow, then worked his way into a run.

Things were going well with Haven. She seemed focused on her work and upbeat. He liked that she'd connected with Alicia and Liz, and was having a good time while she was here with him.

When she came in, she was wearing tight workout pants that stopped just below her knees, and a sports top that hugged her body, giving him a great view of just how fit she was.

By then he was pumped up and running hard, while she smiled at him, slid her earbuds into her ears and got on the elliptical in front of him. She didn't say anything to him, no doubt not wanting to distract him, so he left her alone and tried to focus on his work-out. He kept his pace on his run while Haven started her machine.

But he was distracted, because she had a great ass, and the faster she moved, the more he paid attention to the motion of her legs and butt.

He was done, anyway, so he slowed to an easy jog, letting his heart rate decrease, then walked for ten minutes to finish cooling down and got off the treadmill.

Haven was a distraction. A good one. But he grabbed the towel, wiped off the sweat, and moved over to the weights.

Haven made her way over to the equipment a short while after he'd started lifting.

He stopped and racked his weights. "Do you want me to show you how anything works?"

She shook her head. "I'm pretty familiar with these strength machines. You go on and do your thing. I can find my way around here."

"Okay. If you need any help, just holler."

"Will do."

He did his workout, but also watched Haven.

She was strong and capable on the pulleys as well as the free weights, and like she'd said, she didn't need any help. Still, he enjoyed watching her work out, liked seeing her muscles in movement as she did squats.

She had powerful thighs, though you'd never know it by looking at her. She didn't squat a lot of heavy weight, but she sure could push a lot of reps. Impressed, Trevor went and stood beside her as she finished up a set.

"Can I work in with you?"

She climbed off the machine. "You just want to make me feel bad by resetting the weights."

He laughed. "I'm a guy. And my thighs are a lot bigger than yours."

"Thank God for that. And I just finished my last set."

She started to move away, but he grasped her wrist. "Are you avoiding me, Haven?"

She looked down where his hand was wrapped around her wrist. This time, he didn't let go.

"I'm not avoiding you."

"It feels that way. If I make you uncomfortable, we can set up alternate living arrangements for you while we're working together."

Haven took in a breath. Okay, that had been a lie. Yes, she was uncomfortable. Who wouldn't be, being so close to someone like Trevor, especially after seeing him in such an intimate moment like last night? The problem was, it hadn't made her uncomfortable in the way he thought. It had given her powerful desires she knew she couldn't—shouldn't—act on. And maybe it was time she had a truthful conversation with him about how she felt—and what she wanted from him.

But not now. There were still questions she had, and since today was a free day, she intended to grill him while they still had one-on-one time together.

You're avoiding how you feel, Haven, just like always.

She listened to her inner voice, and agreed, but decided to ignore it.

For the time being, anyway.

"I'm totally fine with our living arrangements. And if it feels like I'm avoiding you, I'm sorry. I know how important your workouts are. I was only trying to stay out of your way."

He relaxed, and let go of her wrist. "What if I like you in my way?"

He wasn't making this easier on her.

"I'm going to go take a shower. How about we meet up for the rest of our Q-and-A after you're finished with your workout?"

He paused, his body still so close to her she could feel the waves of tension coming off him. If she leaned in, she'd touch him. And oh, she'd really like to touch him.

But then he took a step back. "Sure. I should be done here in about an hour, and then I'll take a quick shower and we'll finish what we started."

"Great."

She turned and hightailed it out of there, feeling very much like a coward for not taking Trevor up on what he was so obviously offering.

She wasn't ready.

Not yet.

As she made her way to her wing and her room, she thought about what he'd said.

Yeah, she'd like to finish what they started. Though they hadn't even started yet, had they? So really, what she'd like would be to start something with Trevor.

She took a deep breath, closed the door to her room, and headed into the bathroom to take a shower, deciding it wasn't just men who needed cold showers to keep sexual frustration at bay.

ELEVEN

AFTER TAKING A SHOWER, HAVEN CONTACTED HER producer, filling him in on what she'd been doing. Camera crews would be at the next Rivers game, where she'd do some feed on Trevor and give a rundown on his background while at the game. They'd try to do an interview before the game. Haven had talked to a few of his teammates, who had agreed to give some sound bites as well.

Her producer seemed satisfied with the status, which relieved her. She was nervous about the direction she was taking with this feature, since she'd never done one as detailed as Trevor's was going to be. She'd interviewed athletes postgame before, but those were one- or two-minute pieces, not an entire bio. She was out of her element here, but grateful to have Trevor as her subject. He relaxed her.

Well, sort of. At least professionally, he was making this easy on her. Personally? He made her tense. Nervous. A little breathless whenever she got close to him.

She was going to have to either learn to get a handle on her feelings for him, or figure out a way to have that conversation.

She found him downstairs in the office, so she set up her laptop and organized her notes.

"Ready to get started again?"

He nodded. "Sure."

"I'd like to know about anyone you feel was a mentor to you on your way up the ladder to success. High school coaches, anyone in college."

"Your dad."

She stopped and stared at him. "You don't have to say that just because it's me."

"I'm not saying it just because it's you, Haven. Bill Briscoe saved my ass—more than once—and made it possible for me to have a pro sports career."

She felt the twinge in the vicinity of her heart, but pushed it aside and typed the quote into her laptop. "Okay. Tell me about . . . Bill."

"He took everyone under his wing. He was more than just our dorm parent. He genuinely cared about all of us guys. It made a difference to him that we were educated and also excelled at the sports we played. You know how hard college was for me. I wasn't much into the academic part of it. But Bill pushed me to always do better. He said I wasn't going to play sports the rest of my life, so it mattered that I graduated."

She looked up from her laptop. "And you did."

He laughed. "Yeah. Barely. Thanks to you. And to your—to Bill. Education was always important to him. He always wanted the guys to see a future beyond just a sports career. We talked a lot about what I saw myself doing after I was done with football and baseball."

"Really. And what did you see in your future?"

"Nothing. Sports was always it for me. I don't want to own some car dealership or do sportscasting. It's always been and always will be sports for me. Bill suggested coaching."

"At the pro level?"

"I don't think so. Maybe working with kids somewhere down the road. I want to mold them when they're younger."

She leaned back in the chair and studied him. "I could see that. Kids would look up to you. You could become a teacher, then do coaching."

He laughed. "Yeah, that's not gonna happen."

"Why not?"

"It's just not gonna happen. I'm not teacher material."

"Why would you even think that? You totally could be. All you have to do is go back to school and get the right degree, then you could teach and coach."

"No." He stood and left the room.

Haven looked at the empty doorway, sensing she'd just said something terribly wrong. Trevor had been upset. Or angry. Or something.

But she had no idea what she'd said.

She set her laptop aside and went to find him.

TWELVE

TREVOR LOOKED OUT OVER THE POOL, TRYING TO GET his emotions under control.

It had been stupid to walk out on Haven like that. She'd made a simple suggestion. She didn't know about him, so he could have just nodded and said maybe and left it at that.

Instead, the old insecurities had rushed to the surface. The impatience, the frustration at all the things he couldn't do—would never be able to do—had gotten a stranglehold on him and had taken over, blotting out all his common sense.

He closed his eyes and focused on the things he could do well.

Like play baseball and football.

He was going to have to be very careful in this interview. Haven had a knack for opening him up, bringing out the past, making him answer questions about things he hadn't thought about in a long time. Like hopes and ambitions he thought he'd buried deep.

She was good at her job, probably better than she gave herself credit for. Or maybe it was because the two of them had a natural ability to get into each other's heads. He enjoyed talking to her about anything, and not just himself and his career. He wanted to know what she thought about a lot of things. He wanted to get to know her better. She was so smart.

The exact opposite of him.

He shook his head and stared into the water of the pool, sucking in a deep breath.

Forget it. Let it go.

He heard the back door open and straightened, forcing those thoughts out of his head. It was time to put the mask on again, so Haven wouldn't see, wouldn't know what he was thinking about.

She came up beside him and laid her hand on his arm. "Something I said upset you."

He turned to face her, planting a smile on his face. "No, you didn't. I'm sorry I got up and left. I just needed a break."

He knew from the look on her face that she didn't believe him, but she nodded.

"Okay."

"I don't know about you, but I'm feeling closed in spending the day at the house. Let's take a trip out."

"Sure. Where would you like to go?"

"I'll take you around St. Louis. Show you some of my favorite places."

"That sounds like a plan. I'll bring my camera and we can take some stills."

"Okay."

Their first stop was at the zoo. When they went inside, Haven grinned. "I haven't been to a zoo in years."

"You're missing out. I love the zoo. Though I don't like that the animals are caged." As they walked along, he said, "I took a trip to

Africa a few years ago, went on safari. Seeing animals free like that, living in their natural habitats, was amazing."

"I can only imagine how spectacular that must have been," she said as they stopped at the elephant area.

"The zoo here has excellent conservation programs, though. But there's nothing like seeing a herd of elephants in the wild."

She loved listening to him talk, and wished the camera crew were on board today to film the excitement on his face. She took a few still photos, and she'd make some notes later about their discussion, but the joy on his face as he discussed his trip to Africa was something that couldn't be repeated. She made a mental note to bring it up again during the on-camera interview.

"I had no idea you had such an interest in wildlife conservation."

"Yeah, it's a big deal to me. So many species are endangered. Rhinos are on the brink of extinction because poachers kill them for their horns. Elephants are the same. Humans need to do a better job of protecting animals in the wild. We think zoos are cruel, but in many instances, we're protecting a lot of endangered species that are being threatened. It'd be great if all animals could live free. Unfortunately, that's not the case."

His knowledge of many animal species was fascinating. As they walked along, he talked to her about reptiles and amphibians. She didn't think she'd ever enjoyed a trip to the zoo as much as she had today.

After the zoo, they went over to the Science Center. She really got to geek out there, since they had everything a science nerd would love, from exhibits on math to the human body, fossils, and mummies. She enjoyed the life science exhibits, examining every ecosystem imaginable. She loved that Trevor took his time exploring and seemed to have as much fun as she did. He pored over all the exhibits, the two of them like kids as they stopped and played with everything that was hands-on.

It was wonderful.

"Thank you for bringing me here," she said as, after several hours, they finally left and headed toward the car.

"I'm glad you had fun. It's been a while since I've visited, so it was like a refresher course. Zane and I have come here before, too. He geeks out over it more than I do."

She laughed. "I can imagine. I'm just happy you enjoyed it as much as I did. I felt like a kid again."

He gave her a look, then smiled one of those toe-curling, devastating smiles. "Good. Now, are you hungry?"

"Starving." They'd had a hot dog lunch at the zoo, but she was ready for something more substantial now.

"I know an awesome seafood restaurant."

They got in his car and he drove them just a few miles down the road. When he pulled up out front, the valet opened her door.

"Trevor," the young guy said. "Nice to see you again."

"Hey, Chad." Trevor gave him the keys and led Haven inside, where, once again, everyone seemed to know him well. They were seated right away at a table near the back of the restaurant. Very dark, very private.

"Thanks, Shelly," Trevor said.

"No problem." She laid their menus down. "Lauren just came on duty and she'll be with you shortly."

"Do you know everyone who works here?" she asked him.

He turned to her and shot her a grin. "Pretty much. I come here a lot. I told you, they have great seafood. Oh, and amazing pasta, too."

A petite young woman with short blond hair made her way over to their table. "Hi, Trevor. Great to see you." She turned to Haven. "Hi, I'm Lauren, and I'll be your server tonight."

"Hi, Lauren. I'm Haven."

"Nice to meet you. What can I get you all to drink?"

"I'll have iced tea," Trevor said.

"Same for me."

"Great. I'll bring those right out."

She also told them the specials of the evening before she hurried away to get them their drinks.

Haven opened the menu, but Trevor put his to the side.

"I suppose you have the menu memorized."

He laughed. "Pretty much."

She scanned the menu. There were several items that piqued her interested. "Any recommendations?"

"The salmon is good. So is the lobster risotto. And you can never mess up by going with the scallops."

"Okay. Thanks."

When Lauren came back with their tea, Haven ordered the salmon, and Trevor ordered scallops.

"We need oysters, too," Trevor said.

"Of course you do. I've already ordered them," Lauren said with a grin.

"Thanks."

"They do know you well here, don't they?" Haven asked after Lauren left.

"They fly the oysters in fresh from the Pacific Northwest. Trust me, you're going to love them."

"I trust you. Mind if I ask you some questions while we're waiting?"

He took a sip of his tea. "No. Go ahead."

She fished her notebook out of her bag. "What happens when one team or the other says you have to choose?"

"That hasn't happened yet."

"What if it does?"

"I'll deal with it if and when that day comes. But there's no point in thinking or worrying about something that hasn't happened yet, or something that may not happen. I'm in good shape and so far

I've been able to help both teams during the times I've played with them. It's working."

"Is it? Don't you feel a pull to one sport or another?"

"No."

"You don't have a favorite."

"No."

She made notes as he spoke, but she set her notebook on the table and looked at him. "But surely these teams suffer having a part-time player."

"Have they? Tampa made the playoffs last year. St. Louis won their division. I don't call that suffering."

"But what could those teams do—what kind of player could you be—if you chose just one sport to play? I mean, come on, Trevor. Considering how good you are playing part time for both, if you chose just one you could potentially be a superstar at that one sport. Surely that has to have crossed your mind at some point in your career."

She had to wait for his answer, because Lauren brought their oysters right then.

But she could tell from the smile on his face that he hadn't taken her question seriously.

She wondered if Trevor took anything seriously. Including his career. He was so . . . laid back, so easygoing, seemingly enjoying everything about his life and his jobs.

But her question had been a serious one. And she intended to bring it up again, because she was going to push at him until she got an answer.

TREVOR ENJOYED SEEING THIS SIDE OF HAVEN, WHEN she put on her journalist's hat and dug deep into her question box, drilling at him with probing questions.

Sure, he'd avoided her last question. It wasn't like it hadn't been asked of him before, and he'd given his standard pat answer.

But with Haven, he wanted to think about how to respond, because he wanted to be honest with her. Not with her network, but with her. And he wasn't ready yet to answer.

He didn't mind her grilling him, though. The fiery passion in her eyes was nice to see. It breathed life into her face, into every fiber of her body.

Her mother had been right. He could already see a difference in her. When she had focus, when she was fired up about something, she was much happier. He needed to keep that level of drive within her, keep her mind occupied so she wouldn't dwell on things she couldn't change.

"How's your salmon?" he asked as they ate.

"It's fantastic. Thank you for recommending it. I can see why you eat here so often. How are the scallops?"

"Awesome. Would you like a bite?"

She glanced over at his plate. "I would, actually."

He scooped up a forkful and held it over her plate. She bent and took the fork between her lips. He caught sight of the flick of her tongue underneath his fork. Just a small thing, really, but it made his cock tighten knowing her mouth and her tongue had been on his fork. Her lips were full and pink and he really wanted to see her tongue wrapped around his dick.

Resisting the urge to groan, he asked, "How is it?"

Instead, she let out a soft moan, her eyes floating partially closed. "It's delicious."

The sound of her moans, the way her eyes closed in ecstasy, only made his dick twitch and harden more. "Great. That's great."

He grabbed his glass and took a couple of swallows of iced tea, hoping to douse the flames that were burning him from the inside out.

"Would you like a bite of my salmon?" She held a forkful up to him.

He shook his head. "No, thanks. I've had it before. I know how good it is." And if she kept leaning into him like that, letting him breathe in her citrusy scent, he was going to drag her off her chair and bury his tongue in her mouth right there in the middle of the restaurant.

And now he was hard and uncomfortable and thinking about fucking Haven. While she was completely oblivious to his discomfort while she enjoyed her dinner.

Clearly this whole attraction thing was one-sided, and he was an idiot.

HAVEN CAUGHT THE NOT-SO-SUBTLE WAY TREVOR had been looking at her over dinner. A woman would have to be blind and stupid not to notice when a man was attracted to her, and Haven was neither.

In college, she'd have been giddy over the prospect of a guy like Trevor wanting her. Now, it presented a problem. A huge, complicated problem. On the one hand, she'd love to explore a sexual relationship with him. Or, hell, even one night of awesome sex. But that would simply kill her objectivity on this project, and that was what she'd been struggling with.

Then again, she was ridiculously sexually attracted to him right now. And she could still be objective about this assignment, couldn't she? So even if they did it, they could still work together. Or maybe she was rationalizing the hell out of wanting to sleep with him.

She could just go about this in an adult way and have a discussion with him about the pros and cons of them jumping into bed together. Then again, Trevor was a man with a penis, and she was certain he'd want to go for it, damn the consequences. Penises tended to take charge when it came to sex, and everyone knew a penis had a one-track mind. Of course, her vagina was currently doing all the thinking in this situation, and it wasn't being very rational at the moment, either.

She was overthinking this. So typical for her. Why couldn't she just shut down her brain and let herself feel, then go with her feelings?

Because she'd closed off her feelings, for her own self-preservation. Opening up that wall she'd so firmly shut down was unthinkable.

Not yet. She couldn't.

Sex didn't have to be emotional, though. It could just be physical. Fun and dirty and a release she so desperately needed.

"You've gone quiet over there," Trevor said after Lauren removed their dinner plates.

She finished her tea and nodded. "I've been thinking."

He smiled. "About more probing questions?"

It was time to put all her cards on the table. She was tired of thinking and not doing anything about it. "No. Actually, I was thinking about sex."

She could have laughed at his stunned expression. He looked around. "I don't think we're going to get into my sex life in this interview."

Now she did laugh. "Uh, no. That wasn't exactly what I was thinking about. It was more about—" Now she looked around, then leaned next to him. "You and me having sex."

Trevor signaled for Lauren. When she hurried over, he said, "We need the check. Now."

THIRTEEN

"YOU PICKED A HELL OF A TIME TO BRING UP HAVING sex, Haven," Trevor said, his fingers in a death grip on the steering wheel as he drove the highway toward his house. "I might crash the damn car."

She laughed. "You will not. And I didn't mean we need to have sex right now. I was just . . . pondering."

He shot her a quick glance before turning his gaze firmly back to the bridge. "Well, now the idea is in my head. So you need to decide if that's what you want."

"Of course it's what I want. That's why I was thinking about it. But we can talk about it, if you'd like."

"This is going to be the longest drive I've ever taken. And I don't want to talk about it. I definitely want to have sex with you. Unless you have reservations."

"I do have reservations. We're working together. If we have sex, it could compromise our working relationship."

"You think I won't take you seriously as a journalist if I fuck you."

She appreciated how blunt he was. Also, him just saying the words out loud made her body go up in flames. "Yes."

"One doesn't have anything to do with the other. We're doing an interview together. What we do during our off time is irrelevant. You're still contracted to ask me questions, follow me around, and do the bio."

"That's true."

"And I'm contracted to answer your questions—at least the ones I feel like answering."

She laughed. "So I've noticed."

He reached across the center console and laid his hand on her leg. The heat of his touch sent a shock wave of sensation through her body. "Don't do anything you don't feel comfortable doing, Haven."

She laid her hand over his. "If I weren't comfortable, Trevor, I wouldn't have brought it up. I want this. I want you."

She heard his deep intake of breath.

"I want you, too."

"Then let's do this."

He pressed down on the gas pedal and her lips curved into a smile.

"Try not to get a speeding ticket, okay?"

"I'll try."

In twenty minutes, they pulled into his driveway. Haven unbuckled her seat belt and reached for the handle of the door.

"Just . . . wait," Trevor said.

She did, surprised when he came over to her side of the car. He opened the door, reached for her hand, and pulled her from the car. When he shut the door, she only had a second to take a breath before he cupped the side of her neck, wrapped his arm around her waist, and tugged her close.

"I've been thinking about doing this ever since you got here."

His lips covered hers in a kiss that devastated her senses, turning her world haywire.

It was a soft, exploratory kiss, unbalancing her. Trevor brushed his lips back and forth across hers, and when the tip of his tongue flicked against her mouth, she opened, giving him entrance.

He tasted like after-dinner mints and delicious, hot promise. His mouth was soft and yet hard, masculine. Arousal flamed to life and pulsed a steady beat throughout her body, making her aware of every part of her body—and of Trevor's as well.

He backed her against the car, his body pressing into hers. She felt every inch of hard muscle as he moved against her, cupping her butt to pull her closer to the raging heat that seemed to pour off him until she wasn't sure if it was her, him, or the car.

But judging from her moans and his groans, she was pretty sure the two of them generated a lot more heat than the vehicle. And when he tore his lips from hers and murmured something about moving this inside, she had no objection, just followed mutely along like she was living in some kind of dream.

Maybe this was a dream, because she'd definitely fantasized about doing this with him for a long time.

Trevor certainly hadn't disappointed. That first kiss, if she'd been wearing socks, would have knocked them clear off. It was everything she'd ever thought it would be, and so much more.

He opened the front door and she stepped inside. She didn't make it far, either, because after he closed the door—without turning on the lights—he reached for her, pushing her against the wall in the hallway. And then his fingers tunneled into her hair, his body pressed up against hers. This kiss was more passionate, more oh-my-God, why hadn't she asked for it sooner? She laid her palms against his chest, feeling the fast beat of his heart, the hard plane of muscle, and wanted nothing more than to feel her naked skin against his. Just the thought of it weakened her legs.

She had a very good imagination, and she could already envision their arms and legs tangled together. And as he surged against her, her sex dampened with anticipation. She moaned, and he flicked his tongue against hers, his groan answering her growing impatience.

He moved his hands over her body, lifting the back of her dress to run his fingers over her butt. Everywhere he touched, she tingled, and when he slid his hand inside her panties, she pulled her lips from his and locked gazes with him.

His eyes had gone dark, the desire she felt mirrored in the intensity of his gaze. She traced her fingers over his bottom lip, panting even more now that he dipped his fingers lower, cupping the globes of her ass, drawing her toward the heat, the delicious hardness of his erection. He pressed in, rubbing himself against her clit, and she could swear that if he did that just a few times, she'd come. It had been too long for her, and she was pent-up, needy, and ready to explode.

That was all she needed from him. Just a release of the tension that had been building inside her for what seemed like forever. This wasn't an emotional connection. She refused to let it be. But she knew Trevor, had known him a long time. And maybe that was what was making this so much . . . easier.

At least tonight. And tonight was all she needed from him. Just tonight.

When he swooped her up into his arms and carried her toward her wing, she refused to feel . . . swept away, refused to let the romanticism of the gesture sway her. Instead, she focused on his strength, imagining all that power moving over her, visualizing how it would feel when he was inside her. She knew he would get her there, and she needed it in a hurry.

So when he stopped at her bedroom, she knew she was ready for him. He pushed open her door and stood her next to the bed, immediately taking her mouth in a kiss that was demanding in its urgency. She met him more than halfway, curling her fingers around the nape of his neck to hold him there, as if she were afraid that this was all a dream, and she'd suddenly wake up to find she was imagining it all.

But then he wrapped an arm around her waist and tugged her closer, and he groaned as their bodies met. She realized this was all oh, so deliciously real and she needed it to happen right now.

She was in a hurry, and when she slid her hand between them to cup his erection, she heard his gruff response, reveled in it, and skimmed her hand inside his shorts and underwear to grasp hold of his more than sizable shaft.

He helped her by jerking his shorts and underwear to the ground, stepping out of them, giving her the freedom to wrap her hand fully around the thickness of him, to gaze unabashedly down at his cock.

"Uh, wow, Trevor," she said.

He grinned. Such a male. So proud of what he had.

He had a right to be. She couldn't wait to feel him inside her, bringing her the release she craved.

He leaned against her, giving her free rein to stroke and pet him while he kissed the side of her neck and teased her earlobe with his tongue. And when he pulled the strap of her dress down and kissed that spot between her neck and shoulder, she shivered, so sensitive there that goose bumps broke out on her skin.

He read her body's responses well, because he lingered there, laving his tongue over that spot, drawing her skin into his mouth, teasing her with his teeth until she tilted her head back, moment-arily distracted by what he was doing.

Which gave him the opening to draw the other strap of her dress down, pulling the material over her breasts. He had her bra unhooked and had that removed too before she even noticed what he was doing.

It was like she was in a dreamlike state, as if this weren't really happening.

But it was, and when he turned her to face him and he said, "Look at you, Haven. So sexy. So beautiful," she found it kind of hard to believe those words were being said by Trevor.

But the way he looked at her, the way he skimmed his thumbs over her nipples and cupped her breasts, made her gasp. He made her feel beautiful and wanted. And God, she really needed that tonight.

She really needed him tonight. No one else but him.

He pushed her dress off and it pooled into a puddle at her feet. She stepped out of it, leaving her wearing only her pink string-bikini underwear. She took a step back from him so she could pull them off.

"No," he said, and closed the distance between them. "Let me do that."

"You know I don't need romance."

He quirked a brow at her, then smiled. "Every woman needs romance. Or at least a little seduction."

"I don't. I just need sex." She wasn't sure if she was trying to convince him, or herself. She just wanted a damn orgasm, while trying to keep her emotions closed off.

He let out a soft laugh. "We're definitely going to have sex. But how about you let me work out my seduction moves on you first?"

"Why? Are you out of practice?"

He quirked a smile at her. "Maybe. You let me know how I do, okay?"

She was about to object, to let him know it was okay if they just fucked, but the look he gave her was so sincere, she couldn't help but be moved.

"Okay."

"Good. You seemed like you were in a hurry. Sex should never be hurried."

"Sometimes a quickie is good."

He came toward her, and she couldn't help but lick her lips in anticipation. He had a body that any woman would want. Tall, broad shoulders, wide chest, lean hips, and a cock just meant to give hours of pleasure, provided a man knew what to do with it.

She hoped he knew what to do with it.

"Yeah, a quickie can be good. But not the first time, Haven." He bent and grasped the strings of her underwear, slowly dragging them over her hips and down her legs. She held her breath as she watched, especially when he lingered there, breathing her in. Then he stood, wrapped his arms around her, and lifted her, depositing her on her bed, following her down. He loomed over her, laying his palm flat on her rib cage. "The first time a couple has sex, it should last for hours. There's exploration to be done."

Oh, God. Maybe this hadn't been such a good idea.

FOURTEEN

A QUICKIE? WHAT THE HELL. NO WAY WAS TREVOR giving Haven a quick fuck. Not the first time.

He had no idea what was going on in her head, but when she'd first suggested sex in the restaurant, the idea of banging her in the car in the parking lot had rushed into his head, so yeah, maybe a quickie had been on his mind. At least initially.

But this was Haven, and she deserved better, especially since having sex with her had been on his mind a lot.

The thought of fucking her all night long? Now that was more to his liking. Especially now that he had her naked and stretched out in her bed. She smelled good, her body was smoking hot and curved in all the right places, and his cock was rock hard and ready to give her anything she asked for.

Right now, though, it was time to explore. He rested his head in one of his hands, and used the other hand to roam across her rib cage, heading north to start, over her lush, perfect breasts. Her nipples puckered right away, tightening to dark, upturned peaks as he rolled his palms over them. His gaze drifted to her face. She was watching him. He smiled at her.

"It's okay for you to tell me what you like."

"I like your hands on me."

"Do you like a soft touch, like this?" He rolled his thumb over her nipples, achingly slow and easy. Her breasts rose and fell with her hard breaths.

"Yes."

"Or maybe something with a little more . . . intensity—like this." He caught a nipple between his fingers and pulled, then added some pressure.

"Oh, shit. Oh, yes. I like that, too."

Her bold response made his balls quiver. He leaned over her and caught a nipple between his lips and sucked, rewarded with her gasp, then a very loud moan when he drew her nipple harder into his mouth, increasing the suction. When she held on to his head, arching her back and demanding more, he discovered exactly what Haven liked, so he gave the other nipple the same treatment.

He loved a woman who was vocal, who told him what worked for her and what didn't. A silent woman was very rarely satisfied, because men weren't psychic.

He was looking forward to this exploration, because every sound she made, every "harder," "oh, yes, there," and "oh, my God, yes" was driving him to the brink and making his dick swell with anticipation.

He hoped he'd be able to give Haven exactly what she wanted tonight. He wanted nothing more than to please her.

Haven rocked her hips in time to Trevor sucking her nipples. Her clit tingled, her sex damp with need. And when he pulled away and took her mouth in a kiss that rocked her senses, he moved his hand over her stomach and lower, cupping her sex.

He lifted his head. "You're wet. Are you ready for me?"

"Yes," she said in a breathless voice.

He kept his gaze on her as he dipped his fingers lower, teasing her clit. "I'm going to make you come so many times tonight, Haven, that you're going to beg me to stop."

She swallowed, her throat already dry. "Try me."

His lips curved in a sexy, arrogant, I'm-a-confident-man-and-I'm-about-to-rock-your-fucking-world smile.

She didn't mind that at all. In fact, she found it incredibly arousing at the moment. And when he dipped two fingers inside her and began to pump, at the same time moving the heel of his hand against the most sensitive spot on her, she arched, helping him find the rhythm.

He was so damn cooperative it almost drove her crazy. "There?" he asked.

"Yes."

He didn't need a lot of coaching, either. He was gentle when he needed to be, and then instinctively seemed to know when she needed more pressure, taking her right to the edge in record time. It helped that she trusted him, that this was a man she'd known for so long. He wasn't new.

But he was, wasn't he? They'd been cordial acquaintances before. Verbal sparring partners at best. Tonight, he was going to become her lover, something she'd fantasized about a lot, wondering what it would be like to have Trevor's hands roaming her body, to feel their mouths connect, his tongue tangling with hers. It had been heady fantasies she'd feverishly masturbated to when she'd been in college.

The reality of it was so much better.

Surprisingly, there was no awkwardness between them. They'd gotten naked, he'd taken control, and now she hung on a rack of delicious tension, so close to coming she could fly right now. But she loved Trevor's mastery of her body, the utter bliss she felt as he had his way with her. She wanted a few more seconds of this feeling of absolute euphoria before she let go.

And when she did, she told him.

"Trevor, you're going to make me come so hard."

"Let go for me, Haven. Let me feel it. I want to feel your pussy squeezing my fingers."

She breathed deeply, prolonging the sweet agony for a few more seconds as pleasure tightened within her, then released in waves of undulating pleasure, gripping his wrist as she writhed against him, crying out because it had been so damn long since she'd been with someone who'd made her feel this good.

Her orgasm ripped through every fiber of her. And Trevor held her even while she bucked against him, her nails digging into his arms. It was like an out-of-body experience, like she was flying and she never wanted it to stop.

It took a while for her to settle. When she did, Trevor was right there, watching her, smiling at her, his desire not waned in the least. In fact, the passionate fury in his eyes was even deeper than it had been before.

One orgasm, she'd thought. All she thought she'd needed was one. But it turned out, just seeing the need in his eyes refueled her own. And when he pulled his fingers from her and licked them, her lips parted in surprise, her body clenching in anxious desire.

She sat up and wrapped her hand around the nape of his neck, drawing his mouth to hers for a hot, lengthy kiss that nearly swamped her senses. Trevor's answering groan and the way he swept her away with his hands and his mouth made her realize she'd have to steel her defenses.

Staying emotionally distant from him was going to be difficult. He had a way of taking her under, of making her want him beyond just the physical. He was caring and generous, and as he spread her legs and shifted down to put his mouth on her sex, she threw her hands over her eyes, trying to shut out everything but the way his mouth felt on her pussy, and the way he took her right to the edge again with his lips, his teeth, and his tongue, owning her body instantly in a way no man ever had.

He was relentless in his pursuit of her pleasure, consuming her. She was drowning in every flick of his tongue, every suck of his lips over her clit.

And as she came again, this time crying out in surprise because it happened so damn fast, she grabbed hold of his hair, almost angry with him because he'd possessed her so thoroughly.

She hadn't expected to feel this overwhelmed. She both loved and hated it and didn't know what to do with all these damn feelings.

He came up and kissed her again, and she tasted herself on his lips. And this time, she couldn't fight the emotional response, the hiccup of tears that she pushed back when he wrapped his arms around her and groaned. Because she realized he needed her tonight as much as she needed him.

No. Not emotional. This was just physical. Just a pure, delightful, physical response to two people who enjoyed being together.

And that was how she was going to rationalize getting through this night. Because otherwise she'd never make it. Not with Trevor.

"You okay so far?" he asked, kissing the side of her neck, making those damn goose bumps skitter across her skin again.

She wanted to think she was done with him, that she was satiated and she'd go through the motions to get him off. But she wasn't. His cock lay hard and heavy against her thigh, and all she could think about was getting him inside her, of coming again. And again.

Taking the risk, she met his gaze, losing herself in the green depths of his eyes. "More than okay. I need you inside me."

"I'll be right back."

He was gone only a few seconds. She waited for clarity, for some kind of reasonable logic to enter her head.

She found none, only a ridiculous feeling of loss now that he was gone. She shook it off when he returned with a box of condoms and a silly, boyish look on his face.

"Not sure how many of these we'd need tonight."

She leaned back and spread her legs. "Maybe the whole damn box. Let's get started."

FIFTEEN

TREVOR HAD NEVER BEEN WITH A WOMAN AS RESPON-
sive as Haven. Her taste, her scent, the way she moved and unrav-
eled for him, was unlike anything he'd ever experienced.

The women he'd been with before were practiced. Almost too
damn perfect. It wasn't something he could put a finger on, but it
was like they were trying to meet *his* expectations.

Where was the fun in that?

Haven reached for her own pleasure, and God, he couldn't get
enough of it—of her.

And now she'd opened the box of condoms and held one between
her fingers as she scooted up on the bed and spread her legs. An
invitation. She looked beautiful sitting there, expecting him, waiting for him. He wasn't about to ignore her summons. He was hard,
aching, his balls heavy with come.

He climbed onto the bed and took the packet from her hand.
He applied the condom, acutely aware of the way she watched his

every movement. He kneeled between her legs and slid his fingers into her hair, capturing her lips for a kiss. She grasped his arms and held him there, and when he slid his tongue in her mouth, she sucked.

His balls tightened, his cock lurching toward her like some kind of goddamned divining rod. It knew where it was supposed to be. Her room was thick with the smell of sex—a sweet, musky perfume that made him eager to bury himself inside her and see if she was as sweet and as hot as he'd been imagining.

He moved back and grasped her ankles, then pulled her down the bed, cupping her ankles, sliding his hands over the softness of her flesh as he mapped his fingers over her legs.

And still, she watched him. He didn't mind, loved looking at the darkening color of her eyes, seeing the deepening passion there. He swept his hand over her sex. She was wet, quivering, ready for him.

Yeah, he was ready, too.

He placed the tip of his cock at the entrance to her pussy, eased the first inch in, watching her as he lifted one of her legs and bent her knee to widen her for his entry.

Her breathing quickened as he pushed in. She was slick, her pussy hot as he slid home.

"Yes, Trevor," she whispered, then wrapped her legs around him and brought him all the way in.

He looked at her, the rapture on her face, and then stilled to experience the way she surrounded him. Tight, hot, squeezing his cock and pulsing around him. He had to take a few seconds to breathe in and out, to center himself, because all he wanted to do was let go, to release everything he'd held inside for the past few hours.

But then she reached for his face, tracing her fingertips over the scar above his right eyebrow. It seemed so incongruous to the heat and sexuality that beat between them. He calmed, took a deep breath, and moved within her.

"Damn, Trevor, you're big," she said.

Not the first time he'd heard that. He held his torso off her with the palms of his hands and looked down at her. "Do you need me to stop?"

"No. Don't stop. If you stop I swear to God I'll kill you."

He smiled at her. "Okay, then. You let me know what works for you."

"No problem there. You fucking me is working for me right now. Just keep doing what you're doing."

Again, she gave commands, and he was happy to comply. "I like being inside you, Haven. I like it a lot." He cupped her butt and lifted her hips, then drove in deeper. She gasped, and raked her nails along his forearms.

"Yeah, I like that, too. Do it again."

He did, sliding in, then pulling out, only to ease back in, this time with a little more force. And when he did, he ground against her, making sure to give her clit plenty of attention.

Haven arched her back and widened her legs. "Oh, yes. Like that. A lot more like that. It feels so good."

He loved the sound of her voice when she was lost in the throes of passion. She dropped an octave and added some gravel to her voice. And since she'd tilted her head back, she gave him an opportunity to lick her neck.

"Oh, my God, Trevor. You keep doing that while you're fucking me, you're going to make me come again." This time, her voice begged, and he knew it wasn't a complaint.

"I like the way you taste, Haven," he whispered against her neck. "All over. I like your skin, the way you breathe, and I especially like the way you move when I'm inside you. You make me want to come hard."

She lifted her head and met his gaze, her eyes glazed with passion. "Yes. I want that. I need you to come. I need you to feel what I've felt. It's so good."

And then there were no words because he was lost in her depths, and now it was his turn to do nothing but feel. He knew he could get her there, but as he powered into her with a thrust, she tightened around him and, oh, man, the sounds of her moans and whimpers as she came just wrecked him. That was the end for him, because all he wanted was to let go.

When he released, it was like he'd been catapulted from his own skin. He grabbed hold of Haven and thrust deeply into her when he came. She wrapped her arms and legs around him as he shuddered through an epic climax that left him sweating and shaking, glad he had Haven to hold on to as a lifeline.

His breaths sawed in and out. He took a few more, catching his breath, swiping his hands over her face. She looked up at him, her eyes clear as she smiled at him. He bent and brushed his lips over hers, getting lost in the way she tasted, rolling over and bringing her with him, liking that they were still so intimately connected.

He wasn't sure he wanted to let her go. But he did, pulling her out of the bed with him so they could go into her bathroom and clean up a bit. He glanced at her in the mirror. She looked tired, so he climbed into bed with her and she laid her head on his shoulder. She closed her eyes and she was out within minutes.

He lay there listening to her breathe, enjoying the feel of her body snuggled up next to his.

Eventually, he closed his eyes and drifted off.

SIXTEEN

HAVEN WALKED THE STERILE WHITE CORRIDORS, knowing what waited for her in that room. She dreaded it, but knew she had to go there, to be with her dad.

He needed her, and she'd endure anything just to be there for him. There wasn't much time left.

She took a deep, stabilizing breath and entered the room.

It was empty. She looked all around, but she couldn't find him. "Dad?" She called out, but he didn't answer.

She hurried out of the room, running as fast as she could, but it was like running in mud. Her legs weren't working right.

"Dad? Where are you? I can't find you."

Haven.

She heard his voice calling her name and ran to the sound. But still, she could barely move, let alone run.

Haven.

His voice grew more faint. She struggled, forcing her legs and feet to push harder. This was so damn frustrating. She had to get to him before it was too late.

"I'm coming, Dad. I'm trying to find you. Where are you?"

She felt the wetness of tears roll down her face, knew she wasn't going to reach him in time.

Suddenly, there he was, at the end of the hall. So close, and yet an ocean's distance away, because as she looked at him, so frail, so thin as he reached his arms out for her, she could already see he was disappearing.

"No, Dad, no. Please don't go."

She let out a gasping sob, trying to reach him as he held his arms out.

Haven. I have to go.

"Daddy, no. Please don't leave me."

But it was too late. He was gone.

She dropped to the ground and released the wall of tears.

"Haven. Haven, wake up."

She shot up in bed, still crying, and turned her face into Trevor's shoulder, wrapping her arms around someone solid, someone real.

"Shh, it's okay, honey."

She couldn't even form words right then because the dream had been so vivid to her, the ache of losing her father all over again hurting so badly it made her throat close up, made her heart hurt.

Trevor didn't even ask, just stroked her back and murmured words of comfort as he held tight to her until she cried out the anguish of loss. When the gasping sobs subsided and she had nothing left, he reached over on the nightstand and handed her a box of tissues. She blew her nose and dried her eyes.

And then he held her, not speaking until her breathing returned to normal.

She couldn't talk about it. She hoped to God he wouldn't ask.

Trevor pulled back, his face etched with concern. "I'm going to get you a drink. I'll be right back. Are you going to be okay?"

She nodded.

He slid out of bed and left the bedroom, giving her a few minutes to dash into the bathroom. She flipped on the light, splashed water on her face, blew her nose a few more times, then finally looked up.

God, she looked like she'd been on an all-night bender. Her eyes were tear-stained and swollen, her nose all red, and she looked—awful. How embarrassing to have that nightmare after she and Trevor had just had a fun night together.

She should have known better than to get involved with someone. She just wasn't ready yet. She'd opened up the emotional floodgates and look what happened.

She went back into the bedroom and threw on a pair of sweats and a tank top, then crawled on top of the covers.

Trevor came back in, still gloriously, beautifully naked. For a second, she thought about changing her mind, but refused to waver. She was making the right choice.

The only choice.

"Here, drink this."

"Thanks." She was ridiculously dehydrated after all that crying, so she took a few deep swallows, then set the glass aside. "I'm fine now. And actually really wiped."

He started to climb into bed with her, but she stood. "I think I'd sleep better alone."

He arched a brow. "I thought maybe you'd want to talk about your nightmare."

She let out a short laugh. "That's the last thing I want to talk about. I'd rather forget it, and get some sleep. And you probably should, too. Like, in your own bed."

He didn't move, just sat on the edge of the bed. "What's wrong, Haven?"

"Nothing's wrong. I just need to be alone."

"Something about that dream freaked you out. You should talk about it."

"I don't want to talk about it. I just want to go back to sleep. And honestly, I'm not much for bedmates. Don't take it personally."

"So, you're kicking me out."

"Um . . . yes. Sorry. But it's not you, it's me. Really. I just know I won't get any sleep tonight with you here. It's just a weird quirk of mine. I hope you understand."

Her excuse sounded incredibly lame, even to her own ears.

"Not a problem." He grabbed his clothes and got dressed, then came to her, sliding his hands up and down her arms, generating heat despite her discomfort.

"Are you sure you're going to be okay?"

"I'm fine. Thanks for the water and for . . . you know—being there. It was just a silly nightmare. Zombies or something. I don't even remember most of it now. Honestly." She finished it off with a shrug.

He didn't look like he believed her. "If you're sure."

"Absolutely."

"Okay. I'll see you in the morning."

She was already walking him to her bedroom door. "Okay."

As soon as he left her room, she shut the door and leaned against it, tears pricking her eyes again.

Why did she throw him out? Why couldn't she let him stay and offer her comfort? And why wouldn't she tell him about her dream about her dad?

Because that would have required her to open up emotionally, and she needed to maintain her distance. She'd already made a mistake by having sex with him, and she couldn't afford to get any closer to him.

It was better this way. She pulled off her clothes and climbed back into bed, which now seemed colder, bigger, and emptier without

Trevor's body to warm her, and memories of her father still lingered after her dream.

She was lonely, which was her doing. It was for the best, right?

She knew she'd never go back to sleep the rest of the night.

TREVOR SAT IN HIS ROOM, STARING OUT THE WINDOW. Part of him wanted to go back over to Haven's wing, knock on her door, and make her talk to him about that nightmare.

She'd been upset. More upset than just a run-of-the-mill bad dream. It had to be something deeper, but hell, she'd asked him to leave. What the hell was he supposed to do? Force her to let him stay? He had to go, had to give her the space she'd asked for.

Though he didn't think being alone and upset like that was what she'd really wanted.

He dragged his fingers through his hair and paced his room, wide awake now and knowing he wasn't going to be able to go back to sleep. He grabbed the remote and turned on the TV, clicking through until he found the sports channel. He settled back on the bed and tried to concentrate on the rehash of yesterday's baseball games, but he couldn't concentrate.

His thoughts kept coming back to Haven, on how she'd been crying out in her sleep, how he'd had to wake her and how she'd thrown herself against him, sobbing.

His gut tightened as he remembered how it felt to feel her body wrapped against his while she cried. He'd wanted to offer her comfort, but instead, all she'd wanted was to be left alone.

That wasn't right. No one should be alone when they were hurting like that.

He shouldn't have left her.

Dammit. He didn't know what to do about her—for her.

But he was determined to figure her out.

SEVENTEEN

HAVEN DOVE INTO WORK THE NEXT DAY, DETERMINED to focus on her job and the arriving camera crew and forget all about the bad dream she'd had the night before, as well as the fact that she'd had sex with Trevor.

If she could concentrate on work and nothing but that, she'd be fine.

She staved off the exhaustion from lack of sleep by drinking several cups of coffee and eating the awesome breakfast Hammond had provided. She'd also avoided Trevor by asking the crew to pick her up at the house early that morning so they could go over the battle plan for the interviews and camera shots at the ballpark for the game tonight against Los Angeles. She'd left Trevor a text message telling him she'd meet him at the ballpark later that day.

They were nearing the end of the regular season. The Rivers were doing okay, but still three games out of first place, and the teams in the other division were breathing down their necks trying to get the wild card spot. It wasn't going to be easy for them to make the playoffs. In fact, unless they won every one of their last seven games, it was going to be damned near impossible.

She was going to make that the thrust of her on-camera interview today with Trevor, so they'd have a sound bite to send in for tonight's sportscast as part of a teaser for her upcoming feature, one of the things she'd discussed with her producer. Even though her assignment wasn't going to be completed for a while, her producer wanted to lay the groundwork, to get the audience invested in advance.

No pressure or anything, right?

She went through her notes and she and the crew went over camera angles and where they planned to set up prior to the game. Trevor agreed to meet with her early, before warm-ups, at the field. They'd made arrangements with team management, as well as with a few of the players, so they'd be able to conduct on-camera interviews today.

Her plate was full—exactly what she needed. No time to think about anything personal, which suited her just fine.

Because professionally, things were going smoothly. It was the personal side she'd royally screwed up by sleeping with Trevor last night.

That wouldn't happen again.

When Trevor arrived, he came up to her, his expression filled with concern.

Which was the last thing she needed.

"How are you?" he asked, smoothing his hand up and down her arm.

It was just that kind of gentle care she didn't need. She took a step back, giving him a bright, very professional, not at all personal kind of smile. "I'm doing great today. How are you?"

She could tell he knew something was off, but at least he seemed good-natured about it. "Good. Did you manage any sleep last night?"

Aware of the camera crew lurking nearby, she gave a short nod. "Slept like the dead. I realize you're going to need to get to warm-ups and I have several of your teammates to interview as well today, so let's get your mic on so we can get this interview rolling."

He gave her a sideways look, but then he nodded. "You're the boss."

Grateful he didn't press her any further about last night, she put his mic on, then sat next to him and started the interview. She started with innocuous questions about the current season, including what he thought the Rivers' chances were to make the post-season. Trevor, as always, was filled with confidence about the team's chances and said they'd play as hard as they always had, but it was always a game-by-game situation.

Typical player response, but he gave a great interview and she was grateful for that.

Then she got into some of the background questions she'd asked during the preliminary interviews, about his childhood and the sports he'd played, mainly a reiteration of what they'd already gone over, but this time, on camera. It went well, and it went quickly, so they finished on time.

"Thanks," she said when they were done. "That's all we'll do today. We'll get some shots of you playing tonight's game, and we'll use that as promo for the piece."

"So what are you on to next?" he asked, handing over the mic equipment to one of the crew members.

"I've arranged to interview a few of your teammates. And your coach has agreed to give me a few minutes."

Trevor arched a brow. "You're getting camera time with Manny? How'd you manage that?"

"I asked. I'm very nice, you know."

"Yeah, I know." He started toward her again, but she took a step back.

"We really should get going. There isn't much time and I have a lot to do."

He seemed disappointed. "Good luck with your interviews."

"Thanks. Good luck with the game tonight."

She was being cool and remote and she knew it, but she had to maintain a level of professionalism around the crew. And to protect herself.

She was being ridiculous. But she couldn't help herself. This was who she had to be, how she had to act. She was making the right decision.

Right?

The other interviews went well. She talked with Gavin and Garrett, and they gave great commentary about the team, and Trevor's place in it. They weren't bitter about him only playing part time and both stated he was a valuable asset to the team. They understood when he had to drop out to handle football duties, and they were used to it. The team accommodated him because he was good at what he did, and he didn't act like he was any better than the rest of them.

Actually, none of the guys she interviewed professed any jealousy or bitterness toward Trevor. They teased him on camera about being a hotshot, but, as Gavin said, if you had the skills to back it up, then you should do what makes you happy.

They were good interviews. Maybe her producers wanted some professional jealousy on some of the players' parts, or someone calling out Trevor for being a dick, but clearly that wasn't going to happen. At least not with any of the players she'd talked to so far.

And then she got to his coach. Manny Magee was known to be grouchy, and he hated giving interviews. She was actually surprised he'd agreed to this one, so when he sat down with her, she knew she'd have a limited amount of on-camera time with him.

"Tell me about Trevor Shay."

Manny shrugged. "Good player. Shows up on time, does his job."

"How do you feel about him playing two sports?"

"I hate it."

She knew she'd get blunt honesty from Manny. "So you'd like to have him full time."

"Of course I would. But I'm not gonna get him to play for the Rivers full time. So I'll take what I can get."

"He's that good?"

"He's that good. With someone as talented as Trevor Shay, what coach wouldn't? I'm just glad he's playing for our team and not someone else's, you know what I mean?"

Haven didn't comment, but yes, she did know. They talked about tonight's game and the Rivers' chances to make the playoffs, which they'd use for tonight's clip. Haven thanked Manny for his time, and they finished up.

The camera crew took some shots of the players warming up, including a few close-ups of Trevor fielding the ball and throwing it back. And when he took some swings in the batting cage, Haven stood there with the crew and watched. She couldn't help but be impressed. He was tall, athletic, a strong presence as he knocked the ball with power. And as his muscles flexed, she remembered him moving over her last night, the pure mastery he had over her body.

It was cool outside today, but her body heated as she recalled every moment they'd spent together, the way he had taken her with his mouth, his hands, and his cock.

No. That was definitely not going to happen again, and thinking about him in that way wasn't helping the situation at all.

"I think we have enough shots," she said to her camera guy.

Once the game started, the camera crew worked independently to take some game shots of Trevor, while she did some edits on her laptop up in the club suite. She'd look up on occasion to watch the game. The Rivers were down by three runs in the fifth when Trevor came up to bat.

He took the first pitch, high, barely even moving. He read pitches well. The second was low and in the dirt and Trevor didn't budge, refusing to be fooled into swinging.

He'd been out on a fly ball his first at bat, and had gotten on base with a single in his second, only to be left stranded.

On the third pitch—a decent one—he swung, blasting it foul into right field.

On the fourth pitch, he connected, sending it sailing.

Home run. Too bad no one else was on base because he'd rocketed that pitch into the bleachers. Haven swore she could see the grin on Trevor's face all the way up in the club suites where she was sitting. She cheered along with everyone else, and hoped her camera crew had gotten a decent shot of that home run. She texted down to Andy, her head camera guy, who texted her back that he'd definitely gotten the shot.

Awesome.

Unfortunately, Trevor's solo home run didn't help the Rivers, who ended up losing the game. They'd come back and scored three more runs in the sixth, but Los Angeles had scored two in the eighth, closing the door on the Rivers' attempt to win it, and since Atlanta had won their game tonight, it was looking more and more like the Rivers were not going to make it to the postseason.

But it wasn't over yet, and anything could happen.

She was disappointed for Trevor and for the team, but she still had her job to do.

She met with her camera crew after the game, and they submitted their work to the network in time for the broadcast that night. The crew was finished with the work they'd do for now, and they'd meet up again once Trevor started up in Tampa.

After the game, Trevor was quiet. She stepped up next to him as he walked to the car.

"Tough loss," she said.

"Yeah."

"Great home run, though."

"Thanks. Didn't help the team, though."

She wanted to console him, to put her arm around him and make him feel better, like he'd done for her last night. Her fingers itched to touch him.

Why couldn't she bridge that gap of inches and just lean into him to offer him comfort? What would it cost her to do that?

Nothing.

So why couldn't she make the move? What held her back? Did she think if she touched him, he'd read something into it and want more? More than she was willing to give?

In the end, she couldn't do it, just walked to the car and climbed into her seat, keeping her distance, which felt all kinds of shitty.

"There's still hope for the team, Trevor," she said as they drove back to his house.

"Yeah, there is. Until the last game. Unfortunately, we have a road trip to Atlanta up next, and if we lose even one game to them, we're out of the postseason."

"When does the road series against Atlanta start?"

"Friday."

"Then you'll have to kick ass against Los Angeles and make these games count."

"We'll do that. Believe me, we will."

She did believe him. She was impressed by how fast he shook off the loss, because they went out to eat, and he was his happy, animated self again, signing autographs for fans and joking with the waiter. After dinner, they went back to his house, where she was once again faced with being alone with him.

Maybe it was time she moved into a hotel, to give herself some distance. Instead, when they got inside, she turned to him.

"I have a lot of editing to do. If you don't mind, I'm going to close myself up in the office and work."

"That's fine. I'm going to go watch TV."

He seemed okay with her decision, which relieved her. "Great."

She grabbed her laptop and notes and headed into the office, closing the door behind her. She dove into work, going over her notes, uploading the photos she'd taken, and after several hours, she had made serious progress. She sent the file off to her producer.

She got up and stretched, gathered up her laptop and notes, and turned off the light in the office. She was about to head to bed, but decided to stop in the kitchen for a glass of water first.

It was late, so she didn't expect to find Trevor in there, fixing himself a sandwich.

"Oh. Hey. You're still up?"

He smiled at her. "Yeah. I was watching a movie and I got hungry after." He pointed to the sandwich on his plate. "Want one?"

"No, thanks. I was just going to grab a glass of water before I headed to bed."

"I'll get that for you." He dropped ice into a glass and filled it with water, then handed it to her.

"Thanks. Good night, Trevor." She turned.

"Haven?"

She stopped, her eyes closing for a fraction of a second before turning back to face him. "Yes?"

"What's wrong? Did I do something to upset you?"

Laying her stuff down on the counter, along with the glass, she went over to him, knowing she shouldn't get so close, but unable to help herself. She laid her hand on his forearm, feeling the instant connection, that sizzle of chemistry she couldn't deny, no matter how much she wanted to. "No. Not at all. I'm just . . . tired tonight.

It's been a long day, and I didn't get a lot of sleep last night. I just want to go to bed and crash."

He swept her hair away from her face, and before she could take a cautionary step away, he cupped her face between his hands and brushed his lips across hers. A burst of heat ignited inside her.

"Sleep well tonight. No bad dreams."

With that short kiss he'd awakened all the longing she'd tried to push away, but couldn't. She wanted to linger, to lean against him and soak up his strength. She wanted to get him naked and devour every inch of him right there in his kitchen, then take him to bed with her again so she didn't have to be alone. Instead, she nodded. "Right. No bad dreams. Thanks, Trevor."

She grabbed her stuff and walked down the long hallway toward her wing, feeling the loneliness of another long night wrap around her like a cold chill she wouldn't be able to shake.

It didn't have to be this way, but she had no one to blame but herself for being alone.

When she got to her room, she undressed and got ready for bed, then climbed in, pulling the sheet over herself. She'd already finished work for the day, so there was no appeal to her laptop, though she could surf the net.

She didn't want to, so she decided to read a book instead, settling back against the pillows, hoping getting lost in one of her favorite series would help her unwind and maybe she'd get tired.

An hour later she was still wide awake, and she kept reading the same page over and over again. Not the book's fault, because it was a great romance. The problem was, the characters in the story were hot for each other—and they were actually doing something about it. They were communicating, and having awesome hot sex.

She, on the other hand, kept doing her best to avoid her own feelings, and as a result, she was not having awesome hot sex with a man she should be having awesome hot sex with.

Even fictional characters faced their demons better than she did.

She glared at the book, right now hating those characters, and threw off the covers and got out of bed. She went to the window and stared outside, wishing she were at home.

She missed her mom.

She really missed her dad, missed their long talks. She could use a long talk with him right now.

Not that she could have had a conversation with her dad about Trevor. She and her father could talk about anything—except men and sex. Those conversations had always been reserved for her mom. Sports and television and books and anything else? Her dad. But whenever she'd had boy trouble, he'd grown decidedly uncomfortable and had suggested she talk to her mom.

She looked over at the bedside table. It was late—too late to call her mom, and really, what would she say? That she and Trevor had had sex, and then she'd pushed him away because—well, she didn't even have a valid reason.

That wasn't even the kind of conversation one had with her mother. It was a girlfriend kind of talk. Maybe she could discuss it when she went out with Alicia and Liz later this week. She definitely needed some advice.

Or maybe she should just go with how she felt. And right now she felt alone, and lonely, and felt like spending time with Trevor.

Who'd likely think she was out of her ever-loving mind if she searched him out in the middle of the night after basically ignoring the hell out of him, but she couldn't seem to help herself. She was an indecisive idiot. And maybe he'd tell her to get lost, but that was the risk she was willing to take.

Determined to finally get the hell over herself, she put on a pair of shorts and opened her door.

And nearly jumped out of her skin, because Trevor was right there, his hand raised as if he were about to knock.

EIGHTEEN

TREVOR WAS SHOCKED THAT HAVEN ANSWERED THE door before he even knocked.

He was kind of surprised that he'd made his way over to her wing, and hadn't exactly prepared what he was going to say to her once he got here, but now she'd opened the door, so he'd better start talking.

"Hey," was all that fell out of his mouth. Not exactly earth-shattering or comforting, but it was all he had.

"What are you doing here? Never mind. Come in."

Okay, that went well. At least she hadn't slammed the door in his face.

"I thought you might be sleeping," he said.

"I wasn't. Actually, I was about to come to your room to see if you were still awake. Or, I guess I was going to wake you up if you were asleep." She looked as uncomfortable and awkward as he felt, shifting from foot to foot and looking around the room. "I don't really know what I was going to do once I got to your room. You kind of saved me from having to figure that part out."

He relaxed a little when he realized she was nervous. "Figure what part out?"

"Um, how about we sit down?" She motioned to the two chairs over by the window.

"Sure."

He took a seat, and so did she, then laced her fingers together, still looking as nervous as if she'd been called to the principal's office.

He'd bet Haven had never once been called to the principal's office in all the years she'd gone to school.

He had. Plenty of times.

She didn't say anything, so he guessed it was up to him to say something. "I came to your room to talk to you."

She looked up at him. "Oh. You did? About?"

"About you avoiding me."

She looked down at her hands again. "Yeah, that." And then she lifted her gaze to his. "That's part of the reason I was on my way to talk to you. I'm sorry. The other night when we . . . when we had sex, and I had that nightmare, I backed away."

"I know. What was the nightmare really about?"

She took a deep breath. "It was about my dad. He was in the hospital, and I couldn't get to him. It's a variation on a theme. I've had dreams similar to that one before since he died."

"I'm sorry."

She rubbed her finger across her forehead. "I'm just having a hard time dealing with it. I really miss him."

"I know you do."

"Too much, maybe."

"No such thing as too much, Haven. Maybe the problem is

you've been suppressing your emotions and you haven't let yourself feel the full extent of your grief."

She tilted her head to the side, giving him a look of disbelief. "Oh, believe me, Trevor. I've grieved for my dad."

"Have you? Or did you think you were supposed to just get over it in a week or two and get back to work?"

He saw the truth in her eyes. "What was I supposed to do? I had a job in Dallas back then. I couldn't just take a sabbatical so I could stay home with my mom."

"But you wanted to, didn't you? You felt responsible for her because she's all alone now."

"Yes."

"She's not your responsibility to look after, Haven. She's a grown woman, and if anyone knows how independent Ginger Briscoe is, it's me. It's time you focus on your own needs."

"I'm fine, Trevor. Really."

He stood, took her hand, and pulled her out of her chair, then over to his, setting her on his lap. "You're not fine. You have nightmares. How often?"

He thought for a second there she was going to bolt. Instead, she stayed. "A few a month."

"Always about your dad?"

"Not always."

He swept his thumb across her cheek. "It's no wonder you're such a mess, Haven. You miss your dad. You're not sleeping well. And you never allowed yourself the time to grieve over him."

She let out a sigh. "You know what? You're right. I do miss him. A lot. He was more than just my dad. He was my best friend."

He saw the tears shimmer in her eyes, saw how much she tried to battle them back.

"Just let it go."

"It makes me feel weak. It's been almost a year. I've already cried bucketsful. How much more is there? Shouldn't this . . ." She made a fist and clutched it to her chest. "Shouldn't this pain go away?"

"I don't know. Eventually, it will. But you have to feel however you feel. Trying not to feel is what's hurting you the most."

"Maybe."

"Think of it as honoring your dad whenever you cry for him. You know you'll always miss him, and sometimes you just need to go with your feelings."

Haven felt such a well of emotion at the moment. Not just for her dad, but for Trevor. Most men walled up their emotion, and definitely didn't understand, or even want to be around weepy women. She knew plenty of guys who'd just tell her to suck it up and get over it. But here Trevor was, holding her on his lap and rubbing her back while she tried like hell to hold back the floodgates. And he encouraged her to release it.

She shuddered in a breath, finally tired of the fight. She let the tears fall and lay on his chest, releasing what she felt was a year's full of pain. She clutched his shirt and cried. Not as long as she did the other night after her nightmare, but for about five minutes she had a good, hard cry. And all the while, Trevor stroked her hair and her back and didn't say a word. It was comforting to know he was there for her, and for those few minutes, she wasn't alone.

That was the first time in all these months since she'd lost her dad that she didn't feel alone in this. She pulled back, using his shirt to wipe her eyes.

"I made a mess of you," she said.

"That's what I'm here for."

She splayed her hands across his chest. "You should take off your shirt."

"Why? Do you need to blow your nose in it?"

She laughed. It felt really good to laugh, to release the tension after an emotional cry. "Maybe."

And when Trevor pulled off his shirt and handed it to her, she was way more interested in his naked chest than she was in his shirt. It felt cathartic, that she could move on from grieving to something infinitely more appealing. She tossed the shirt on the floor and snaked her fingers over the warmth of his bare skin. "I might need a little more comforting."

"Is that right?"

"Yes." She moved over him, straddling his lap now. "A different kind of comforting."

Trevor grasped her hips, his fingers digging into her flesh, causing an uproar in her nerve endings.

"Well, you know I'm here for you, Haven. Whatever you need."

She pulled off her tank top, baring her breasts. "Anything?"

His eyes gleamed hot and dark as his gaze zeroed in on her quickly tightening nipples. "Anything. Do you need me to make you feel good?"

"Oh, yes."

He cupped her breasts, using his thumbs to draw lazy circles over her nipples. She grabbed his shoulders and held on while he pulled her forward, drawing one taut peak between his lips. She gasped as he sucked and rolled his tongue over the bud until she felt it between her legs, her sex throbbing with need. And when he released, he pleasured the other nipple as well, making her moan with delight.

Haven threaded her fingers in Trevor's hair and pulled his head forward, needing his mouth on hers. He wound his hand around the nape of her neck, instantly making that connection the moment their lips touched, holding her there while he explored her mouth with a deep, soul-searching kiss that fueled her fire to scorching levels. Every part of her felt him, tasted him, breathed him in as he took command with that kiss, sliding his tongue over hers, nipping at her lips, his hand cupping her butt to anchor her as he stood, carrying her to the bed.

He sat her down on the edge of the bed, then pulled off her shorts and underwear, his hands taking a slow, leisurely cruise along her legs before parting her thighs. He nestled down between them and put his mouth on her sex.

Sensation exploded as his mouth found her clit, his tongue slipping along her folds, taking her right to the very height of pleasure as he relentlessly pursued every inch of her pussy. She threw her arms over her head, abandoning herself to the extremes of indulgence, letting herself get carried away by Trevor's mastery of her body.

She needed this rush of bliss, this total recklessness of heady pleasure, her mind emptied of heavy thoughts, her body tuned in to Trevor's tongue and mouth. She delighted in every stroke of his tongue, her hips rising toward him with every suck of his mouth around her clit.

She was going to come. Everything tightened within her as he flicked his tongue over the tight, pulsing knot, the current center of her universe. And when he grabbed the hood of her clit and sucked, she climaxed, holding his head there while she undulated against his expert mouth, wave after wave of orgasm making her gasp until she felt like her breath had been stolen from her.

Shattered, she finally rested her hips against the mattress, catching her breath from that phenomenal orgasm. She lifted her head to see Trevor drop his shorts and climb onto the bed next to her.

"I didn't bring condoms with me. I had no intention of coming here to have sex with you tonight."

She rolled over onto her side, her fingers playing with his very fine chest. "It wasn't my intention, either. But I don't want you to leave and go get them."

She moved her hand upward, over his jaw, then leaned in to brush her lips against his. His mouth was wet—from her—taking her right to the edge of desire once again.

She pushed him onto his back and climbed on top of him, deepening the kiss, tangling her fingers in his hair, tugging just a little as she felt the edge of need take over.

Too bad about that lack-of-condom thing, because right now she'd like nothing more than to slide his hard cock inside her.

But she could do something to take the edge off—at least for him—just as he'd done for her.

She kissed her way along his jaw, his neck, flicking her tongue along the column of his ear before snaking her tongue down the very muscular line from his neck to his shoulder, using both her hands and her mouth to map his body.

And what a body he had. She used her own to slide down over his magnificent chest and rock-hard abs, stopping to tease her tongue over his nipples, causing him to suck in a hard breath, his cock lurching between them. He obviously liked that, which made her smile.

And when it was her turn to spread his legs, when she reached his cock and cradled the shaft between her hands, he propped his head between his hands and looked down at her, giving her one very hot, one very primal male smile.

But she was the one who held all the power at the moment, a very heady feeling, especially when she flicked her tongue across the wide, soft head of his cock and saw the way his lips parted, heard his raspy breathing. She knew she had him when she got up on all fours and turned sideways so Trevor could watch her take his cock between her parted lips and slide her mouth down over it, inch by slow inch.

* * *

"FUCK," HE WHISPERED. "OH, FUCK YES, JUST LIKE that, Haven."

Trevor swallowed, but there was nothing to lubricate his throat. He'd gone sand dry watching Haven take his cock in between her beautiful lips. He gripped the sheets and held on when his shaft disappeared and she seemed to swallow him whole. Watching it and feeling it was like nothing short of a mixture of pure heaven and utter sweet hell, because he could erupt. Right now, right this instant, with Haven's hot mouth surrounding his dick, squeezing him as she tightened her hold on him, her tongue flicking around him as she lifted off him, his cock wet from her mouth, then went down on him again.

Sweat broke out on his brow when she cradled his balls in her hand, giving them a light squeeze while at the same time rolling her tongue around the crest. He'd never wanted anything more than to shoot his load right into her sweet mouth, and never wanted to hold on more so he could watch his cock disappear once more between her full lips, to feel the incredible pressure of her clamping down around his shaft and squeezing while she tightened her grip around the base and pumped his cock into her mouth.

Christ, she was beautiful when she sucked him, occasionally gazing up at him, letting him know she had him, that she was with him, that she was going to give him exactly what he needed.

He reached out to sweep his hand over her soft hair. "Haven. You're going to make me come, honey. Like right now."

It was all the warning he could give her, because he began to pump with her, to lift his hips and drive his cock deeper into the recesses of her mouth. She stayed with him, continuing to grip his shaft and force it deeper into her mouth.

He felt the stirrings of orgasm rise up from the base of his balls.

He arched, let out a harsh groan, and erupted, his gaze glued to Haven's sweet mouth as he jettisoned what felt like gallons of come into her mouth. It was the sweetest climax ever as he watched her throat work while she swallowed everything he had to give, until he was spent, emptied, his legs shaking from the force of his orgasm. She licked the head of his cock, taking every drop he had.

It was a damn good thing he was lying on the bed, because she'd zapped his energy. He wasn't sure his legs would even work. She moved up beside him and he wrapped an arm around her to pull her close, then tipped her lips to his to kiss her.

"Thank you," he said.

"Mmm, you're most welcome. Just returning the favor."

He held her there next to him for a few minutes, then said, "So, not kicking me out this time?"

She tilted her head back and gave him a sleepy smile. "No. Not this time. I'd like you to stay."

He pulled the covers up over them both. "I'm not going anywhere. But, Haven?"

"Yes?"

"We need to get a box of condoms for your room." Because he would have liked to be inside her tonight. Not that he was complaining about the way she'd pleasured him. Damn, she'd been sweet. She had a perfect mouth.

She let out a short laugh. "Yes. Box of condoms. We'll take care of that tomorrow."

He liked the sound of that. He settled in against the pillows and closed his eyes.

NINETEEN

HAVEN WAS ALL ALONE IN TREVOR'S HOUSE SINCE HE was traveling to Atlanta today.

She'd stayed behind to finish up her work here with the camera crew. And tonight she was going out with Alicia and Liz and some of the other Riley women, so she told Trevor she'd meet him in Atlanta tomorrow. It wasn't like she'd be missing anything today anyway, since it was only a travel day for the team.

But she did miss Trevor. They hadn't spent much time together the past couple of days. He'd had back-to-back games finishing up the series with Los Angeles, where they'd won the last two games, giving them hope facing Atlanta, which was a make-or-break series for them. Though they hadn't had much alone time, and she'd had late nights getting her edits finished so she could send her work to the studio, she'd gotten some great interview stuff with Trevor on camera.

Now she had a chance to relax, to chill out with the girls tonight before heading out to Atlanta tomorrow. She was actually looking forward to it after several days of hard work.

She took a shower and chose a skirt and a black-and-white button-down sweater over a tank, then slid into her wedged heels. She did her hair and makeup and headed downstairs, just in time for the doorbell to ring.

Alicia was at the door, looking gorgeous in jeans, black boots, and a leather jacket.

"You look stunning," Haven said. "Maybe I should change clothes."

Alicia laughed. "Are you kidding? You look fabulous. Let's go."

She climbed into the backseat of the car. Liz was in front, applying lipstick.

"Hey," Liz said from behind the wheel. "You ready for this night?"

"Absolutely. How about you?"

"You have no idea. The baby was a terror for the past few days. She had shots."

"Aww, the poor thing."

"I know. My mother-in-law is keeping her tonight and will love on her and not mind at all that she's a screaming banshee. Me? I need a freaking break, especially with Gavin being out of town the next few days on a road trip."

"You know what I love about you, Liz?" Alicia asked as they pulled through the gate and onto the street.

"What's that?"

"That you're not one of those, 'Oooh, my baby is the most perfect thing I've ever created, sleeps all through the night and never cries' type of moms."

Liz snorted. "Girl, please. That baby has a set of lungs on her.

She poops. She vomits. She doesn't sleep. Sometimes I think she's possessed. It's a good thing Gavin and I love her to pieces. Otherwise she'd end up in a basket on someone's doorstep."

Haven laughed. "She sounds like a normal baby to me."

"Oh, she totally is," Liz said, pulling onto the highway. "But she's hardly the type of baby you see on television. No one tells you about all the screaming. And the throw-up."

"I consider myself warned," Alicia said. "How about you, Haven?"

"Totally." Though Haven doubted she'd have to worry about having a baby anytime soon.

But the thought entered her head. She was approaching thirty, and hadn't had a serious enough relationship—talking marriage and having children—in her entire life. Maybe it was time she started getting that kind of serious with someone, consider settling down and having some babies.

Then again, this wasn't really the right time. She was embarking on the career she'd always wanted. She wasn't in a committed relationship. Hell, she wasn't even dating anyone. She was having sex with Trevor, and even though he'd played a part in her dreams and fantasies for so many years, he was hardly the guy she was going to marry and have children with.

He was way too busy with his career as well, and, like her, he hadn't ever had that kind of a relationship, either.

Besides, she wasn't ready yet. She was totally a career woman now. Life in the big city, traveling all over the country.

This was her dream, and she was living her dream.

Right?

They started out at Kemoll's downtown, a place Liz assured her was one of the best Italian restaurants in the city.

It sounded fabulous to Haven. One, because she was starving, and two, because she loved Italian food.

Once inside, where Liz had made a reservation, they were met by Jenna, Gavin's sister, and Tara, Liz's sister-in-law. Tara was married to Gavin's brother, Mick, who was currently playing football for San Francisco. Jenna's husband, Tyler, played hockey for the St. Louis Ice.

"Savannah can't make it tonight. She's out of town working a consulting gig for some big-shot Hollywood star," Liz explained as they got to their seats. "Savannah is married to Alicia's brother, Cole, who plays for the Traders."

Haven blinked. "You all make my head spin. And I'm sorry I won't get to meet Savannah tonight."

"Some other time," Jenna said with a grin. "I think there are enough of us here that we'll make a party of it."

"Who's minding your club tonight, Jenna?" Alicia asked.

"My assistant manager. She's doing a great job, so I can take a few days off now and then." Jenna turned to Haven. "I have a music club that I started up last year. It's doing pretty well."

"I heard about it," Haven said. "It sounds amazing. And congratulations."

"Thanks. It's been fun. It hardly seems like work when there's music involved."

"Jenna sings beautifully," Liz said. "I keep pushing her to record her music and go for a record deal. She's resisting me."

Jenna waved her hand. "I'm happy where I am, staying an amateur."

"Now I'm really curious," Haven said. "I'm going to have to stop at your club and hear you sing."

"You're welcome anytime."

Their waitress came by and took drink orders.

"Just sparkling water for me," Liz said. "I'm the designated driver tonight."

They decided on a bottle of cabernet to share and a couple of appetizers as well.

"I hear you're profiling Trevor Shay," Tara said. "That must be interesting. I know Mick has talked about playing against him in football. He's quite the athlete."

"He's definitely interesting. We've captured a lot of him on film and I haven't run out of interview questions for him yet."

"Haven's actually known him for a lot of years. They went to the same college, and her parents were his dorm parents," Alicia said.

"Oh, really?" Jenna said. "So you're friends with him. That probably helps."

"It has."

Their waitress brought the wine and poured for everyone. It was incredible, and Haven felt immediately more relaxed after a few sips.

"Or are you and Trevor more than friends yet?" Liz asked with a waggle of her brow.

"Oh, is there something going on between the two of you?" Tara asked.

"Liz," Alicia said. "You're such a busybody."

"That's me, honey. Always up in everyone's business. But that night we were all together at your place, Alicia, I definitely saw some sparks when Trevor and Haven looked at each other. I'm just doing follow-up."

"I have . . . no comment," Haven said, returning Liz's smile over the rim of her wineglass.

"I think that means yes," Jenna said.

Haven should have been uncomfortable with the line of questioning. But actually, she enjoyed it, liked the ease and camaraderie with these women. They weren't mean-spirited, they were fun and genuinely curious. And God, she liked having women friends to talk to.

They ordered dinner, and she loved that everyone selected something different. She was going to enjoy seeing their food.

"Mick's got three road games in a row," Tara said as she took a bite of her salad. "Which means I'm going to have to rely on Mom to help me with Sam. Thank God I have her. If we hadn't made the move to come back here, I don't know what I would have done. I have to deal with my business, which is picking up a lot, and I love having the little guy, but now that Nathan is off at college, I'm kind of on my own when Mick is out of town."

Tara shifted to look at Haven. "Nathan is my other son. I had him when I was very young, well before I met Mick. So yes, I have one kid in college, plus a toddler. I know, it sounds insane."

Haven grinned. "It sounds like a beautiful family. You're very lucky."

"Thanks. I feel that way. Crazy sometimes, but still, so happy." Tara turned back to Liz. "Anyway, I'm kind of on my own when Mick is out of town."

"I know what you mean," Liz said. "Since Genevieve arrived, it's been great, but I'm still on maternity leave. As soon as I go back to work—which will be all too soon for my liking—I'm going to have to give serious thought to hiring a nanny." She finished that off by scrunching her nose.

"You know Gavin's mom will be happy to help out," Tara said. "She's offered to babysit."

"I know she has, but she's already watching Sam, and I don't want to burden her with an infant. Besides, Genevieve is a handful. To burden her with an infant when she's already watching a toddler? I don't know."

"Uncle Jimmy can deal with Sam while Aunt Kathleen takes care of the baby," Alicia said. "I think they could do it."

"They could, and they wouldn't balk. I'll have to talk to Gavin about it. Plus, he'll be available to watch the baby once baseball season is over with, but that's only a few months."

"And babies need consistency," Jenna said. Then she shrugged. "Or at least that's what I've heard. Since I'm not a mom, I'm just offering useless advice."

Tara laughed. "Your advice is never useless. Everyone's welcome to weigh in."

Jenna waved her hands. "No, thanks. I have enough issues just trying to decide what kind of vodka to order for my bar. I'll leave the baby stuff for you and Liz to deal with."

"Well, now that you and Tyler have been married almost a year, when will—"

"Not yet," Jenna said, cutting Tara off midsentence. "We're not ready for babies yet. I want a couple of years with just him and me together as a married couple before we start popping out babies."

"Fine." Tara affected a pout. "I'll ask again this time next year."

Jenna laughed. "You do that."

"See how much fun this is, Haven?" Liz said. "We used to talk about men and sex. Now it's babies."

"We still talk about men and sex. We just haven't finished the wine yet, and Liz isn't drinking because she's driving—and breast-feeding."

Liz frowned at Alicia. "So you're saying I'm the drunken insti-gator of all the men-and-sex conversations?"

"Typically, yes." Tara gave her a direct look.

"I'll have you know I don't need to be drunk to talk about sex. As a matter of fact, Gavin and I just recently jumped back on the sex train, postbaby. And it was about damn time."

Haven was very much enjoying this conversation. She could understand why they were all so close.

"Really," Tara said. "And how did that go?"

"I was a little leery at first. I mean, after you poke a seven-pound infant out of your vagina, things are a little tender down there at first. When I first had Genevieve I told Gavin his cock was never coming near me again."

Tara laughed. "I remember having a similar conversation with Mick after Sam was born."

"This isn't making me want to have children anytime soon," Jenna said with a grimace at Haven and Alicia.

"Or, quite possibly, ever," Haven added.

Alicia clinked her glass with Haven's. "Seriously."

"Oh, but it gets better," Liz said. "Everything healed up and I got horny again."

"Of course you did," Alicia said with an added eye roll.

"And let me tell you, the first time having sex when you haven't had sex for about eight weeks?" Liz waggled her brows. "It was like a fireworks show. I can't tell you how many orgasms I had."

Alicia leaned over toward Haven. "You'll get used to Liz. She's very descriptive about her sex life."

"And she forces us all to talk about ours," Jenna added.

Liz snorted. "Oh, right. I force you. You love talking about all that hot sex you and your hockey stud have."

Jenna studied her fingernails. "It's not my fault. You bring out the worst in me."

Haven laughed. She had no idea she was going to have so much fun listening to women talk about sex and babies.

They ate, and drank more wine. Every course was amazing. Haven had the veal, which was tender and delicious. By the time she finished eating, she was full and desperately needed to get up and walk around a bit. She was thankful their next trip was to a club Liz had picked out for them, and even more grateful when Liz said she planned for them to dance their asses off tonight, because she needed to burn some calories.

They'd spent several hours drinking wine and talking about their careers, their men, and life in general.

"Don't think we didn't notice you didn't get put on the hot seat yet, Haven," Liz said as they settled in at their table in the VIP section of the club. "Just because we're all used to talking nonstop doesn't mean we aren't going to grill you about your relationship with Trevor."

She'd just received another glass of wine from their waitress at the club, and they were far enough away from the music and the dance floor that they could hold a conversation.

"I'm sure I have no idea what you mean. I don't have a relationship with Trevor."

"You two were eyeing each other that night like two kids about to devour their favorite candy," Alicia said.

"He is pretty delicious candy," Tara said with a gleam in her eye. "So what's going on? *Is* there something going on?"

All sets of eyes focused squarely on her. And Haven wasn't sure she was ready to talk about her and Trevor just yet. Or even if there was anything to talk about.

"Honestly? I don't know."

"Honey, you're either in his pants or you aren't," Jenna said with a wry grin. "Have you seen the goods?"

Haven laughed and set her wineglass down. "I didn't know we were being that direct."

"Have you even been listening to our conversations?" Liz asked. "Of course we're that direct. We talk cock around here, Haven. And we want all the intimate details."

"You really don't have to divulge any information if you don't want to," Alicia said.

"Yes, she does. We all have to," Jenna said. "It would be totally unfair if Haven was allowed—I don't remember what you call it— oh yeah. Privacy." Jenna stuck her tongue out at Liz.

Liz laughed. "Oh, come on. It's more fun when we all share."

"I think my husband begs to differ," Tara said. "Mick says you all know way too much about our sex life and his cock."

Haven laughed out loud at that one. "I think I'll definitely keep my mouth shut, then. I don't think we want Trevor's cock the topic of discussion tonight."

"So you have seen it, then," Jenna said, a smug smile on her face. "Do tell."

Haven blushed crimson, and despite the wicked cold air-conditioning in the club, she felt hot all over.

"I don't think you need to say a word, Haven. From your pink cheeks, you're busted." Tara shook her head. "It's obvious you and Trevor have torn up the sheets."

She laid her face in her hands. "I swore I wasn't going to say a word."

"And you didn't, so don't worry. All the sex talk on ladies' night out is secretly held among us all," Alicia said. "It's our code of honor."

"True." Liz stood. "And why are we talking about sex when we could be out on the dance floor?"

Jenna gaped at her. "Because *you* brought it up?"

"Did not. Now get your asses up and let's shake them like crazy and make all the guys here jealous."

Haven followed the rest of them onto the dance floor. The music was loud, the place was crowded as hell, but Liz made people get out of their way and they formed a circle. Haven lost herself in the driving beat and they stayed out there for about four songs until her throat was parched and she had worked up a sweat. She and Jenna went and grabbed a seat, then signaled the waitress for two sparkling waters.

"Hey, don't feel pressured about Trevor," Jenna said after they downed a few sips of water.

Haven frowned. "In what way?"

"Oh, you know. We like to have fun, but you don't have to answer all our pushy questions about him. Just tell everyone to fuck off and mind their own business."

Haven laughed. "I don't mind, really. There's not much going on anyway. We're working together and trying to figure out what else there is. I don't think there's anything. Maybe just sex."

"Good sex, I hope."

Haven couldn't help but smile. "That part needs no figuring out."

"Then let the rest of it play out and see what happens. Don't expend a lot of energy trying to examine it a hundred different ways."

Haven shrugged. "I'm not. I'm just going with it. I spent way too much time backing away from it. Now I'm plunging into the deep end and seeing where it goes. Even if it's just for the duration of the time we have together, I'm all in."

"Good for you. Life is short, honey. Live it fully and without regrets."

No one knew that better than Haven.

They went back out on the dance floor, and despite some very intent looks from several incredibly good-looking guys, they were mostly left alone, which suited Haven just fine. It was obvious the women were out for girls'-night-only fun, and wow, did Haven have fun. She never got tipsy because she danced her ass off most of the night, sweating out any alcohol she consumed.

These women could party. She'd never laughed—or danced—so much. By the time Liz dropped her off a little after one in the morning, she was exhilarated, and more than a bit exhausted.

She went to her room and got ready for bed, then grabbed her phone to check messages.

There was one from Trevor. He'd texted her several hours earlier.

Hope you're having a good time tonight. Thinking about you.

Her heart squeezed. It was way too late to send him a return message, but she couldn't resist.

Had a great time. Just got home. Sleep well tonight. Thought about you a lot, too.

Her finger hovered on the send button. She shouldn't, but she did, then set the phone on her nightstand.

She was surprised when she got a return text.

You were out late.

She smiled and returned the text. *These women party hard.*

She hit send.

A few seconds later, her phone rang, startling her.

"Hey," Trevor said when she picked up.

"Hi." She couldn't believe the thrill she felt hearing his voice. She wasn't a teenager anymore, and hadn't been one for a long time. But still, she fully admitted she was deep in lust with this man. "You're up late."

"The phone woke me."

"Sorry," she said. "I knew I shouldn't have sent that text."

"It's okay. I'm glad you sent it."

"Don't you have a roommate when you're on the road?"

"I'm out in the hall."

She laughed. "Better not get in trouble for breaking curfew."

"I don't think loitering in the hall is considered breaking curfew. You tucked in safe in bed now?"

"Yes."

"I can't wait to see you tomorrow."

She took a deep breath. "Me, too. Too bad I can't be your roommate."

"Yeah. Too bad about that. Also too bad I have a roommate tonight, or we could have some serious phone sex."

"Trevor." Her body swelled with instant need.

"Something to think about for the next time we're alone."

"You're good at tormenting me."

"Call it foreplay."

"Uh-huh."

"Hey, you can always get yourself off and tell me about it later."

"I could, couldn't I? After all, I don't have a roommate."

His voice lowered. "And now my dick is hard."

She slid down under the covers. "And I'm wet, thinking about you being hard."

"What are you going to do about it?" he asked.

"I don't know." She petted her pussy, wishing he were there to take care of things.

"Make yourself come, Haven. Let me hear it."

She sucked in a breath. "And then what will you do?"

"Then after we hang up I'll sneak into the bathroom and jack off. Really quietly."

Just the thought of him doing that was enough to ratchet up her desire to unbearable levels.

"Hang on a second." She pulled off the covers, and shimmied out of her underwear. "Okay."

"Are you naked?"

"From the waist down. How about you?"

He laughed. "Uh, no. But I'm hard. Really hard, and picturing you on your bed. Spread your legs for me, Haven."

She really wished she could see him. That he could see her. But that would be unwise, especially with him loitering in the hallway. With an erection. She spread her legs, her hand immediately drifting toward her pussy, gliding over her flesh. "I'm touching myself. I wish it was you touching me."

"I wish I could put my hands on you right now. Or my mouth. I want to make you come."

And he could do it so easily, too. She closed her eyes and imagined him between her legs, his fingers and mouth doing delicious things to her. Instead, she used her own fingers, brushing over her clit. She knew her own body, knew what it took to bring herself to a lightning-fast orgasm.

"Haven, I hear your breathing. Do you know what that does to me?"

"Yes. I do."

"Tell me what you're doing."

"I'm rubbing my clit. Slow to start, then giving it a little pressure. Going a little faster now. God, Trevor, just hearing your voice—I need to come so badly."

"Put your fingers inside your pussy for me. Don't come just yet." She dipped a finger inside. "I'm so wet. I want your cock in me."

Now it was Trevor's breath she heard. "I want that, too. Soon, babe. Fuck yourself for me."

She did, her breath catching as she imagined Trevor's thick cock sliding in and out of her. "Trevor. This is so good. Fuck me, Trevor."

"Christ, Haven. My cock is so hard. Do you know how much I want to be there? How much I want to lick and suck your pussy and make you come? Take your fingers out and lick them. Taste yourself for me."

She shuddered at the hushed tone in his voice, knowing what it cost him to be out there in the hall, hard and aching. She removed her fingers, sucked her juices off each one, let him hear her until she heard him groan.

"It tastes like pussy, Trevor. Like my pussy. Why aren't you here to make me come?"

"I wish I was. Now you have to do it. Make yourself come. Let me hear it."

She was so ready, so far gone, she plunged her fingers back into her pussy and lifted her hips, grinding the heel of her hand against her sex. "I'm going to come for you. Are you ready?"

"Fuck, yes. Do it."

She felt her pussy squeeze tight around her fingers as the first stirrings of orgasm wrapped around her, chilling her skin, blinding her to everything but the bolts of intense pleasure lighting her up.

"I'm coming, Trevor. I'm coming." She let out a harsh cry as her climax blasted through her. She heard every one of Trevor's coaxing words as she rocked through her orgasm, shuddering until she fell to the mattress, spent and perspiring.

"That, Haven, was incredible."

She smiled. "Thanks for the coaching."

"And now if I don't get into my room and jack off, I'm going to burst out here in the hall."

"Think of me when your hand is wrapped around your cock, okay?"

"Honey, you're all I'm going to think about. And I'll probably bite my tongue clean off trying not to shout when I shoot my load."

She grinned. "Good. But don't bite your tongue. I'll see you tomorrow, Trevor."

"'Night, Haven."

She hung up, and spent the next few minutes just lying there, imagining Trevor stroking his cock and getting off while thinking about her. They were some very fun, very hot thoughts.

She finally got up, cleaned up, then climbed back into bed, a lot more relaxed and ready to go to sleep.

She couldn't wait until tomorrow.

TWENTY

TREVOR—HELL, THE ENTIRE TEAM—HAD NEVER PLAYED three worse games.

The three games they needed to be at their very best, and they'd sucked. They couldn't manufacture runs when they needed them the most, they'd made stupid mental errors on defense that had cost them runs, and they'd lost close games they shouldn't have lost.

They won only one game in Atlanta, and that one by only one run, which meant they'd been eliminated from postseason play. And they had no one to blame but themselves.

Trevor's own production had been shit. It was like his bat had taken a vacation. He'd left runners on base, couldn't get on base when it had been most critical, and he'd struck out with the fucking bases loaded.

God, he'd been terrible. Hell, the whole goddamned team had played badly.

He'd never felt shittier, even though Manny had given them a pep talk after tonight's game in Atlanta, telling them sometimes tough losses came at the worst possible time, and this year, the worst possible time had come now, at the end of the season when they'd needed to win.

Trevor had planned to play in the postseason, had already made plans to talk to Tampa about delaying his start with them.

Now, his baseball season was over, and he wasn't sure he was prepared to deal with that.

Even worse, Haven hovered in the locker room with her camera crew. And while he was happy to see her, the last goddamned thing he wanted right now was another fucking camera stuck in his face.

He saw the sympathy on her face, and he knew she wanted to hug him, but she had her job to do, just like he'd had his to do.

Though he'd royally blown his.

And still, she hovered, as if this were the last place she wanted to be right now, too. Well, he wasn't going to invite her over to talk to him. He wasn't feeling particularly generous at the moment. She was going to have to either grow some balls, stick the camera in his face, and do her job, or hide in the corner all night long. Either way, in about five minutes he was headed to the shower, and her opportunity to do the interview would be lost.

He unlaced his shoes and bent over, but couldn't resist taking a peek at her from the corner of his eye.

She was still there, avoiding everyone.

Sink or swim, sweetheart. Come on, Haven, where's your courage?

Finally, she pushed off the wall and came toward him, the cameraman directly behind her.

"Trevor."

He lifted his gaze to hers. "Yeah."

"I'm sorry about the loss, and I can't even imagine how shitty you must feel right now, but I'd like to get a few minutes of you on camera."

"Sure."

With an audible sigh, she motioned to the cameraman, who started filming. Haven sat next to him.

"This was the last game of the season for you and for the Rivers tonight, Trevor. How do you feel about the loss?"

"How do I feel? Right now I feel like—" He was about to say *shit*, but he knew that wouldn't fly. "I feel bad. I feel bad for the team. Like I let them down."

"It wasn't just you out there playing, though. Why do you feel personally responsible?"

"I didn't do my part. I played like shit." She could edit that out later. Or maybe she wouldn't. At this point he didn't care.

"You take the game seriously."

He shot her a look. "Hell, yes, I do. This is my career. I love this game. Every guy on the team does. We hate losing, especially when getting into the postseason was within our grasp."

"There were some tough calls out there, and every game was close."

"And we made a lot of mistakes. I made a lot of mistakes. I struck out with the bases loaded. That right there was the potential to turn that game around."

"So you take personal responsibility for losing tonight's game."

"I do." He looked around. "Talk to any guy on the team tonight and every one of them will say the same thing." He paused to take a breath. "Look, I know I tout myself as some kind of superstar. That I play two sports and I like to think I do both of them well. But at the end of the day, we're a team. We win as a team and we lose as a team. And right now we the team think this sucks. And we're going to continue to think it sucks until the start of next season, when we get together again, bound and determined to take the team all the way to the postseason again."

She didn't say anything else, so he stood. "I'm going to hit the showers."

HAVEN FELT AWFUL FOR TREVOR—FOR THE ENTIRE Rivers team. It had been a grueling series with Atlanta. Both teams played tough. Both had exhilarating highs and both made mistakes. It could have gone either way. Unfortunately, this year it had gone Atlanta's way, and they would be heading to the postseason, while the Rivers players would be going home.

The first thing she'd wanted to do in the locker room was put her arms around Trevor, tell him she knew how it felt, and commiserate with him. But with her camera guy in tow, she had to keep her professional face on and grill him about the game, about how it felt to be on the losing end this year.

She'd hated every minute of it, but it was her job and she'd had no choice. She told her camera guy to send her the film and she'd edit it later, then she waited outside for Trevor.

It was a while before he came out—before they all came out. Alicia and Liz were waiting out there with her. Liz had the baby with her, and oh, God, she was so precious, with red hair and the biggest green eyes Haven had ever seen. Liz even let Haven hold her, and Genevieve just looked up at her with those beautiful eyes.

"You don't mind if I kidnap your daughter and take her with me, do you?"

"Not at all. But I will kill you," Liz said. "And so will Gavin, who's going to be in a bad mood for a month at least after that loss."

"No, he won't," Alicia said. "Because you have Genevieve to take his mind off losing the postseason."

Liz smiled. "That's very true. I'll remind him he has more time with his daughter now."

"She's an incredible consolation prize," Haven said, handing Genevieve back to Liz.

"Thank you. I'm glad she's with me on this road trip. I hesitated bringing her along, but she really is going to be a great comfort to her daddy right now."

The guys spilled out. It was a quiet group, all of them going to their families for comfort. Garrett slung his arm around Alicia, who gave him a big kiss. Gavin took Genevieve from Liz and cuddled her close, kissing the baby on the top of the head before brushing his lips across Liz's. Trevor finally came out and met Haven.

They visited with everyone for a few minutes, then said their good-byes and headed toward the team bus. Trevor hung outside with her.

"I'm sorry about the interview," she said.

He frowned at her. "Never apologize for doing your job. You did what you had to do."

"You could have refused. But it was an insightful interview into a player's emotions after a particularly tough end-of-season loss. I know it was brutal, but you were very honest and I appreciate you giving me the time."

"You're welcome. And you need to toughen up."

"Excuse me?"

"I thought you were going to hide in the corner of the locker room all night. It was a perfect opportunity to interview some of the players. As well as me."

"You were all down."

"And easy prey for a reporter. A lot of us were vulnerable and ready to spill our guts about how we felt right then. You could have swooped in and gotten some great interviews. You blew it."

She sighed at the realization. "I know. I need to work on that."

"Yeah, you do." He looked toward the door. "I have to go with the team."

"Yes, you do. And I need to catch my flight back to St. Louis. I'll see you back there."

"Okay."

She watched him get on the bus, then got in her rental car and headed for the airport. She worked on the flight, writing some copy from her notes. By the time they landed, she was tired. She took a taxi back to the house.

Trevor wasn't back yet. She knew his flight left after hers, and they probably had some team stuff to deal with, so she didn't expect him back until late. She unpacked and got into bed, turned out the light, and was asleep within minutes.

She woke to the feel of a warm body next to hers, a hard cock brushing up against her butt, and a very large callused hand massaging her breast and teasing her nipple.

She stretched, rubbing her butt up against Trevor's cock, arching against his hand. He pulled the strap of her tank top down, exposing her breast so he could tease and pluck at her nipple.

She was still only half awake, and this was a languorous, decadent interlude. She let Trevor take the lead while she rode along in hazy pleasure.

He seemed in no hurry, playing with her nipples until she writhed against him in desperate need. Only then did he slide his hand inside her panties, cupping her sex. Her clit was tingling, and the touch of his warm hand sent every fiber of her body into overdrive.

He never said a word to her. It was just touching, and the sound of their breath—hers ragged and panting as he took her right to the edge of orgasm. And when she plunged over she gripped his arm, holding him there while she shattered with loud moans. It felt so good to have him make her come, to feel his hands on her body while his was stretched out behind her.

While she recovered from that amazing orgasm, she heard him tear the condom wrapper open and wriggled out of her underwear. He lifted her leg, resting it on top of his, then entered her from behind, capturing her breast once again in his hand as he thrust his cock inside her.

And still, no words had been spoken between them. She didn't need him to say a word, because they were communicating with their bodies, with the way he captured her nipple between his fingers and tugged, sending shocks of pleasure straight to her core while at the same time pulling his cock partway out and then slowly inching his way inside her again.

It was sweet, slow torture. She felt every inch of him as he entered her and withdrew, over and over again. And when she reached down to strum her clit, all she heard was his satisfied "mmm" of approval.

This was just what she'd needed, what she craved the most. Not a fast, frenzied fucking, but this easy lovemaking, the way his hands made a slow map of her body as if he had all night to touch her, to kiss the nape of her neck and take a love bite that sent chills coursing over every inch of her skin. She increased the pressure on her clit and her body responded, tightening around his cock.

In answer, he groaned, gripping her hip and pushing deeper into her. Only now, toward the end, did it become something harder, something more than just two people lazily fucking. Now, they were reaching the end, both of them searching for their climax. And as she bucked back against him and he used his hand to push her forward so he could thrust deeper inside her, she craved it, needed him to thrust, to give her exactly what she needed to come.

And when she did, she tilted her head back, crying out as her climax gripped her in the throes of ecstasy. And as Trevor clasped her tightly to him, his body shuddering with hers, she'd never felt anything like these lightninglike pulses that shocked her with such incredible pleasure.

After, he kissed her shoulder, her back, and they returned to utter laziness. Part of it was the depletion of her energy reserves. The other part was a genuine joy to feel him holding her again. She'd missed him while they were apart. She didn't dare tell him that, though, because it implied she cared about him in ways even she couldn't admit—wouldn't admit.

This was just fun and games. This was just for now.

So she'd leave it at that.

She half turned and wound her arm around his neck, offering up her lips for the kiss she needed. He gave her that and more, cupping her face and kissing her until her world spun.

"Welcome home," she said when he finally pulled back.

"Thanks. I missed you." He withdrew and gave her a playful slap on the butt, then disappeared into the bathroom.

The words spilled from his lips so easily.

Why had they been so hard for her to say?

TWENTY-ONE

HAVEN HADN'T BEEN HOME IN A WHILE. SHE'D LEFT Oklahoma when she'd gotten the job offer from the network, had settled into her apartment in New York, and had stayed there, determined to make it work.

She'd almost quit, had almost packed up her things several times, determined to find a job back home. It had been her mother who'd forced her to stay in New York, had told her she should at least try before she gave it up.

And then the assignment to do Trevor's feature story had come up.

Now, she still wasn't certain this was the job she wanted to do for the rest of her life, but at least she was working.

"Excited to see home again?" Trevor asked as they pulled off the turnpike.

"Yes." She was looking forward to seeing her mom. And dreading the visit home at the same time. For so many reasons, including reliving her father's last days. She couldn't help but feel the shroud of overwhelming sadness wash over her, remembering the last time she was here. She'd left a couple of weeks after her father died. She'd had to go back to Dallas—back to her job. She'd wanted to stay longer, but her mom had insisted she start working again. And then she'd gotten the new job in New York, and it had been a whirlwind of packing and travel, forcing her to put away her grief to deal with later.

Life went on, her mom said. And so did work. Even her mom had returned to work. *It's what we do*, she'd said.

But Haven hadn't felt much like working. All she'd wanted to do was be with her mom and try to make sense of a world without her father in it.

Nothing had made sense back then.

It still didn't. Not without Dad. She still missed his counsel, still couldn't believe she couldn't pick up the phone and send him a text message, or call and talk to him whenever she felt like it.

He'd have been devastated about the Rivers' loss. She'd have commiserated with him. They'd have talked about what went wrong, what the Rivers could have done better, and how they'd come back stronger next season. Her dad would have likely called Trevor as well, would give him a pep talk and tell him how well he'd played this season.

She wondered if Trevor was missing her dad. She wouldn't ask him.

She took a deep breath.

"You okay over there?" Trevor asked.

"I'm fine. Just tired."

"Oh, come on. You can't be tired. Let's get pumped here. I'm looking forward to seeing your mom."

She liked his enthusiasm, but she knew why. "You're looking forward to eating my mom's cooking."

Trevor grinned. "Yeah, there's that, too."

The camera crew was going to meet them down here tomorrow. Today, they'd have a reprieve, and she could focus on seeing her mom.

When they pulled onto the campus and she saw the familiar buildings and the streets where she'd grown up, she felt both a sense of calm and a melancholy she couldn't shake. Everything was the same, and yet it was never going to be the same again.

She used to look forward to coming home, mainly because it was home. Mom and Dad were there, and she'd always felt safe and welcome here. The one thing she could always count on was a sense of family, of routine.

Now? It just felt . . . lonely. She didn't know how her mother dealt with this every day.

But when they pulled into the driveway and she saw her mom come outside, her lips tilted.

Yes, this was still home. Mom was here. As soon as Trevor put the car in park, she unbuckled her seat belt and opened the door. Her mom came down the driveway and Haven threw herself into her mother's waiting arms.

A hug had never felt so good.

"Oh, Haven, I missed you so much."

She might never move from the comforting, welcoming feel of her mom's embrace.

"I've missed you, too."

Her mom took her hands and took a step back. "You look good. But you've lost weight."

"No, I haven't."

"Yes, you have. A mother knows these things."

A mother—her mother—always thought she wasn't eating enough. It was just her way of wanting to feed her constantly. Not that Haven minded that, since she loved home cooking.

As she stepped back, she realized her mother was the one who'd lost weight. But not in a bad way. "You look awesome."

Her mother grinned. "Thanks, honey."

"And you," her mom said, turning her attention to Trevor, who'd been patiently standing by Haven's side. "You come here and give me a giant hug."

Trevor scooped up Haven's mom into a giant bear hug. "Hi, Miss Ginger. It's good to see you."

"Oh, you, too. You look amazing as always."

"So do you," he said after he set her down. "I'll grab our bags while you two go inside."

Haven walked in with her mom. "I made stew. It's a little chilly out here today. It's definitely startin' to feel like fall—finally."

"Stew sounds great, Mom." She set her purse by the front door and followed the incredible smell into the kitchen.

"There's a pitcher of sweet tea on the table."

There always was. The only thing different was her dad's place at the head of the table was now empty. Haven's heart squeezed, but she tamped down that tug of painful emotion and pulled her chair out and took a seat. She poured a glass of tea and took several sips.

Her mom looked good as she bustled around the kitchen. Really good. Other than that, nothing much seemed to have changed. It had been a couple of months since she'd been back home.

She felt guilty about that. She spoke to her mother frequently on the phone, and she'd wanted to get back, but between ending her job in Dallas and starting the new one in New York, she'd been busy.

And maybe avoiding.

"I put your things up in your room, Haven," Trevor said as he made his way into the kitchen.

"Thanks."

"Did you put your stuff in the guest room, Trevor?" Haven's mom asked.

"Yes, ma'am. Thanks for letting me bunk here."

"It's no problem. There's no reason for you to stay at a hotel when we have plenty of room here. Isn't that right, Haven?"

Haven cast a quick glance at Trevor, who slid her a half smile.

"Right, Mom."

"I hope you're both hungry, because supper is ready."

"I'm starving," Trevor said.

"He's been anticipating your cooking the entire trip over here."

Her mom beamed a wide smile. "I'm glad to hear that. Haven, why don't you set the table, and Trevor, you can bring the pot of stew over. I'll get the bread out of the oven."

They dug in, and Trevor filled her mom in on baseball.

"I'm sure sorry to hear about the end of your season, Trevor. I know how hard you all worked. I watched all the games, and you gave it your best shot. There's nothin' more you could have done."

"I know, but it sure feels sh— It sure feels bad to have lost it right there at the end."

"I know it does, honey. And I also know how competitive you are. If Bill were here, he would have been just as disappointed as you are. But he would have been proud of you."

Trevor gave her a gentle smile. "Thank you, Miss Ginger. I appreciate you saying that."

"So now you're off to play football with Tampa?"

"Yes, ma'am. Looking forward to it, too."

"I just don't know how you change gears like that. From baseball to football in an instant."

"It's pretty easy. I've been following the team. They're doing good. They'll do even better once I'm there."

Haven rolled her eyes. Her mother laughed.

"I've always liked your confidence, Trevor. That's why you're so good at what you do."

"And what about you, Miss Ginger? What are you up to these days?"

"Oh, a lot, actually. Since Bill passed away, I'm no longer a dorm parent."

Haven's head shot up. "What? Why not?"

"They need a man and a woman for the position, and without your dad, I could no longer meet the requirements."

Trevor frowned. "So . . . what? They just fired you?"

"Now calm down. They did not just fire me. I've been working part time in admissions, but I've gone back to school to get my teaching credential. I used to teach a long time ago. Maybe you don't remember that, Haven."

Haven's stomach had knotted up with worry. "I remember you telling me that before you and Dad started as dorm parents, you taught high school."

"I did. High school English. It's been a while so I need to brush up, but I've decided I want to teach again."

"Good for you, Miss Ginger," Trevor said. "I think you'd make an excellent teacher. Kids really flock to you, and you have a great understanding of their emotions."

"Thank you, Trevor. I'm excited. For the first time since Bill died, something has lit a fire under me."

Haven had no idea about any of this. She felt so out of touch with her mom and what had been going on. She reached across the table and squeezed her mother's hand. "You're sure this is what you want to do?"

"Yes. I've also renewed my gym membership. I go almost every day with Wanda Dixon and Cathlyn Simms. We started out on the cardio equipment and took up weights. We also take a Zumba class. Now that is fun."

Haven blinked. Her mom at the gym? It was like she didn't even know her anymore. No wonder she looked so different. Her cheeks were rosy and she was smiling a lot.

"That's awesome, Miss Ginger. Exercise is great for you. You must feel really good."

Her mom nodded at Trevor. "I feel amazing. I've lost fifteen pounds, and I've been sleeping better than I have in years."

"That's just . . . great." Haven wanted to be happy for her mom. She really did. But something didn't feel right.

"And then there's this book club I joined as well. We meet once a week on Thursday nights. I'm reading a lot again. It's so refreshing. So eye-opening."

Haven leaned back in her chair, unable to fight the tears.

Her mom frowned. "Haven, what's wrong?"

"Wow. It's a good thing Dad died, so you could have this whole new life, isn't it, Mom?"

"Haven. Honey, it's not like that at all."

"Isn't it? Your life improved after he died, didn't it? Look at all the fun you're having now." She pushed back from the table. "Excuse me. I need some air."

She fled the kitchen and grabbed the car keys Trevor had left on the table by the front door. Without thinking, she got in the car and backed down the driveway, knowing only that she had to get out of there, had to get away from her house and her mother and everything that just wasn't the same anymore.

Not only was Dad not there, leaving a gaping hole in her life, but now her mother was this completely different person.

Did everything have to change? Everyone?

She had to go see her dad and try to make sense of all of this.

TREVOR COULDN'T BELIEVE THE WORDS THAT HAD spilled out of Haven's mouth. She was always so sweet, so sensitive to everyone around her, especially her mother.

But she'd just cut down her mom, and in the cruelest way possible.

"Miss Ginger. I'm sorry. You have to know she didn't mean it."

Tears welled in Ginger's eyes. "Oh, honey. I know she didn't. This past year has been so hard for her. She was so close to Bill and losing him devastated her. God, it devastated me. I could barely function the first couple of months after he was gone. I don't know what I would have done without Haven, without my friends and family. But Haven, she pulled it all inside and wanted me to think she was fine. She felt she had to be the strong one for me when I knew deep down inside she wasn't all right. That's why I called you."

"I'm glad you did. But I thought she was coming out of it, that she was through the worst of it."

Ginger nodded. "I think she wanted to walk into her house and see that nothing had changed. It's bad enough her daddy isn't here anymore. And now everything else is different, including me."

Trevor felt the need to defend Ginger. "You have a right to move on with your life."

"I know that, and you know that. But I don't think she understands just yet that Bill is, was, and always will be the great love of my life. And whether my weight or my occupation changes, how I feel about him never will."

She pushed back from the chair. "I need to go talk to her."

Trevor stood. "I'll go with you."

She laid her hand on his chest. "No, honey. This one I have to do alone. I'll bring her back with me."

Trevor watched Ginger grab her keys and walk out the door, wishing there was something he could do to help.

But Ginger was probably right. This conversation had to be between mother and daughter. And he couldn't intervene.

He'd never felt more helpless.

TWENTY-TWO

HAVEN SAT ON THE CEMENT BENCH THEY'D ERECTED in front of her father's grave, staring at the headstone marked with his name, his dates of birth and death, and the words *Husband, Father, Friend To So Many* etched on his tombstone.

She swiped at the tears, knowing how her dad would tell her not to cry over him.

"I'm sorry, Daddy. I know you'd be mad at me for the things I said to Mom. But it's like she's forgotten you. She's got this whole new life now. It's like she's moved on, and I can't seem to do that. I guess I'm not as strong. I need your help."

She shuddered as she inhaled, wishing like anything she could feel her dad's big strong arms around her right now. Just one more time.

"Remember when we'd sit in the living room and watch football together? Remember the popcorn fights? Mom would get so mad at us about that."

"That's because I'd have to do all the vacuuming, and a week later I'd still find popcorn kernels."

She half turned to find her mother standing just behind her. She came and sat on the bench next to her.

"I'm sorry for what I said to you. It was rude and unforgivable," Haven said.

Her mother put her arm around her. "You have no need to apologize. You were always taught to say what was on your mind."

"Not like that. It was disrespectful. Please forgive me."

"You're forgiven. I know what I'm doing must seem to you like I've moved on from your father, when nothing could be further from the truth, Haven." Her mother stared at the headstone, and Haven saw tears shimmer in her eyes. "God, I loved that man with all my heart and soul. There will never be a love in my life like him. He was the first, the last, and everything to me."

Haven sniffled, and then she realized that her mother had buried the love of her life. It had been utterly and completely cruel of her to throw those words at her mother. Haven had lost her father, but her mother had lost the man she had loved for more than thirty-three years. She took her mother's hand and squeezed it.

"But your father made me promise that I wouldn't stop living, that I'd continue to follow my dreams. And I did promise him that. When the school told me about the dorm parent situation, I figured I'd make good on that promise and go back to school—back to teaching again. I'd gotten a little complacent. And if I sit in that house and wallow about losing your father, I'll lose myself as well, Haven. I can't do that. I have to keep living. Not just for you, but for myself. And for your dad."

Haven nodded. "I know you do."

Her mother turned to her. "And so do you. Your father would be so disappointed in you if you allowed your world to stop because he died."

Haven inhaled on a sob. "I know he would. But I miss him so much."

"We still have each other. For as long as I'm alive, we'll still have each other. But you have to go out and find your life, my sweet baby girl. Promise me you'll do that."

Her mother wrapped her up in her arms. And just like that, she felt the warmth of love surrounding her. It was as if for that moment, she felt her dad's presence there, as well. Maybe it was just her imagination, or wishful thinking, but a sense of well-being enveloped her.

"I will. I promise, Mom. Things will be better now. For both of us."

She looked at her dad's headstone, and for the first time since he died, she was able to think about the future without that future feeling empty.

Okay, Dad. For you. For Mom. It's time for all of us to move on.

TREVOR PUT AWAY THE LEFTOVER STEW AND DID THE dishes, and even made another pitcher of tea, needing to keep his hands and his mind occupied while he waited for Haven and her mom to get back. When he heard the car doors, he wiped his hands on the dish towel and pulled out clean glasses in case they wanted a drink.

Haven was the first to show up in the kitchen.

She arched a brow. "You did dishes?"

"Yeah. Are you still hungry?"

"No, I'm fine."

"How about some tea? I made more of that."

"Aren't you all domestic. I'd love a glass of tea."

He poured her a glass and handed it to her. "Where's your mom?"

"She went upstairs."

"Are you okay? Are the two of you okay?"

"We're good now. Thanks."

He took a seat next to her. "Do you want to talk about it?"

She took a couple of swallows of tea. "Not particularly, other than to apologize to you as well. I wasn't my best today, but things are going to be better now."

She didn't owe him any explanation. That was between her and her mother. "You don't have to apologize to me, Haven. I told you before that you're allowed to feel however you feel."

"Thanks for that. But I was rude, especially to my mom."

"You settled that, though, didn't you?"

"Yes."

"Okay, then. Nothing more to talk about."

She took a deep breath. "I thought we might go for a walk, if that's all right with you."

He nodded. "Sure."

She grabbed her zip-up hoodie and he pulled on his sweatshirt before they stepped outside.

Trevor felt the chill in the air, even through his sweatshirt. It made him think of football. Crave it. He wanted to be in Tampa, with his team. Much as he'd hated losing to Atlanta, to be shut out of postseason baseball, he had to switch his mind-set.

Tampa had already played three games without him. He had to get his ass in gear and his body ready for football. He was already in shape, but football was a different game.

"You're quiet," Haven said.

"Thinking about football."

Her lips curved. "Already making the switch mentally?"

"Yeah."

"And you're ready to play."

He shifted his focus to her. Her eyes were red rimmed and swol-

len. Time to shut off thoughts of himself and his game. "I'm ready
to play. How about you?"

"What about me?"

"How do you feel?"

They'd arrived at a public park just outside campus, so he took
her hand and led her to one of the picnic benches. They sat on top
of the bench.

"I feel fine now. I went to the cemetery. I talked to my mom,
and I know this sounds silly, but I also talked to my dad. Everything feels clearer to me."

"Good."

"I guess I was stuck in the past and I didn't want anything to
change. I didn't want my dad to have died." She looked over at him.
"I've been in denial, refusing to face a life without him."

He swept her hair away from her face. "It's been hard for you."

"Yeah, it has been. And that I can face now. It's been hard. It
probably always will be. I think that's what was so hard about seeing my mom tonight. She was moving forward, and it appeared to
be so easy for her."

"It's not easy for her, Haven. You have to realize that."

"I do now. It was petty and childish of me to say those things to
her, to accuse her of not mourning my father. She loved him. With
everything she had, she loved him every day they were together.
She still does."

He nodded and scooted closer to her. "You both did. He was a
very lucky man to have both of you."

"He had so many people who loved him. You, all the guys."

"Yeah, we did. It was hard losing the postseason and not getting
that phone call from him telling me everything was going to be
okay. I miss him, too."

"I know you do. He left a legacy, Trevor. People will remember him."

Her voice was stronger now, her eyes clearer.

"Of course we will. I couldn't have survived college without him. He was more like a father to me than my father ever was."

"Thanks for that. It means a lot to me to hear it."

"It's the truth."

"I guess it was just hard for me to let go of his memory."

He tilted her face to his. "You never have to do that. Don't even try. You just have to let go of the pain."

She nodded. "You're right." She leaned her head against his shoulder. For a while, they just sat there side by side, his arm around her in the dark. A few students walked by, no doubt heading back and forth to the nearby library, which was open all night.

God, he sure as hell didn't miss college, at least not the academic part. That had been hell for him. He missed playing, though.

Haven shivered next to him.

"Ready to head back? It's getting cold out here," he said.

"Okay."

He slid off the table, then grasped Haven around the waist, pulling her into his arms. She nestled against him, then wrapped her arms around him and laid her head on his chest. She tilted her head back and looked up at him.

"Thanks for being here with me and for not thinking I'm some giant mess of a crazy, raving bitch."

He laughed. "I don't think that about you."

"Oh, please. Even I think that about me."

"Well, you're wrong." He tipped her chin up with his fingers, then brushed his lips across hers. "I think you're honest with your emotions."

"I wasn't. I was running hot and cold, not facing them."

"You're more honest than most women I know, Haven."

"I'm going to try to be more honest in the future. I have to be. Running from how I feel has been tearing me apart."

Now he cupped her face in his hands. "You should never run from how you feel."

She leaned further into him, laying her hands on his chest. "You feel pretty good. And I'm definitely not running now."

He laughed, then tugged her close and kissed her, liking the way she molded her body to his. If they were alone—and they were anything but alone right now—he'd make her feel all kinds of things. Because she sure as hell was making him feel things, especially rubbing her body against his like she was.

"You need to stop," he finally said, leaning his forehead against hers.

Her breath came out in a rush. "I want you. Can we make that happen?"

He looked around. They weren't alone and he didn't think getting arrested for indecent exposure would be a good idea. "Not here. Do you think we could manage quiet sex in the house with your mom around?"

She let out a short laugh. "Probably not, but we can try."

They hurried back to the house. Haven looked at the upstairs window. "Her room is dark. Either she's downstairs waiting up for us, or she's gone to bed already."

They opened the door, and the only light on was a small lamp in the living room.

"She used to leave that lamp on for me when I was out at night. She's gone to bed," Haven said in a whispered voice. "You go ahead and go up to your room. It's the farthest from hers. I'll get ready for bed, then I'll meet you in yours."

He nodded, tiptoeing up the stairs, trying to make as little noise as possible. He went into his room, brushed his teeth, and climbed out of his pants and shirt. Fifteen minutes later, Haven opened the door and gently closed it. She wore very short pajama bottoms and a skimpy tank top.

"She's a pretty heavy sleeper. I think we'll be okay."

She came toward him and climbed on the bed, straddling him. "I need to be with you."

She kept her voice low, and he just knew it was going to be the hardest thing to stay quiet. With her planted squarely on his quickly hardening cock, it took all the restraint he had not to groan. He fit his hands to her hips and took in the sight of her, her cheeks pink from their walk. She'd washed her face, so she wore no makeup. He liked that she came to him that way, that she didn't think it was necessary to be all made up like so many of the women he'd dated. Haven was confident in her looks, in her body, and as he swept his hand over the nape of her neck and pulled her down for a kiss, he tasted the mint of her toothpaste, his tongue sliding alongside hers.

She whimpered, the sound caught on a heaving whisper as he rolled with her, tucking her underneath him so he could stretch his body out, feel her legs against his, her breasts rubbing his chest. She teased her leg alongside his. It was like silk rubbing against him, and made his dick pound.

He lifted his head. "You're making this harder."

She reached between them, cupping his erection. "You mean I'm making this harder."

He sucked in a breath. "Yeah. That. Definitely that."

"I have a tiny little secret to confess," she said.

He paused, looked down at her. "Oh, yeah? What's that?"

"I've never had sex in this house before."

He grinned. "Well, it's about damn time you do. Want me to sneak you into your bedroom so you can fulfill all your teen girl fantasies?"

She let out a snort. "No. Definitely not. Besides, I didn't have teen girl fantasies about having sex in my room."

He trailed his fingers along the side of her breast. "So, you waited until college, huh?"

Her gaze stayed on his face, but her breathing quickened when he brushed the palm of his hand back and forth over her breast. Her nipple hardened through the material of her top.

"Maybe."

"Were any of those college girl fantasies about me?"

"No."

She'd answered way too fast. "You're lying. You wanted me." He rolled to her side, then drew the straps of her tank down, baring her breasts. He bent and caught one hard nipple in his mouth, flicking his tongue back and forth until she arched against him.

"I definitely didn't want you."

He smiled against the softness of her skin, using his teeth to tease her. "Yeah, you did. It's okay to admit it."

"You were annoying."

"I was charming and irresistible."

She frowned. "Maybe to most of the female population on campus. Definitely not to me. To me, you were annoying."

He slid his hand over her rib cage and down her stomach, loving the silken feel of her skin under his hands. When he dipped his fingers inside her panties and found her hot and wet, a moan escaped her lips.

"Am I annoying you now?"

"Yes. But in a much more pleasant way."

He rolled her bottoms off and spread her legs, sliding down her body to put his mouth on her. All he could hear was her breathing as he pleasured her, and the occasional gasps and moans he knew she was trying hard to suppress. He loved her taste, the way her hips moved as she directed him right where she wanted him.

"Oh, Trevor, you're going to make me come. I need to come. Please."

He laid his tongue on her clit and took her over the edge, her body shaking with her orgasm. He didn't give her time to recover, just slipped off his boxers and put on the condom, then entered her with her body still vibrating.

Her pussy contracted around his cock, squeezing him in a death grip that shook his resolve as he pushed deep inside her. He stilled, lifting up to look at her. Her eyes were deep pools of stormy blue, her hands pulling him down, her legs wrapping around him.

"Harder," she whispered. "I want to feel you deep."

"You want deep?"

"Yes."

He pulled out and flipped her over, shoved a pillow under her stomach and spread her legs and entered her.

She gasped, and lifted her butt, pushing back against him.

"More," she whispered.

He wanted to give her more, wanted to give her hard, fast, and as deep as he could sink into her, but the damn bed squeaked. So instead, he gave her slow and deep, feeling every bit of her each time he inched into her body. Her heat surrounded him, every muscle quivering around his cock until sweat beaded and ran down his back. And still, he held on to her hips, watching her ass move as he pumped ever so slowly in, then eased out, until she moaned and tossed her head back, rocking that sweet ass against him.

He leaned over her. "Do you know how badly I want to shove my cock deep into you? Do you know how much I want to give it to you hard and fast until you scream?"

"Yes," she said. "As much as I want it."

"Damn bed," he muttered, then reached underneath her, finding her clit. "But I am going to make you come, Haven. And then I'm going to come hard inside you."

She tightened around him as he stroked her clit, her pussy gripping him in a vise that made him grit his teeth and fight not to come. Not yet. Not until Haven did.

"Trevor. Trevor, yes. Make me come."

He swept his fingers back and forth over her clit, felt the contracting of her pussy around his cock.

"I'm coming. Oh, I'm coming, Trevor."

Hell, yes, she was. And he felt it tear through him at the same time. He wrapped an arm around her, holding on to her as he shuddered through his own release, thrusting deeply into her over and over again, not caring that the bed made noise, that he groaned, that she let out a soft cry as they came together.

Fuck, it was good, so damn good that he lost all sense of awareness except for the feel of Haven shuddering against him, her body squeezing every drop of come he had until she collapsed. He rolled to his side, drawing her against him, both of them damp with perspiration from the effort.

Trevor swept Haven's bangs away from her forehead and she reached out to rub her fingers over his lips. He grasped her wrist and kissed each fingertip, then took her mouth in a deep kiss that made his cock fire to life again.

Yeah, his cock might want round two, but he needed a few minutes.

"I sure as hell hope my mother doesn't come running down the hall to see what all that noise was about," Haven finally said.

"Me, too. But if she does, I promise to throw you on the floor on the other side of the bed, toss a blanket over you, then tell her I was thrashing around because I was having a nightmare."

Her lips curved. "How chivalrous of you to protect my virtue like that."

"Just the kind of guy I am, babe."

"Speaking of my virtue—or lack thereof—I should go back to my room. Otherwise, I'm going to be tempted to cuddle up next to you and fall asleep. And then there'd definitely be some explaining to do in the morning."

Trevor took a deep breath. "I'd like you to sleep here with me tonight. But yeah, you probably should."

Haven got out of bed and bent over to find her clothes. He took a few minutes to appreciate the feminine lines of her back and of course, her great ass and legs.

After disposing of the condom, he put on his boxers and walked her to the bedroom door, pulled her into his arms, and gave her a long, deep kiss that made his cock go steely hard. When he pulled away, Haven licked her lips.

"Thanks for that. Now I'll never get to sleep tonight. Then again," she said, cupping his erection, "it looks like you won't, either."

He took a deep breath. "Yeah, but I'll have great dreams."

She quirked a sexy smile and reached for the doorknob. "Pleasant dreams, Trevor."

TWENTY-THREE

OVER BREAKFAST THE NEXT MORNING, HAVEN PLAYED it very cool. She was polite and tried to act normal. Her mother asked her if she slept well, no doubt referring to her breakdown from the night before.

She had slept well, thanks to Trevor, and she'd told her mother she had no trouble sleeping.

Trevor had been all smiles and, as always, was charming with her mother. He even helped her make breakfast while Haven sipped coffee at the kitchen table. Haven told her mom about Trevor's house in St. Louis, and about Hammond. Her mother was fascinated about the house, and Haven showed her photos. Trevor invited her up for a visit. The whole thing was oddly . . . comfortable, and yet uncomfortable at the same time. It was as if she were sharing her boyfriend with her mother.

Which she clearly was not, since Trevor wasn't her boyfriend.

But she liked seeing him working side by side with her mom,

cooking bacon while her mom had fixed eggs and biscuits. She could almost envision the two of them together. Trevor had always been close to her mom—and her dad. He hadn't been lying to her when he'd told her they were like parents to him when he'd been in college. He'd been around a lot back then, but back then she'd been wholly distracted by him because she'd had such a crush on him and hadn't known how to act around him.

Not that she had a better handle on that now. But maybe she was at least starting to figure out how to separate the professional from the personal.

Today—last night—had been personal. When they started working on the interview again, it would be professional. It seemed they could both juggle it, which was a good thing.

Her mind shifted to the professional. She wished he'd open up to her about his family. She wanted to know more about his childhood. Now that she'd met Zane, she was curious about his parents. Why didn't he want to talk about them? Why wouldn't he let her interview them? Part of a human interest story on an athlete was childhood background. It helped shape who that athlete was today. Trevor's not talking about his parents was going to leave a giant gap in the story, and that didn't sit right with Haven.

As someone who cared about him, she took a step back. As a professional reporter, she was going to have to push him on this.

She pondered it over breakfast, during which she and Trevor exchanged glances. She also noticed her mother shooting very knowing looks at both her and Trevor, so maybe their tryst last night hadn't been as secret as she first thought. At least her mother was smiling whenever she looked her way.

Then again, the last thing she wanted her mom to think was that she had some personal relationship going with Trevor, because it wasn't a relationship.

It was just sex. She was doing a good job compartmentalizing it there.

Okay, maybe it was becoming more than just sex, at least to Haven. But she wasn't going to allow herself to make it more than a fling, an interlude, something fun to do while she was on this assignment. She had enough to handle with getting her career on track and putting this whole grief nightmare to rest. Anything else would be too much.

Trevor was too much, and he'd made no indication he was even interested in a relationship. The last thing she wanted was to get hurt, and have more emotional turmoil to wrestle with.

No, she was better off putting Trevor firmly in the "fun to have sex with" box and leaving him there. So when he turned his sexy grin in her direction, his eyes capturing her with their intensity, she put a lock on her heart.

She could so easily get lost in him.

She could so easily love him.

ADMITTEDLY, TREVOR HAD FUN REVISITING HIS COLlege campus for the day with Haven and the camera crew. They met with both his football and baseball coaches and Haven conducted short interviews while they reminisced. It was great to catch up with the coaches. He also got to talk to a few of his teachers, who were kind enough to say nice things about him even though he knew he'd given them all headaches. He walked them around campus and showed them some of his favorite hangouts, and they went out on the football field. He even took a few passes from some of the current football team out on the field.

That was fun, and Haven said they got some good shots. Now they wanted to do some interviews in town at some of his favorite local haunts.

"Let's stop there," Haven said, pointing out a local luncheon-ette. "This is a familiar hangout for a lot of the sports teams. I called ahead, and Ralph said we could film inside."

Trevor grinned. "I haven't had a cheeseburger in here in a long time."

"And it just so happens it's around the lunch hour."

He gave her a sidelong look. "It's like you planned it this way."

"It is, isn't it," she said with a waggle of her brows.

Ralph had been the owner and manager of the luncheonette forever—at least according to Ralph. He was in his late sixties now, and beamed a smile at them as they walked in. Ralph looked like he ate at least two cheeseburgers a day, but he still had plenty of energy as he hurried from behind the counter with his arms out-stretched to pull Trevor into a big bear hug.

"Trevor Shay. It's about time you showed your face here again."

"It's good to be here. I'm hungry."

"Haven called and said you'd be coming in. I'll put those burg-ers on right now. Still with grilled onions and pickles, no mustard?"

The one thing everyone liked about Ralph was that once you became a regular, he never forgot your likes and dislikes. "Still the same."

Trevor and Haven made their way to the corner booth. It was just after the peak lunch crowd, so the place wasn't as crowded as it normally would be, since most of the students would be back in class by now.

Even Andy, the camera guy, ordered a cheeseburger and put the camera down while they ate.

"Ralph makes the best fries you'll ever eat," Trevor told Andy.

"This is truth," Haven said, shoving two in her mouth.

Andy agreed, and they enjoyed an interview-free lunch. Ralph even came over and sat with them, reliving old times, including Trevor's junior year, when the team won the national championship.

He pointed out a picture on the wall of the team. Trevor grinned, remembering when they'd all come in and signed that photo for Ralph.

"It's one of my prized possessions," Ralph said.

After lunch, Andy grabbed the camera, and Haven asked questions about the diner.

"What makes Ralph's a special memory for you?"

"My roommates—Garrett Scott, Gray Preston, and Drew Hogan—we'd all hang out here when we didn't have class or sports practice. The burgers are great, and all our friends would be here. It was a good spot."

"To meet girls?"

Trevor grinned. "Well, that, too, but it's off campus, and everyone from the college comes here. It's a tradition. Me and the guys made it a point to meet here every Monday afternoon after practice. Unless one of us had a game, we were here."

He looked around, the memories as thick as gnats invading the field on a hot summer night. He could still see them all sitting in this very booth—younger versions of all of them—laughing like crazy, girls surrounding them. God, life had been great back then. "We'd sit here and plan out our futures, talk about where we were gonna be in ten years."

"And has it worked out the way you thought it would?"

He looked at Haven. "Better in a lot of ways. I'm fortunate to be living my dream, playing in two sports. And I have your father—Bill Briscoe—to thank for much of that."

Haven paused for a second, giving him an unguarded glimpse of both her pain and her gratitude at his statement. "And why is that?"

"Bill and Ginger Briscoe were the dorm parents for the sports dorm. But they were a lot more than that to all of us. To me. I struggled academically and emotionally. Bill was tough when I needed someone to be tough on me, and listened when I needed an adult to talk to. I wasn't the easiest kid back then, but he really under-stood me. He gave me space when I needed it, and he sure as hell knew when to rein me in. I'm not lying when I say I wouldn't be who I am today without him."

"Okay, let's cut here," Haven said, then turned to Trevor. "Thank you."

"Just stating the truth."

After thanking Ralph for the lunch and saying good-bye, they headed over to one of the bars. It wasn't open yet, so they did an interview outside, where Trevor told some tales about some out-landish antics he and the guys had gotten into on some wild week-end nights after games. He had Haven and Andy laughing when he told them the story about sneaking a very drunken but just-a-month-from-age-twenty-one underage Drew out of the bar one night when the cops came in because the bar was over capacity. It had been a big win for the football team, so it seemed like everyone on campus had crowded into the bar that night to celebrate.

"We threw him out the bathroom window."

Haven's eyes had widened. "Did he get hurt?"

"Nah. He landed on top of the Dumpster, then rolled off that and onto the ground in the alley. Then we hurried out the back and dragged him back to the car."

He could tell Haven fought to keep a straight face. "Poor Drew."

"He was fine. Drunks are very resilient."

They wrapped up and Andy left them back at the house. It was hard saying good-bye to Ginger, but Trevor had to get on a plane and head to Tampa. He had deadlines to make and he needed to get ready to play.

He and Haven got in the car and made the drive back to St. Louis.

"How do you think it went?" she asked as they drove along the turnpike.

He turned to her. "How do I think what—oh, the interview stuff? Fine, I guess. How do *you* think it went?"

"It's good. Really good, Trevor."

He liked hearing the confidence in her voice, was happy to see her focused on work.

"Trevor, this piece would be so rich if we could touch on your early family life, if we could talk to your parents."

He gripped the steering wheel. There was so much she didn't know, so much about him—about his past and, hell, even his current life—that she was unaware of. Dipping into the past would only open old wounds and possibly expose his secret. That he would never do. It was too much of a risk. "No."

"I don't understand. Is there something you're ashamed of? A lot of players have ugly childhoods, you know. You've risen above it, become a success. We could—"

"I don't want to talk about this, Haven."

"You don't trust me."

He shook his head, trying to keep his focus on the road. "Let's not talk about this while I'm trying to drive. I need to focus."

"Okay."

He'd put her off, for now.

But he knew she was going to bring it up again.

And he was going to shut her down again.

And he'd keep doing it.

For his own preservation, and for the safety of the secret he'd held all these years.

TWENTY-FOUR

THE BALL SAILED THROUGH THE AIR IN A PERFECT arc. Trevor never once took his eyes off it, though part of him recognized the safety on a path to his position. He dug in and pushed, racing to beat the corner to the first down line.

He reached for the ball and it landed right at his chest. The safety slammed into him and pushed him out of bounds. Holding tight to the ball, Trevor rolled to the ground.

The whistle blew, and Barrett Cassidy held out his hand. Trevor grabbed it and Barrett hauled him up.

"A few more steps, I would've had ya," Barrett said.

Trevor laughed. "You'd like to think so, wouldn't you?" Trevor slapped Barrett's helmet and the two of them trotted back to the line of scrimmage.

"Good catch," his coach said as the offense regrouped.

It was a grueling practice. It might be early October, but in Tampa, it was still hot. Sweat dripped down Trevor's neck, but he had to focus. He was playing catch-up with the team that already had played three games. They'd won two, lost the last one. He had to meet rookies and reinsert himself with his teammates again.

Nothing he wasn't used to, but it always took him a while to change gears from baseball to football.

He caught sight of Haven walking the side of the field. Andy the camera guy was there, too, taking shots of him at practice.

He hadn't seen much of her since they'd gotten back to St. Louis. He'd packed up and grabbed a flight right away, while she'd stayed behind to finish up footage to send in to her studio.

It had been three days. He'd missed her. He'd invited her to stay at his place, but she hadn't answered him. She'd told him she was arriving today, so she must have come right to the field.

He wanted some alone time with her, but damned if he knew when he was going to get it. That was why he was hoping she'd stay with him at the house.

After practice ended, he stopped and talked to his coach, George, for a few minutes.

"There's a rookie tight end that wants your job this year," George told him.

"Warrell Timmons," Trevor said. "Kind of a hotshot punk."

George laughed. "He's good."

"Not as good as I am."

George slapped him on the back. "That's what I like about you, Trevor. You're always so modest."

"You don't like me because I'm modest, George. You like me because I'm one of the best tight ends you've ever had."

"True. So why don't you give up baseball and play for us full time? You're not getting any younger and I'm tired of having to wait for you."

"Hey. I've got plenty of playing years ahead of me."

"So you say. But football's a hard game."

"Not for me it isn't."

"Those young kids like Timmons are coming up all the time. One of these days, one of them is going to push you right out."

Any other guy would be offended—or maybe paranoid. But Trevor knew his coach. There was a place for him on this team as long as he stayed healthy, kept his stats up, and wanted to play here. And every year some new hotshot like Warrell Timmons tried to shove Trevor out of the way. He knew he couldn't devote the entire season to playing for Tampa, so they had to develop new players at the tight end position.

And maybe Trevor couldn't spend the entire season playing, but he was good at helping the new guys.

"So you want me to spend some time with this kid?"

"If you wouldn't mind. Knock that chip off his shoulder and show him how the position is supposed to be played. Right now he has a God complex. He could do no wrong at the collegiate level. But you know how it is when you come to the pros."

Trevor cracked a smile. "I do. Consider it done."

This should be fun.

"But Trevor?"

"Yeah."

"Don't be too hard on the kid. He's had it rough, so he's over-compensating by playing the tough, cocky rookie, you know?"

Trevor scratched the side of his nose, remembering exactly what that was like. "Yeah, Coach, I know."

"Figured you did. This is his dream and I know that. I've tried to talk to him, but he's not getting rid of the attitude."

Trevor nodded. "Gotcha, Coach. I'll handle him."

Instead of walking off the field, Trevor went over to where Warrell was gathering up his stuff.

"Good practice today."

The kid stood, straightening himself, trying to tower over Trevor, which was hard to do considering Trevor's height.

"Uh, thanks. You, too. You know, for an older guy."

Trevor laughed. Yeah, he popped attitude, all right. "Think you can beat me?"

Warrell puffed his chest out. "Know I can."

"Good. Let's put you to the test. If you have any energy left after practice."

"I've got plenty to spare, old man. Do you?"

"More than you. Let's do this."

Trevor called the receivers coach over, and they went through a series of drills. Warrell had great reflexes, but he was still young and didn't know the playbook as well as Trevor did, so on a wide-out, one of the quarterbacks threw both of them a six-nine-six, and Trevor cut across the field, making a sweet catch and a run into the end zone, leaving Warrell in the dust.

They went through several formations, and while he was good, and had the potential to be great, it was obvious Warrell wasn't yet at Trevor's skill level. He had the stamina of youth, but not the experience.

And Trevor didn't intend to cut him any slack. The best way for Warrell to learn was to play with the best. And Trevor knew he was one of the best.

When the coach whistled for them to finish, they headed to the drink table.

"You're good," Trevor said. "Not as good as me, but you're still good."

Obviously not ready to back down yet, Warrell lifted his chin. "I'll get there. Once I learn all the plays, I'll give you a run."

Trevor grinned. "Well, you can try."

"Hey, you'll be off playing baseball, and I'll be here soaking up all the limelight and stealing the starting tight end spot right out from under you."

"Sure, kid. You keep thinking that."

Yeah, he had a chip all right. Trevor would keep working on him. He'd come around.

TWENTY-FIVE

HAVEN SHOULD HAVE KNOWN TREVOR WOULD OWN two houses.

Why she expected he'd have some condo here in Tampa she didn't know, but that was what she'd anticipated when she plugged his address into the GPS of her rental car. Instead, she ended up here at the water's edge on the other side of Tampa, in Clearwater.

The views of the water as she'd driven along were gorgeous. The sun hit the bay, glinting like blue diamonds. What she wouldn't give to live in a place like this. She'd grown up in Oklahoma, where there were plenty of lakes to hang out at in the summer, but nothing like this kind of water with endless views. She wished she hadn't been driving, so she could have gawked more.

She'd always loved the water. So had her dad. She and her parents would take the boat out onto the lake in the summer. God, that had been fun when she was a kid.

She pulled up in front of the house. It nestled against the water, so the location was perfect, but still, she'd expected something entirely different for Trevor.

This place was not at all like the grand old mansion–type house he owned in St. Louis, either.

This was a baby blue frame house with white shutters. An older home, it looked a little run-down, but wow, the views of the water were spectacular. And she'd only seen the front.

Trevor had given her a set of keys at practice and told her to let herself in and make herself at home.

Actually, she'd planned to stay at a hotel, but hell, she'd missed him, and he said there was a guest house if she really wanted to stay in that, but there were also two guest bedrooms on a separate floor from the master as well.

What she really wanted was to stay in his room.

In his bed.

She'd figure all that out later. She stuck her key in the door and opened it.

Uh, wow. The inside was totally different from the outside.

Like . . . night-and-day different. There were dark wood floors all through the house, and as she made her way through the foyer, she stopped to take in the open-concept floor space, which opened up the entire downstairs, from the kitchen all the way through the spacious dining room and into the huge family room. There were floor-to-ceiling windows that overlooked the deck and the water. She went to the doors and saw a pool and a boat dock.

"Amazing," she said to herself, then turned and went into the kitchen, which she was certain was larger than her old apartment back in Dallas. Stainless-steel appliances filled the space, along with beautiful maple cabinetry, and, as she ran her fingertips over the gorgeous granite countertops, she wondered if she could just hang out in the kitchen the entire time she was here. It was a cook's paradise, and she'd love to cook on that amazing stove.

She continued the tour into the next room, which was a workroom, complete with a built-in wall desk that ran along all four walls.

She went outside, grabbed a suitcase, and rolled it up to the second floor.

Uh, wow. Each bedroom was huge, but she took the one with the view of the water. She didn't want to make presumptions. Maybe Trevor didn't want her in his bedroom, and she wasn't about to make that decision without his input.

Besides, this room was awesome.

She stepped outside the room and saw stairs leading to a third level, so she wandered up. The door was shut and she assumed it was Trevor's room. She felt weird about invading his privacy without him being there, so she went back to the other level.

Not that she had any complaints, since the bedroom she'd chosen was plenty big enough for her, and also had a walk-out deck overlooking the water, and an oversized bathroom. She'd definitely enjoy that room.

She dragged her other suitcase upstairs and unpacked. Since she had no idea what time Trevor would be back, she decided she might as well make herself at home. She changed into her swimsuit, put on her cover-up and slid into her sandals, then grabbed her notebook and went downstairs to browse the kitchen.

She opened the fridge and her eyes widened. Not only was it completely stocked, it was . . . ridiculously organized. Drinks were lined up side by side on the top shelf, juices on one side, milk, beer and soda on the other. Then condiments were loaded in the door, by color or something. Lunchmeats were in color-coded containers. It looked like an OCD paradise in the refrigerator. But it was well stocked with food of all types, plenty to drink, and a lot of fresh fruits and vegetables. After familiarizing herself with what was in all the cabinets, she made herself a glass of iced tea, then headed outside onto the deck.

It was hot, but there was a breeze coming in from the water. She pulled up one of the chairs and spread out the towel she'd found in the cabinet on the deck. Obviously, Trevor thought of everything. Or he had someone else think of everything. She'd put sunblock on before she'd put on her bikini, so she slid on her sunglasses and started making some notes.

It wasn't long before the beautiful day distracted her. She laid her notebook down and stared out over the pool, the heat outside making her sweat. But as her gaze drifted, she caught sight of the boat, her mind awash in memories of her and her mom and dad taking the boat out in the summer. Her dad would drive the boat while she and her mom water-skied or rode on the tube. Sometimes, they'd go fishing.

She felt a small pang in her chest, but this time, the memories were sweet ones instead of painful.

She exhaled in relief. Maybe things were getting better.

The sun heated her skin, so she set the notebook on the table and took off her sunglasses, then dove into the pool. The water was cool, refreshing, and she swam a few laps before pulling up on the steps.

This place was idyllic. She saw several boats going by. The location of this house was ideal. Trevor had really done well for himself. She was happy for him.

She got out of the pool and sat, letting the sun dry her. She was going to reach for her notes again, but she yawned, put her sunglasses on, and tilted the chair down, flipping onto her stomach. She'd gotten up before the sun came up this morning to take an early flight, and she was exhausted. Maybe she'd take a short nap.

She closed her eyes, the sound of the water and the boats going by lulling her to sleep.

* * *

TREVOR PARKED IN THE GARAGE AND GRABBED HIS team workout bag out of the backseat, then headed inside, tossing his bag on the nearby table by the door. He saw a purse on the counter.

Haven was here. Good.

"Haven?" He went straight for the fridge to grab an energy drink. It was hot at the team facility today, and he was drained. He unscrewed the cap and took a long swallow as he made his way into the office.

She wasn't there, so he went upstairs.

She'd arrived, because he saw her things in the bedroom.

The guest bedroom. Huh. He wondered why.

He'd have to fix that.

He went downstairs.

"Haven?"

Still, no answer. He went to the back door and looked out, smiling as he saw her lying facedown on one of the lounges.

Obviously making herself at home, just the way he wanted her to feel.

He dashed upstairs, changed into his swim trunks, and came back down, quietly opening the French doors leading to the deck.

It was obvious Haven was asleep. Her arm hung over the edge of the chaise longue, and she was facing him, but she didn't move when he stepped outside.

And damn, she looked good with all that skin available to look at, her red-and-white dotted bikini barely covering her gorgeous body. She was well tanned, and she had a fine ass and long legs. She'd undone the top, so her smooth back was exposed.

He'd missed her. It had only been a couple of days, but dammit, he'd missed seeing her, missed touching her, kissing her, and feeling her body against his when he went to sleep at night.

He didn't like being separated from her.

And he didn't like what that meant. He enjoyed being single. And he had a secret he needed to keep, which meant he couldn't become attached to a woman. Because getting involved meant trusting someone with that secret.

He had never let anyone in—at least not a woman he cared about. Only a couple of people outside the family knew, and they were business associates. They were paid very well to keep his confidence. He didn't think a woman he was in a relationship with would ever understand the closely guarded secret he'd held for so many years.

Maybe Haven would, but he wasn't ready to take that chance yet.

But Haven had shared her grief with him. She'd allowed him to see her vulnerable and in pain. Maybe . . .

No. Besides, what she'd shared had been different. He didn't even want to think about all the ramifications of sharing his secret.

Taking a deep breath, he ran and jumped into the pool, deliberately making a loud splash before diving deep and skimming the bottom. When he surfaced, Haven was sitting at the edge of the pool, smiling at him.

"Now there's an entrance. Sorry, I fell asleep."

He pulled himself up on his elbows, resting against the side of the pool next to her. "Long day?"

"I got up early. How was your day?"

"Good. Tough practice, and it was hot out there. I'm used to it, though."

She tilted her head to look at him. "I'm sure you are, being a superstar and all."

He grinned. "Yeah, that's me."

"Nice place, by the way."

"Did you give yourself the tour?"

"I did. It's a very impressive house. I was surprised by the outside. It didn't look like you at all."

He arched a brow. "Yeah? What did you expect?"

"I don't know. Something . . . mansionlike. Like your other place."

He gave her a look and she laughed. "Seriously, I'm surprised you have two houses. I thought maybe you'd have a condo here."

"I just wanted a place by the water. This house was a dump when I bought it. I had it redone on the inside. It's still a work in progress."

"It's beautiful. And I can tell it suits you."

He couldn't help but enjoy the compliment, especially from her. "Is your room okay?"

"My room is fantastic. The deck is amazing, and the bathroom is incredible. So is your kitchen. I hate my apartment in New York. The kitchen is awful in there. It's a tight squeeze, with a midget refrigerator and no counter space, which always makes me sad because I love to cook. I get so tired of eating take-out food."

"And I love to eat. You're welcome to use any part of the house you want. Especially the kitchen."

"Awesome. I assume you don't have a chef here like you do in St. Louis?"

"No. Hammond stays there and doesn't travel with me."

"Too bad. I was getting spoiled by his cooking. But it'll give me a chance to play in your kitchen."

"I'll look forward to that."

"So you invited me here to do your cooking for you."

He laughed. "Yeah, that was the only reason."

She pulled her sunglasses off. "I can see I'm going to have to keep an eye on you."

He loved looking at her eyes. With her sunglasses off, and her hair previously wet from swimming, she was makeup free and looked gorgeous.

"I missed you," he said, tracing his finger over her kneecap.

She took a deep breath. "Did you?"

"Yeah."

Dangerous territory, that he shouldn't be venturing into. Getting emotionally involved with Haven was only going to cause trouble, because once she was finished with this assignment, he was going to have to let her go.

And he would let her go. He'd have to.

But right now he couldn't help himself, especially since she was staring back at him, making him want to climb out of the water, run his hands over her body, and kiss her until this fire that had barely banked with his swim in the pool consumed them both.

"Well." She laid her palms on the tops of her thighs. "Speaking of food, I'm kind of starving here. How about you?"

He was starving for a taste of her, but he could wait. "Yeah. I'm hungry. I can take you out to eat."

She shook her head. "If you don't mind, I'd rather eat here. You have plenty of food in your refrigerator, and like I said, I'm kind of geeking out over your kitchen."

"I'm not going to object if you want to cook."

"Great. I'm going to run upstairs and take a quick shower and change clothes, then I'll be back to get started on dinner."

"I'll do the same."

He climbed out of the pool, then pulled her to her feet. They dried off, then went inside.

"Meet you in the kitchen," she said.

Haven disappeared upstairs. Trevor looked around, wondering if having Haven stay here had been a good idea.

He wanted his hands on her. He wanted her in his bed every night.

But soon enough, he was going to need her out of his life.

Shit. He was starting to wonder if he really knew what he wanted.

He dragged his fingers through his hair and started up the stairs to take a shower.

TWENTY-SIX

HAVEN MADE CHICKEN STIR-FRY FOR DINNER, ALONG with rice. They were eating in the dining room at a beautiful table Trevor had told her he'd found at a garage sale down the street from his house and rehabbed himself.

That had been a surprise to hear. She was learning all kinds of things about Trevor she hadn't known before.

She loved the table. It bore scars from years of use, but he'd obviously sanded it and stained it a gorgeous dark color.

The man had many talents.

"You didn't put your things in my room today," he said.

She looked up at him. "Your door was closed, and the other rooms were open. I just figured you didn't want me to invade your bedroom."

He gave her a direct look. "Haven. First, if there's something I want or don't want, I have no trouble telling you. And second, believe me, I want you in my bed."

Her body fused with heat. "Okay, then."

He took a sip of water, then added, "Provided that's where you want to be."

"Oh, I want to be there."

His eyes gleamed dark, a promise of what was to come. "That's settled then."

"I might leave my things in the guest bedroom, though. I kind of dig that shower."

"You haven't seen the one in my room yet."

She arched a brow. "Really. It couldn't possibly be any better."

"Oh, but it could."

"Now you're teasing me." She scooped up a forkful of chicken and vegetables and waved it in his direction. "It's like you're trying to entice me into your bedroom."

"Do I need a fancy shower to entice you into my bedroom?"

Her lips curved. "Not really. I'm pretty easy."

He laughed. "You are, huh?"

"Where you're concerned, I am."

"Noted. I'll be sure to see just how easy you are after dinner."

"You do that."

They finished eating, and Trevor helped her with the dishes. Actually, he nudged her to the side and scrubbed the wok, then loaded the dishes into the dishwasher while she cleaned the table and put away leftovers.

Maybe he was in a hurry to give her that tour of his shower. She grinned at the thought.

But after dinner, he poured her a glass of wine, grabbed a bottle of water for himself, and took her outside.

It was so much warmer down here than it had been when they'd left St. Louis. She didn't even need to wear a jacket outside. She curled up on one of the chaise longues and they watched the sun filter over the water.

"There's a great place in Tampa for us to watch the sunset. I'll take you there one night."

She sipped her wine, a delicious chardonnay with just a touch of tartness. "I'd like that. Thank you. But I don't need you to entertain me, Trevor. I know we're both here to work."

"But I like Tampa. And you need to see the beach here."

"Okay. And when do you think we'll have all this time to do all these things?"

"I don't play all the time, Miss Briscoe. I'll have plenty of time to wine and dine you and play tour guide."

She rolled the wine around in her glass and shot him a half smile. "You mean when you're not trying to seduce me into your shower?"

"There'll be plenty of time for that, too."

"You must not work very hard at this football thing."

He laughed. "I guess you'll just have to train your camera on me and see."

"I'll definitely be doing that on Sunday."

"Good. You'll get to see one hell of a show."

She liked his confidence, saw the excitement on his face. "You're eager to play, aren't you?"

His lips curved. "Yeah. I wish I was playing postseason baseball right now, but I have to deal with the reality of that, so I'm tuned into football and ready to get going."

"I'm looking forward to seeing you in a game situation. Up close."

He turned to face her. "You've never watched me play in a game, have you?"

"No. I saw you in college, but that was different. And of course I've watched you on TV, but that's not the same thing. I'm excited about being at the game Sunday."

He laid his water on the table. "Come over here, Haven. I have something else that'll excite you."

Smiling, she set her wineglass down and went over to where he was sitting on the chaise, straddling his lap. She'd thrown on a short skirt after her shower, along with a T-shirt. He pressed his fingers into her hips and lifted his gaze to hers.

"Now *this* excites me."

She leaned forward and rested her forearms on his chest. "Does it?"

"Yeah. It's been too long since you've been close to me like this. And I like seeing your legs."

He was all hard muscle, his heart beating a fast rhythm against her breast as she wound her arms around his neck. "Like this?"

"Yeah. But with fewer clothes." He cupped her butt and pulled her against what was quickly becoming a delicious erection. She loved that he got hard so fast for her, that he seemed to want her with a need that equaled her own furious desire for him. And when he grasped her around the waist and pulled her upward so they could kiss, those familiar butterflies danced in her stomach.

She nestled her knees against his hips, rubbing her pussy against the sweet steel of his cock, using that friction to give her the pulse of pleasure she needed to tell him exactly how much she'd missed being this close to him.

And when he reached down and slid his hands under her skirt, pulling it up so he could slide his fingers inside her underwear, she gasped.

"You do realize we're outside."

"No one's going to see."

"Right. Except people riding by in their boats."

He lifted his head. "I don't see anyone going by in a boat."

He dipped his hand inside her panties, smoothing his fingers over the curve of her buttocks. "I like when you wear skirts. Easy access."

"It might have been the reason I chose the skirt."

"I like the way you think, Haven." He teased his fingers down the crack of her buttocks, causing her to gasp as he mapped her body in ways that had become all too easy and familiar, and yet so incredibly hot. He knew her so well, knew how to raise her temperature to unbearable levels. And when he eased in farther, tucking a finger inside her pussy, she lifted, giving him access.

She'd give him anything, even outside like this, just to make those incredible sensations continue.

"You're wet. Hot," he said, his gaze holding hers as he moved his finger in and out of her. "And tight. Ready for my cock. You need to come, Haven?"

"Oh, yes. Please."

"Lean back and let me make you come. Then I'm going to fuck you out here."

The thought of it tightened her. She hadn't had a lot of sex in public places, but she was definitely up for it with Trevor. He made her feel safe. He'd occasionally take a look around to make sure no one was driving by in a boat, but she felt the sense of privacy his property provided for them. And she was aching and more than ready for an orgasm.

She leaned back, bracing herself on her hands on either side of Trevor's knees. He raised her skirt, smoothing his fingers over her satin panties.

"These are going to have to go," he said, reaching up to grab the material at her hips. With a strong grip, he ripped her underwear, giving her a devilish smile as he pulled the material away and tossed it onto the deck.

"I can't believe you just did that."

"You're going to appreciate it when I do this." He gently strummed his thumb over her clit, then slid a finger inside her with the other hand, fucking her while he rubbed her, evoking delicious sensations.

He was right. She didn't care about the ripped panties, only that he continue touching her, that he stroke her until she was mindless, until she arched against him, wordlessly begging for more of the sweet slide of his fingers over her aching flesh.

Haven pushed against his hand, letting her legs fall over the edge of the chaise to give Trevor better access. His fingers performed magic on her, taking her right to the precipice in record time. The most erotic thing was his gaze focused on hers, the eye contact that made their connection almost painfully intimate, especially here, where she felt more exposed than ever. And yet she couldn't tear her gaze away from him as she climaxed, letting out a long moan as he thrust his finger inside and she clenched around him in the throes of one amazing orgasm.

When she came down from the shuddering high, Trevor lifted up and swept his hands around her neck, pulling her forward for a shattering kiss that made her quiver all over.

She clasped her hands over his wrists. "You give me goose bumps."

"The good kind, I hope."

She rubbed her hand over his erection. "The best kind. The kind that makes me want you inside me so you can give me even more."

He drew in a sharp breath, then shifted, pulling a condom out of his pocket. "Let's get you on me."

She smiled, grasped the condom, and opened the wrapper while Trevor undid his zipper and took out his cock. Now it was Haven's turn to take in a breath. She wrapped her hand around his shaft. "Not only have I missed you, I've missed this."

"I feel so used."

She laughed. "Do you?"

"No. Go ahead and use me. Climb onto my cock and fuck me all you want."

She rolled the condom on, then lifted up onto her knees, fitting his cock at the entrance to her pussy.

"That's it," Trevor said, holding the base of his cock so she could balance herself. "Slide onto me."

She inched down, feeling every delicious inch of him fit inside her. She lifted her skirt so he could watch, his gaze filled with so much heat it made her nerve endings tingle.

"Every time is like the first time," she said, in awe that she felt such magic with him. More than physical, she shared a connection with him that she didn't dare try to fathom. Right now she only wanted to enjoy this moment, this sensual delight that enveloped her in its grasp and made her sex quiver and tighten around his cock.

Trevor slid his hands under her skirt, finding her clit and rubbing his fingers ever so lightly over her as she began to move back and forth. It was like a dance between the two of them, her body so in tune with his that she knew exactly how to rock against him to give them both the kind of pleasure that would make this good for them.

"Yeah, babe, just like that," he said, gripping one of her hips while he continued to master her clit in a way that sent her spiraling into an orgasm. She held on to his arms and rolled through the climax that surprised her, shaking with the aftereffects. She climbed ever higher as she increased her movements, wanting him to go with her next time.

And when he lifted her T-shirt and dragged it over her head, drawing the cup of her bra down to capture her nipple between his lips to suck, she'd never felt such extraordinary sensations before. She grasped his hair and tugged, holding on for dear life as she squeezed his cock with her pussy muscles and rocked against him.

"You're going to make me come, Haven. I'm going to come hard in you."

She kissed him, taking possession, her tongue flicking out to tease and tangle with his. "Yes. I need you to come with me."

He cupped her butt and thrust into her, making her burst, and this time, he buried his face in her neck and came with her, both of them shuddering. She was wrapped around him, holding him tight when she rocked through yet another pulsing orgasm, this time feeling his body thunder with hers.

The aftermath was just as sweet as Trevor smoothed out her skirt and swept his hands over her back, kissing her neck and lips. They were tangled up, seemingly everywhere, but Haven liked it like that. And when he stood, he carried her inside, taking them upstairs, to his room this time.

She barely registered his impressive king-sized bed as he walked through on his way to the bathroom.

He was right. It was one hell of a shower. All marble tiles and so many sprays that six people could shower in there. He turned it on and pulled her inside.

"Just how many people shower in here at one time?" she asked as she stepped under one of the sprays to wet her hair.

He laughed. "Just me."

She wasn't going to probe any further, because she didn't care who'd been here before her. Especially when he washed her hair and soaped her body, lingering on all the good spots. And when he dropped to his knees, spread her legs, and used his mouth to give her yet another mind-blowing orgasm, she was pretty sure she'd blown every brain cell she had left.

After, he used an oversized towel to dry her off, then guided her to his bed, and pulled her next to him.

Exhausted and spent, she was asleep as soon as he threw the covers over them both.

TWENTY-SEVEN

THERE WAS NOTHING BETTER THAN TO BE IN FULL uniform and pads, with the sound of a full stadium cheering you on, to get your adrenaline going.

Trevor had missed playing with the Hawks, but he was glad to be here today. The crowd noise was deafening, and it pumped him up to hear their cheers when he was introduced as he ran out of the tunnel.

Trevor was more than ready to play this game against New Orleans. It was going to be a tough one, but his team had practiced hard, and they were prepared against a tough opponent.

He'd been keeping his eye on JW Zeman, Tampa's quarterback. JW had been drafted out of Notre Dame two years ago in the first round, a promising athlete with an incredible arm. He'd shown great leadership potential right away, and he'd done well his first year. The team expected great things from him, especially this year now that they'd shored up the offensive line and had added depth in other areas.

JW and Trevor had hooked up right away on offense. The kid threw the ball hard and long, and had a confidence a lot of young quarterbacks didn't show as rookies. Even better, JW liked throwing to his tight ends, which benefited Trevor.

"You ready for this?" JW asked as they stood on the sidelines, watching Tampa get ready to kick off to New Orleans.

"I'm always ready. How's the arm?"

"Itching to throw."

Trevor grinned. "Let's kick their asses, then."

Tampa kicked off and defense took the field after the return. He liked the defense this year. With free agency and the rookies they'd drafted, they'd filled some holes. They were tough, and New Orleans made only one first down before they were forced to punt the ball back to Tampa.

Trevor went in on the first series, though the first attempt was a running play that netted them only four yards. On second series, JW threw it to Brady McCall, the wide receiver, for a first down.

Trevor came out after that, and they pulled two running attacks in a row, bringing up a third and short. Trevor came back in and JW threw him a sideline pass that Trevor caught for a first down. Damn, but it felt good to catch the ball, to hear the crowd involvement. He dashed off to the sidelines and waited for his next chance to go in as they continued to move the ball down the field. He went in and out during the plays, catching the ball whenever it was thrown to him. The one thing he'd always prided himself on was his ability to get his hands on the ball. He rarely dropped it. Hell, he didn't drop it.

He was in at second and goal, the ball on the nine-yard line. He pushed off on his route, wide open in the end zone. JW looked left at the wide receiver, then dropped it into Trevor's hands.

Touchdown, baby. They all did a quick celebration in the end zone, but it was back to work.

New Orleans managed a field goal late in the first quarter, but Tampa's running backs tore up the clock and JW sneaked one in just as the half ended, putting them up by eleven points.

Good, so far, and defense was working New Orleans.

Second half they broke it open, scoring three touchdowns. Their defense shut down New Orleans's passing game. Even the rookies got in a little work, but Trevor could tell that rookie receiver Warrell Timmons wasn't happy Trevor had scored two touchdowns, while he had only gotten into the game late.

The only thing that mattered was the team had won.

Still, he'd promised the coach he'd work on the kid's attitude, so after they did interviews, Trevor went up to him.

"You got some play time in today."

"A little."

"You looked good out there. And you'll get more."

Warrell shrugged. Tension rolled off the kid in waves. Trevor could tell he was pissed.

"Hey, I'm going to have some of the team over for a barbecue at my place this week since it's a bye week. You interested?"

Warrell looked at him as if he didn't quite believe he'd been included. "I . . . dunno. Maybe. Where?"

"I have a house on the water. Give me your number and I'll text you directions."

"I'm after your job, you know."

"So you keep telling me. But you still gotta eat, right?"

For the first time, Warrell offered up a hint of a smile. "Yeah."

"Okay, then."

They traded numbers, and Trevor told him he'd text him with the information. He hadn't planned on a barbecue, but it was a good idea, and it would give Haven access to some of the players, which would be good for her job.

Now he just had to round up some of the guys, who he knew would show up on short notice. Coach would take care of inviting the rookies.

This should be fun.

TWENTY-EIGHT

"DO YOU ALWAYS THROW IMPROMPTU PARTIES LIKE this?" Haven asked as she sat at Trevor's dining room table making notes.

They'd been busy since his game Sunday. She'd done interviews and they'd done camera shots before, during, and after the game. God, he'd looked delicious in that uniform. And he'd played amazingly. He was lightning fast and so accurate. She'd been an absolute squealing fan girl during the game, unable to peel her attention away from Trevor.

So much for being an objective reporter.

"Sometimes. I hadn't planned on it for this week. It just kind of . . . came up, and with this being a bye week, it seemed convenient."

"I see." Just kind of came up? As if this kind of thing happened all the time.

Maybe in his world they did.

"Okay, so what are you going to do? Do we need to go to the store and get food?"

"Nah. I'll have it catered. I already made a call."

"You did." Of course he did. Because people like Trevor could make that happen on short notice.

"And what brought this on?" she asked.

"Warrell Timmons." He was scrolling through his phone, barely paying attention to her.

"The rookie tight end?"

"Yeah."

"You're having a barbecue because of Warrell Timmons? Why?"

He looked up at her. "What?"

"What does Warrell Timmons have to do with you hosting a barbecue?"

"Oh. He has some chip-on-his-shoulder issues and they need to get knocked off."

"By inviting him to a barbecue."

"Well . . . yeah."

She blinked, not able to make the connection. It must be a guy thing. "Okay. So we don't need to go buy food."

"No. But I need to figure out a way to make sure he and I spend some time together. I know how these events go. All the rookies will band together in a herd."

Haven leaned back in her chair, pondering how to make that not happen. "What about games?"

He looked up from his phone. "Huh?"

"You know. Games. Organize people into groups and play games. Forced proximity and bonding and all that." Then it hit her. "Oh, like a scavenger hunt."

His lips curved. "That might be fun."

"It would be. You have the land here. And you can extend it beyond just indoors and on your property. There's the nearby marina within walking distance. It would give you some bonding time with Timmons, too. Put people into groups of two or three."

"Yeah, me and Timmons, plus the wideouts. Groups of four."

"I can assign the groups and manage the hunt."

"You'd do that?"

"Of course. It'll be fun."

Now it was Trevor who wore the thoughtful look for a few minutes. "Okay, that's doable. We'll need prizes. I'll offer up a fishing expedition for the winners."

"I'm sure they'd love that."

"I'll make a call and get the prize arranged."

"And I'll put together the teams. Do you know who's coming?"

"Not yet, but I'll get it figured out. You might have to do the judging."

"That's not a problem."

Now she was excited. She'd organized events like this for her sorority in college, but she hadn't done so in a long time. She had no idea how receptive a bunch of football players would be, but she thought it was a great idea. And if team building was the objective, she couldn't think of a better way to get it done than this.

She was glad Trevor was on board with the idea.

She spent the remainder of the day making up her list of items for the hunt, trying to keep everything football related, since that would be more fun for the team. She had to leave Trevor out of the setup since he'd be participating, so she went shopping, then put the list together, and the clues, and ran into town to make copies.

"I brought burgers and fries."

She looked up, realizing it must have been hours later. Trevor was in the kitchen and she inhaled the smell of the food.

"Oh, that smells really good." She stuffed the sheets in the folder and came into the kitchen. "What time is it?"

"Eight thirty. You were at that for a long time."

"It's all organized now, though."

"Thanks for doing it. I hadn't realized it was going to take so long. Sorry to put all that on you."

"Are you kidding? I'm having a blast. This is going to be fun." She took the plate he offered. "At least it's going to be fun for me. I hope it is for your teammates."

"Trust me. We're all a bunch of kids. And we're competitive. Everyone's going to love this."

"Did you get the prize organized?"

"I got several, actually. I did the deep-sea fishing expedition for the first-place winners, and gift cards for dinner out at some of the nice restaurants for second and third place."

"Awesome."

He handed her the gift certificate for the fishing expedition as well as the gift cards. "I'll let you handle those."

"Okay."

They ate dinner. Haven didn't realize how hungry she was until she'd devoured her dinner. She'd lost all track of time buying the items to hide as well as putting the clues and the lists together.

"You got everything you need?" Trevor asked. "And you had enough money for the stuff?"

"Plenty. You gave me several hundred dollars. Which reminds me, I put your change on the counter."

"That's fine. I don't suppose you want to show me the list in advance."

"No, I don't. Surely you don't want an early advantage in the game."

He grabbed her plate and got up from the table, a subtle smile on his face. "Would I do that?"

"To gain an edge over your competitors? I'm sure you would. In fact, I think I'll take all of my notes upstairs and hide them in my room."

She slid out of her chair and took her folder, dashed up to her room, and hid the folder in the closet, along with the bag of scavenger hunt items for tomorrow.

When she came downstairs, Trevor was leaning against the counter. "So, I should sneak into your room tonight and rifle through your things?"

She crossed her arms. "Do I really need to lock my door?"

He laughed. "No. You're safe, and so is the sanctity of your scavenger hunt."

"Good to know. You ready to get back to work?"

"Come on. Let's go out on the deck. We'll have a beer and relax. You've done enough work today."

"I've still got some energy left."

"And it's going to be a long day tomorrow. Turn it off for tonight."

"All right."

He grabbed a couple of beers from the refrigerator and they walked outside. The night was warm, but there was a breeze coming in off the water. The moon was nearly full, casting a bright light on the deck. They pulled up chairs and Haven took a seat, then a long draw of the beer Trevor handed her.

It felt good to relax and enjoy the view of the water. Trevor seemed at ease. Then again, when didn't he? With as much as he had going on, he never seemed nervous or anxious.

"I like your life," she said.

He turned his head to look at her. "Yeah? What about it?"

"I don't know. It's just so . . . relaxing. You always seem so calm."

He laughed. "Not always. Tonight it is. I guess I just don't let things get to me."

She leaned back and took another swallow of her beer, studying him. "But how do you manage that? I don't know that I could juggle two different careers like you do and not be stressed about it."

He shrugged. "I'm used to it. I've been doing it for years. It gets a little hectic at times, like now, when I'm making the transition, and sometimes I feel like I need to pull out of baseball early and start the football season at the beginning. It's always a juggling act. I feel that pull, you know?"

She filed that comment away to jot down. "Then why do both, Trevor? You've been at this for seven years now. Isn't it time to give one up?"

"Why would I do that, when I still enjoy playing both sports? And how could I choose which one to play?"

"You do realize at some point you're going to have to make a choice."

"Why?"

She could tell by the look on his face and the sincerity in his voice that he really believed he could continue to play both sports. "I don't know. Because playing sports is tough on a body. And you're getting up there in age."

He laughed. "Now you sound like my competition."

"You're going to be . . . what? Thirty this year?" She took a swallow of beer and set the bottle down on the table.

"I am. Do I look like I'm slowing down?"

"Not really."

"I could bench press you, Miss Briscoe." He squinted, as if guessing her weight.

"Don't even think about it."

He stood and came over, scooping her out of the chair before she could even object.

"God, you're light."

"Trevor, seriously. Put me down."

"What do you weigh? Like a hundred pounds?"

"Uh, more than that."

"I could probably press you over my head." He started to lift her higher.

"Let's not." She laid her palm on his chest. "Please put me down. I get your point. You're strong. It's obvious from looking at your muscles that you take good care of your body."

He set her feet on the ground, but didn't let go of her. "So, you've been looking at my body, huh?"

She rolled her eyes and pushed at him. "You know I do. But purely from a . . . research perspective."

"Uh-huh. I've been looking at your body, too. And not at all from a research perspective."

"And here we are working together. You're being very unprofessional."

"This shouldn't surprise you."

He carried her through the doors and up the stairs.

"You could put me down," she said.

He looked down at her. "Why would I do that?"

"Because I'm heavy?"

He laughed and continued up, bypassing her room. "Now you're insulting me." He pushed open the door to his room, then set her on the bed, climbing on top of her. "You think you're too heavy for me to carry up the stairs?"

"I didn't exactly say that."

"You implied. Should we get into that bench-pressing discussion and my age again?"

"Fine. Though I think you do that to change the topic."

He pulled off her capris, then her underwear, nuzzling her inner thigh with his lips. "Speaking of changing the subject . . ."

He was very distracting, and when he put his mouth on her sex, whatever they'd been discussing dissolved in a puddle of desire. She lifted, reaching for his head, tangling her fingers in his hair while he plied her senseless with his amazing tongue and mouth. She was on the very brink of orgasm when he suddenly stopped.

She lifted up on her elbows, dazed with desire, her pussy throbbing as she watched him drop his shorts and climb onto his knees.

"Now suck me."

Shuddering, she put her mouth around him as he fed his cock between her lips.

"I love watching your mouth work, Haven, the way you wrap your tongue around the head of my cock and suck me hard."

She loved the way his voice went deep when she gave him pleasure. And when he dipped his fingers where his mouth had been, rubbing her clit as she sucked him, she wasn't sure which of them was going to come first.

But then he pulled his cock out of her mouth, leaving her wanting more of the salty taste of him in her mouth.

Until he climbed down between her legs again, picking up where he'd left off before, this time tucking two fingers inside of her to go with the delicious sensations of his tongue and lips over her clit.

The delay had only heightened her desire. She was going to come this time, and nothing was going to stop it. She could feel every fiber, every nerve ending pulse and tingle as her orgasm rushed through her body. She lifted her hips against his face and let out a cry of pleasure that made even her legs tremble as she came with a wild burst, then wave after wave of sensation. And through it all, Trevor continued to pump his fingers in and out of her, driving that sensation even higher, prolonging her climax until she dropped her hips to the bed, completely satiated.

Only then did he pull his fingers from her, lick them clean, and once again move to her head, cradling it in his hand as he fed his cock to her.

She wanted to give him the same pleasure he'd given her. Despite her body still trembling with the aftereffects of that amazing orgasm, she took his cock in her hands and stroked him while she licked and sucked the wide, soft head, then took him wholly in her mouth.

"Oh, fuck," he said, driving his cock deeper in her mouth. She took hold of him, squeezing the base, cradling his balls and giving them a gentle massage before pulling back, rolling her tongue across his shaft.

She loved the look on his face, the way his breathing quickened, letting her know she was giving him the ultimate in pleasure. She wanted to make this good for him, as good as what he'd given her. She flattened her tongue against the head of his cock, then swirled around the crest before covering her lips over his cockhead and sucking him in, inch by slow inch, giving him harder pressure now.

"That's going to make me come, babe," he said, pulling out, then thrusting his cock into her mouth faster and faster.

She wanted this, wanted him to explode just as she had.

She flicked her tongue across the head, then clamped down on his cock and gave him the suction he needed. He groaned and said the sweetest word in the softest voice, so incongruent with this shattering moment.

"Haven."

He cupped the back of her head, releasing a hot spurt of come onto her tongue. She swallowed as he emptied into her mouth.

She felt his whole body shake with his orgasm.

She knew how that felt, that amazing flood of release that catapulted you to another place. She held tight to him, letting him shudder through it, licking his cock until it went soft before she released him.

He dropped down beside her, cupping her face in his hands to kiss her.

They rolled over on their backs and stared up at the ceiling.

"Okay, now I might be a little out of breath. But I think my brains also might be leaking out of my ears."

She laughed. "That good, huh?"

"Yeah. That good."

She flipped over on her side and rested her head in her hand, content to just look at him. He really was an amazingly beautiful man. If she could go back in time and tell her younger self that she'd be here in bed naked with Trevor Shay, her younger self would laugh at her and tell her there was no way in hell that was ever going to happen, because Trevor was way out of her league.

Yet, here she was. And Trevor seemed . . . content. Happy. No mention of other girls or a desire to be with anyone else.

What did that mean?

Probably nothing. But he'd been so sweet to her this whole time, as if she were the only one who mattered to him.

God knew he mattered to her. She was his for the duration of this assignment.

After that, he'd move on. She knew he would. They had said no words of commitment to each other. He'd go do his thing, and so would she. She'd do well to remember that he wasn't a relationship kind of guy. And she had a career path to think about.

But for now, she sure was having fun.

TWENTY-NINE

IT HAD BEEN A BUSY DAY, AND EVEN THOUGH HAVEN hadn't gone to practice with Trevor, she'd been occupied preparing for the scavenger hunt tonight. All the items had been sufficiently hidden. She'd noted all of their whereabouts and updated her master list. Now all that was left was the party tonight, which she hoped was as fun as she thought it was going to be.

It was almost a shame she was going to be in charge of the scavenger hunt, and unable to take part in it, because she would have loved to play side by side with Trevor. But she still intended to have a great time managing the festivities.

The caterers were setting up in the expansive dining room, as well as the breakfast bar in the kitchen. An extremely competent staff of four people who clearly knew what they were doing put up tables and covered Trevor's dining room table to serve the food. Trevor also informed her he was going to have bar service.

Bar service. Sure . . . why not?

This was so far outside the realm of her life, but hey, at least it made for interesting observations about his.

He threw impromptu parties for his teammates. And, he'd explained to her, because the rookie tight end had some kind of attitude issue.

She couldn't quite make the connection between the rookie's problem and inviting him to a party.

Maybe that was a guy thing. If it were her and one of her coworkers was copping 'tude, she'd ignore them. Or tell them to fuck off.

But that was her, and in her world, things were obviously different.

Men were certainly different. She'd showered after her day of running around, curled her hair and done her makeup, then put on a sundress and sandals. Though why she was primping she had no idea. Especially since she came downstairs and saw Trevor in a pair of shorts and a sleeveless shirt, which showcased his awesome arms. Once again, his body took center stage.

The guy was ripped. She was going to have to quit ogling all the photos she'd taken of him. It was kind of obsessive, in a weird stalker-girlfriend kind of way.

She laughed at herself.

"You're all dressed up," he said as he looked up and smiled at her. "You look beautiful."

Okay, worth the compliment, though it shouldn't matter to her. "Thank you. Obviously, considering how you're dressed, this is very low-key."

"Very. The guys know not to dress up, but you'll see some of the women dressed like you."

"Is that right."

"Yeah."

"And there will be actual women here?" She'd gone over the list of attendees with him, and he'd given her names of couples, so she hoped he wasn't wrong about that.

"Promise. Most of the guys will bring wives or girlfriends. Unless they're not seeing anyone."

"Okay." Not that she cared. In the sportscasting world, she'd have to get used to being around athletes, and a lot of those athletes were going to be men.

"Which, I guess, makes you my date for the night."

She felt a little flutter in the vicinity of her stomach. "I'm not your date. I'm a sports reporter, remember?"

He leaned in, and she caught his just-showered scent. Resisting the urge to breathe deeply, she took a step back. She had to act like a professional tonight. Not Trevor's girlfriend.

"Can't you be both?"

She wanted to be. "I don't know, Trevor. I think we have to maintain a separation."

"We'll be co-hosts of the party tonight. I'll introduce you to the guys on the team. I've already told them about the story you're doing. You can grill them about me."

She couldn't really object to that. "That works."

When the guests started to arrive, Trevor was right. Guys brought women with them. And the offensive coach came, too—a guy in his forties named George, if Haven recalled her research correctly. He'd brought his wife, Amanda, a slim brunette with a great smile.

"And who is this, Trevor?" Amanda asked, smiling at Haven.

"This is Haven Briscoe. She's a sports reporter, and she's doing some work with me."

Amanda turned to Haven and shook her hand. "It's very nice to meet you, Haven. Just what our Trevor here needs—more attention."

Haven laughed. "Well, you might be right about that, but I do what my bosses tell me."

"And here I thought you might be Trevor's girlfriend, that someone finally tamed the wild animal."

"Sorry. That wouldn't be me." She wondered why Amanda referred to Trevor as a wild animal.

And there went her thoughts again, that visual of his hips moving up and down while he stroked his cock. The way he thrust when he was inside her. The room grew warmer.

Focus, Haven. And not on your very vivid imagination.

"Oh, well. Surely some woman someday will get you to settle down and decide that football is the one sport you should be playing."

Trevor laughed and put his arm around Amanda. "Has George been feeding you those lines, Amanda?"

"Not at all. I've got a perfectly good mind of my own. And you should know by now that all of us here in Tampa want you here permanently."

Trevor kissed her cheek. "Thanks for that. It means a lot to me."

Haven stood next to Trevor as a few other coaches and several players started filing in. Trevor introduced her to Warrell Timmons, the tight end rookie. He'd come by himself and looked rather uncomfortable.

He was a very attractive young man. Super tall, like Trevor, but a little bit leaner, not as much muscle. He had beautiful dark skin, gorgeous light brown eyes, and a nice smile that he didn't use but once, and that was when he politely flashed it after he'd been introduced to her. After that he made his way into the living area, where Trevor told her a lot of the rookies were huddled.

"I mean to break up that party," Trevor said, motioning to the rookies. "It's good they're bonding, but I want to get Warrell comfortable with me, and get the other rookies meshing with the veterans."

"We'll take care of that with the scavenger hunt after dinner."

"You're right about that," Trevor said, resting his hand at the small of her back. "Come on. Let's go get something to drink."

She asked for a glass of wine from the bartender, and Trevor grabbed a beer. They made their way around the room, and Trevor talked to a few of the guys while Haven wandered off to visit with some of the other players. Trevor liked that Haven was independent, that she didn't cling to his side like a lot of the women he'd dated always seemed to do.

When the catering manager found him and told him the food was ready, he announced it to the crowd, and they all made their way to the tables. There was barbecued beef and chicken, along with potato salad and coleslaw, fruit salad and beans. Everyone filled their plates.

He found Haven talking to Barrett Cassidy, the safety on the team, and Barrett's brother Grant, who played quarterback for St. Louis.

"You're on a bye this week, too?" he asked Grant as he took a seat next to them.

"Yeah. Thought I'd take a trip out here and enjoy the warm weather, see one of my brothers."

"You came out here to see the bikini babes, not me," Barrett said.

Grant grinned. "Maybe."

"I've discovered Grant and his brother Barrett are part of a family dynasty of football players," Haven said. "They have two more brothers."

"Tucker doesn't count. He plays baseball," Barrett said.

Grant leaned back and shot his brother a look. "I'm going to tell him you said that."

Barrett shrugged. "Like he hasn't heard it before?" He took a long swallow of beer.

Trevor laughed. He knew all the Cassidy brothers. They were a tight-knit group, and they were all kick-ass athletes.

"Haven and I were doing a little trash-talking about the University of Oklahoma versus Texas, where I went to school," Grant said. "It's a hell of a rivalry, as you know."

Trevor looked over at Haven, who cast a smile at him. "I have to defend the alma mater."

He laughed. "I guess you do."

"I hear there are games in store for us tonight, Trevor," Barrett said. "Is that right?"

"Think of it as a team-building exercise."

Grant nodded. "Sounds fun, seeing as how your team needs all that building."

Barrett shoved an elbow in his brother's ribs.

"Hey," Grant said. "That hurt."

"You quarterbacks," Barrett said. "Such pussies."

"I'm totally up for it," Grant said. "And if you and I aren't on the same team, Trevor, be prepared to have your ass kicked."

Trevor knew these guys would be competitive. "We'll see about that, won't we?"

"Will you be playing, Haven?" Barrett asked. "Because the Cassidy brothers will kick your butt, too."

Haven laughed. "Unfortunately, no. I'll be ringleading this circus tonight."

Barrett cast a glance over at Trevor. "How much did you have to pay her to get her to agree to that?"

After taking a sip of beer, Trevor said, "Surprisingly, she volunteered."

"You poor thing," Barrett said. "You have no idea what you've signed up for."

Haven laughed. "I think I can handle this rowdy bunch. Besides, you're all going to be way too busy to give me a hard time."

Haven excused herself after dinner, and they let everyone socialize a bit while the caterers cleaned up dinner. Trevor noticed

Haven was taking down everyone's names, and she'd wandered off into the office. When she came back, she got everyone's attention and herded them all into the living room.

"Trevor and I have cooked up something very special—and hopefully fun for you for tonight. Trevor, do you want to tell everyone about it?"

He didn't. Too many details, and he didn't want to screw it up and get things wrong. "You go ahead, Haven. You're doing a fine job."

"Okay. We're going to have a scavenger hunt. And the best part is, there are prizes at the end. You're all going to be paired up in teams. There are forty items in total that have been hidden. These items could be hidden somewhere on the property here, on the street, or in town. You'll be given a list of these items, as well as clues where to find them. You have one hour and one hour only. At the end of the hour you're to report back here. The team that has found the most items will be declared the winner."

"What are the prizes?" one of the guys asked.

"The prize for the first-place team is a deep-sea fishing expedition."

Lots of oohs, aahs, and applause on that one. Trevor loved to fish, and he knew several of the guys did, too.

"There are also prizes for second- and third-place teams, too, which is dinner at some of Tampa's finest restaurants. So let's get started.

"I'll announce the names on each team," Haven said. "Once everyone's together with their teams, I'll hand out your tote bags you'll be using to accumulate the items, and your list of items and clues."

She started calling names. True to what they discussed, Trevor and Warrell were on the same team, along with wide receiver Elvin Detteridge and Elvin's girlfriend, Allison.

One rookie was paired with at least one veteran. Trevor made sure to have Haven mix it up that way, so the rookies weren't paired up.

Haven had worked that out well.

Once all the teams were formed, Haven handed them their bag with clues and the list. "Good luck," she said, offering him a smile.

"Thanks."

He turned to Warrell, Elvin, and Allison and pulled out the clues and items list. "You ready to kick some butt?"

Allison nodded. "Absolutely. Let's see what we've got here."

She took the list. "Oh, these are all football items. Awesome."

"How about we let Allison be in charge of reading the clues," Trevor suggested. "And who has a good sense of direction?"

"Well, this is your home," Elvin said. "You should be able to tell from the clues where this stuff might be."

"That's true," Allison said. "I think we ended up on the best team, having Trevor with us."

Warrell had yet to say anything.

"I don't know about that," Trevor said. "Knowing Haven, she wouldn't deliberately give anyone an advantage. Besides, she doesn't live here, so she wouldn't know to mark a spot that I would be familiar with."

"Oh," Allison said. "Good point."

"Ready, everyone?" Haven had her phone out. "I'm starting the countdown. Ten . . . nine . . . eight . . ."

Trevor turned to Warrell. "Let's win this, okay?"

Warrell gave a short nod. "Sure."

When Haven gave the go signal, everyone scrambled. Some out the back door, some out the front.

"Let's not start with the first clue," Allison said. "Everyone will start with that. Let's work our way up from the bottom."

"That sounds like a good plan," Elvin said, then looked to Trevor and Warrell.

"Works for me," Warrell said.

They made their way down to the marina based on one of the clues, and found a team keychain hanging on the bell at the entrance to the harbor.

"Score one for our team," Allison said with a triumphant fist pump. She slid the keychain into the tote bag. "Okay, next clue."

Thirty minutes later, they had three of the items, but were stumped on one of the clues.

"'If it quacks like a duck . . .'? What the hell does that even mean?" Warrell asked.

"There aren't any duck ponds around here," Trevor said, trying to think.

"How do you know for sure? Do you hang out at all the ponds?" Warrell asked.

"Well . . . no."

"Let's head down to the lake over there. Maybe we'll see some ducks," Allison suggested.

"Okay." But he didn't think they'd find anything there.

They ran into a few of the other teams, but no one followed them. They all looked like they were hard at work doing their own thing. He didn't want to be distracted, though.

They'd been working on the clues, but damn that Haven, these were hard.

When they got down to the lake, they all looked around, even splitting up to wander the area.

They came up with nothing.

"It's not here," Elvin said.

Then it hit him. "Duck's Bar. Just up the street and around the corner."

Hopefully no one else had come up with the clue. They ran, and Warrell asked the bartender, who pulled out the team football from behind the bar.

"Awesome," Elvin said. "That's four items for us."

"How are we doing for time?" Allison asked.

Warrell pulled out his phone. "Fifteen minutes left."

"Let's check out the next clue." Allison went over the list. "Or maybe we should split up. Elvin and I will do one, and you and Warrell can do another. It'll double our chances to get more items."

Trevor nodded. "That works."

Allison read them their clue—"Find me at the bottom of the barrel."

"We'll meet up back at the house with five minutes left," Allison said. Then they dashed off in another direction.

"Okay, what do you think that means," Trevor asked.

"You got me." Warrell looked around. "I don't see any barrels around here."

They started walking along the marina, both of them searching opposite sides of the road. "Keep your eyes open for a barrel. There has to be one—"

Of course. He didn't know why it hadn't occurred to him right away. "We have to get back to the house. There's a barrel at the end of my dock. "

They made a run for it. When they got back to the house, Trevor stopped Warrell. "Play it cool. We don't want anyone to notice where we're going."

Warrell nodded. They grabbed a beer, then went out onto the deck. Trevor motioned with his head toward the barrel, and Warrell went over there, stuck his hand inside, and, grinning at Trevor, fished out a team bobblehead.

Yes.

By then Allison and Elvin had made their way back. "Find any-thing?"

Trevor produced the bobblehead.

"Awesome," Allison said. "We had no luck at all with our clue."

"But we have five," Trevor said. "That's pretty good."

"But is it good enough? There are forty items in total."

"And a lot of teams," Trevor added. "So we'll see."

They hung out and waited, watching as the rest of the teams showed up. Trevor had no idea who would win.

"What do you think?" he asked as he and Warrell hung out, drinking beers.

"I dunno. No one looks like they have a bag stuffed full. I think we got a shot."

"Me, too."

"Okay, everyone," Haven said. "Time's up. Turn your bags in."

Allison turned in their tote bag. Trevor watched as Haven gathered all the bags and started counting up items. He had to admit, he'd had fun. He went back to his group and finished his beer.

"We did good. No matter what happens, we did good. We're a great team."

"You're right," Elvin said. "We killed it. And from the looks of some of those bags Haven is emptying, we did better than a lot of the other teams."

Trevor clinked his beer against theirs, then looked over at Warrell, who finally seemed relaxed. He even grinned.

Everyone mingled and had snacks and drinks while Haven tallied up the winners. When she announced that she was ready, people started gathering around.

"Third-place winners of gift cards to some of Tampa's finest restaurants are Vivian and Louis Trammell, and Sue and JW."

Rounds of applause went up.

"Second-place winners of gift cards are Trevor, Elvin and Allison, and Warrell."

"Hey, that's us," Trevor said.

"Dammit, I wanted to win," Elvin said.

Warrell laughed at that. "Don't we all."

But they took their gift cards. "Thanks," Trevor said as Haven handed him the gift card.

"You're welcome. You all did very well."

"And the winning team, with ten items found, is Coach George and his wife, Amanda, along with Barrett and Grant Cassidy."

"I didn't know the Cassidys could run that fast," someone shouted amid the applause.

"I will kick your ass in practice next week," Barrett said, pointing a finger and glaring at one of the guys.

Trevor laughed. Everyone gave the winning teams cheers. And Coach was grinning.

It was a good win, because Trevor knew how much Coach loved deep-sea fishing. So did the Cassidy brothers.

"Thanks for this, Trevor," George said, waving the gift certificate. "I'm going to enjoy it."

"So will I," Amanda said, sliding the certificate into her purse. "While he's off fishing for the day, I'll be at the spa."

Haven had moved in next to Trevor. "Sounds like a win-win for everyone, then."

"More so for me, I think," Amanda said with a wide smile. "I do love my spa days."

"I don't know. I do love my fishing." George put his arm around Amanda. "But yeah, spa day for you, babe."

The party started to wind down. Trevor saw everyone out, surprised when Warrell came up to him.

"I actually had a good time. Thanks for inviting me."

"Thanks for coming. I think our team did good."

Warrell nodded. "We did. And I'm still planning to beat your ass on the field."

"I'll be looking forward to it."

Warrell grinned. "See you on Monday at practice."

After the caterers and bartenders cleaned up and left, Trevor locked the door and grabbed a bottle of water. Haven was busily putting away all of the scavenger hunt stuff.

"My cleaning staff is coming tomorrow. They can take care of that."

She looked up at him. "So can I. This will only take a few minutes to put away."

He walked over to her and took her hand. "You've done enough work tonight. Let's go outside. You should put your feet up and relax. I feel like all you did was work during the party."

She laughed. "It was hardly work. I mostly sat and had wine while the rest of you ran off and did the scavenger hunt thing. And I got to visit with Luisa Wilson."

"Oh, Mowery's wife?"

"Yes. She's like eight months pregnant. She said her ankles were swollen and she wasn't up to dashing around doing the scavenger hunt, so she stayed behind while her husband went off and did the hunt. She and I talked. She's very nice."

"Yeah, she is. Do you want more wine?"

"Sure."

"What are you having?"

"I can get it."

He gave her a look. "What are you having?"

"The sauvignon blanc."

He went to the refrigerator, studied the bottles for a minute, then pulled one out. "This one?"

"Yes."

He uncorked it and poured her a glass, then motioned for her to join him as he headed out the back door. She'd long ago kicked off her sandals, so she padded out to the deck barefoot.

He liked her feet, liked her painted pink toenails. And when she went and sat by the pool and slid her legs in the water, he kicked off his tennis shoes, pulled off his socks, and sat next to her, handing her the glass of wine.

She took a sip, then sighed. "Mmm. This is good." She turned her head to look at him. "How did it go with Warrell?"

"Good. He loosened up some."

"I'm glad."

"Me, too. I think it might help him at practice and in game situations to realize we're all not the enemy."

"I hope so."

"Thank you again for organizing all this tonight."

"You're welcome. It was fun for me."

"It was work."

"Work can sometimes be fun."

He liked hearing her say that. It was the attitude he was trying to cultivate. Though tonight hadn't been part of her job. "Did you get to talk to any of the players—actual work-type stuff?"

"No. I didn't want to break up what was a relaxing, fun night with reporter questions. I'll leave that for another time, when I'm working in my official capacity."

He shifted so he could look directly at her. "No one would have minded, you know."

"Maybe. Maybe not. But you can lose trust if you start pummeling people with questions while they're trying to kick back and have a good time. This just wasn't the right venue for me to go after people with questions about you or the team."

"Okay. You know what's best." He paused for a minute, then smiled. "So does this mean if I'm kicking back and having a good time, you won't ask me questions?"

She laughed. "Nice try. And no. It doesn't work that way, since you're the reason I'm here."

"Well, it is all about me."

Now she rolled her eyes. "Modest as always."

"You know me so well."

"Actually, there's a lot more I need to know about you."

"For the story."

She wanted to know more about his past. Yes, for the interview, but also because she was curious about him—about his past, and how he came to be. "What if I said my reasons were personal?"

He laughed. "I wouldn't believe you."

She cocked her head to the side. "Why not? Is it so hard to believe I want to know more about you because I care about you?"

He didn't answer her for a few seconds, then he turned to look at her. "We're just having fun here, Haven, right?"

She frowned. "What do you mean?"

"You and me. Nothing serious, right?"

His words stung. They shouldn't have, but they did. She should have known better than to open herself up to getting hurt. But a simple question and she'd done that.

She hid that sting behind a casual smile. "Of course. You have two careers that keep you more than busy. I have a new career that will have me traveling everywhere. Neither one of us is looking for a romantic relationship. Like you said, we're just having fun here, Trevor. And when this interview is over, I'm walking away."

He looked at her, and for the life of her she couldn't fathom what she saw behind his eyes. She wished it weren't so dark outside.

"Right. That's exactly what I want, too."

She got up and grabbed a towel to dry her feet and legs. "I'm glad we both want the same thing. I'd hate for there to be anything awkward—you know—when this is over."

He looked over his shoulder. "Where are you going?"

"It was a super busy day and I'm kind of tired tonight. I'm going to head up to bed."

His lips curved. "My bed, I hope."

She paused. "Actually, I have a few hours of writing to do on the interview. I could use some quiet time, so I can get through this as quickly as possible. I think I'm going to close myself up in the guest room tonight. I hope you don't mind."

He gave her a curious look. "Sure. I'll see you tomorrow."

"Okay." In her best this-is-all-just-casual-between-us voice, she said, "See you tomorrow, Trevor."

She hurried upstairs, closed the door, and leaned against it, trying to calm her rapid pulse.

Stupid. She was so stupid.

She had fallen in love with him.

Again.

And it was totally, utterly one-sided.

Again.

When will you ever get smart, Haven?

He will never love you.

TREVOR HAD NO IDEA WHY HE'D SAID WHAT HE'D SAID to Haven.

Correction. He knew exactly why he'd pushed her away.

She'd said she cared.

He couldn't afford to let a woman—to let Haven—get close enough to care about him.

Because she wanted to know more about him, which meant exploring his past. And that meant exposing secrets—secrets he wasn't ready to trust anyone with.

Or was he ready?

No. He couldn't. Just the thought of it . . . what she might think if he told her . . .

She wouldn't understand. She'd think less of him. Or even

worse, she'd try to help, and no one could help him, because no one could know.

He took a long swallow of his beer and rolled the bottle around in his hands.

The problem was, she wasn't the only one who cared. He'd gotten used to having her in his life. In his house. He missed her when she wasn't around. He loved having her body next to his at night. He enjoyed her laugh, her sense of humor, her counsel. He'd grown closer to Haven than any other woman in his life before.

Was that love? He didn't know.

Maybe it was, because when he thought about her, everything inside him tightened with lust, with emotion, with a sense that if he didn't have her next to him all the time, something was missing.

But still, he kept a part of himself removed from her.

He couldn't tell her about that part. It would change her feelings for him.

And that meant there could be no relationship, which was why he'd spent all these years alone.

With no answers to his dilemma in sight, he stared out into the darkness.

THIRTY

HAVEN DIDN'T QUITE KNOW WHAT TO MAKE OF SOME of the other players offering themselves up for interviews about Trevor. But as she sat there and watched the team practice, she noticed Trevor would talk to one of the players, who would nod, and then later on make his way over to her.

She rolled her eyes, feeling manipulated and irritated. Who was in charge of this interview, anyway? So whenever one of the guys came over and offered himself up, she politely turned him down, telling him she'd look him up later if she had any questions about Trevor.

Damn the man for always wanting to control things. Maybe she'd put *that* in her bio piece about him.

God forbid he should hand over the reins of control to a woman, letting her be in charge.

Though he hadn't minded whenever she'd wanted to climb on top of him during sex. She'd been in charge then, hadn't she?

As she saw him dash down the field, the ball sailing in the air and landing in Trevor's arms, goose bumps pricked her skin. She vividly recalled herself naked, riding Trevor's lean hips while he dug his fingers into her flesh, urging her to take them both right to the edge, then over. Her nipples tightened, her pussy quivering with the need to—

Dammit. Shaking herself out of her self-induced sex dream, she forced her attention on Trevor's confident jaunt back to the huddle. She caught him taking a quick glance up at her sitting on the sidelines. He gave her a knowing smile, almost as if he'd been aware of what she'd been thinking.

No way. It wasn't like her body was giving off sexual pheromones or she was holding up an *I Need to Get Laid* sign or anything. He had just smiled at her. That was all it had been. Like a *Hi, how's it going?* kind of thing.

Right?

It had just been one night apart. And maybe she hadn't slept much and she'd stared out at the dark water outside her window instead of sleeping, lost in her own thoughts. She could have been cuddled up next to Trevor's warm body, or mixed in a tangle of arms and legs, her body moving under—or over—his, wildly crying out in orgasm, instead of sleeping in a cold bed all by herself.

She might as well get used to that, because as soon as the interview was over, that was what she'd be doing every night.

Forcing her thoughts back to her work, she fixed her attention on the notes she'd spent the past few hours making, then put her laptop aside and grabbed her camera. Andy was working film, but she wanted some still shots as well.

She walked the sidelines, framing Trevor as he stood in the huddle. As tall as he was, it was easy to pick him out of all the amazingly athletic players. Or maybe it was just that she could easily call him out. Either way, she grabbed a shot of him bending over in the huddle, and then getting into position as the offense readied for the next play. He charged down the sideline and she took several pictures, getting one of him making a spectacular grab, his body stretched out, his feet leaving the ground as he reached up for the ball.

That was going to be a great still shot. She took several more, just of him, and of him with his team, before going back to her seat.

After practice, she waited for him to shower, then met him at the entrance.

"Good practice?" she asked.

"Yeah. I think we're ready for Dallas this weekend."

"Good."

"I'm going to hit the showers. Oh, and Larry, the receivers coach, has invited a bunch of the receivers to dinner at his place tonight. It's going to be relaxed, talk strategy. Guys are bringing wives and girlfriends."

"I'm not a girlfriend. And obviously not a wife."

"No, but you have to eat, right?"

After their conversation last night, she didn't know how she felt about going with him. But declining would be petty, and she wasn't petty. Besides, it would give her an opportunity to see him in action—at least socially—with the other receivers, and the job came first. "Yes, I do have to eat."

"So that's a yes?"

"Sure."

"Great. I'll meet you back at the house. Dinner's at seven."

She left and headed back to the house. She had a few things to talk to him about. She had a great idea she'd come up with during her hours of nonsleep last night, when she'd gone over his bio and reviewed his charity work. She thought it would be a great piece for the interview and she knew he'd love the idea, because it would feature one of his charities. She couldn't wait to run it by him.

She met with Andy to make arrangements for him to send her the film he'd taken. They were going to meet up again in Dallas this weekend for the game.

She drove back to the house and worked more on her notes so she could send them in to her production team. She was in the dining room, working on her laptop, when Trevor came home.

"Hey," he said, laying his bag down in the kitchen.

"Hey yourself."

"Are you working?"

"Yes. Finishing up some notes and uploading some photos I took of you and the team today. Would you like to see them?"

"Yeah." He leaned over her while she showed him the photos. This was actually the first time he'd reviewed her work.

"These are good. You're a great photographer, Haven."

She tilted her head back to smile at him. "Thanks."

"Could you send me a couple of the pics you don't use?"

"Sure. Are you going to frame them and hang them on your wall?"

He laughed. "No. But I'll send them to the person who handles my PR and she can use them."

"I see."

The doorbell rang, and Trevor went to the door. He came back with a man who looked to be in his midthirties, dressed in a dark suit. He was quite good-looking in a *GQ* kind of way, with short sandy blond hair, deep blue eyes, and black Clark Kent glasses.

"Haven, this is my lawyer, Bradley Rayburn."

She got up from the table and held out her hand. "Nice to meet you, Bradley."

"Call me Brad. Nice to meet you, too, Haven. You must be the person interviewing Trevor for the network feature story."

"I am."

"How's that going?"

"It's going very well. As you know, Trevor is quite the subject." She cast a smile Trevor's way.

Brad grinned. "Yeah, he is."

Brad put his briefcase on the table, opened it, and pulled out a file folder. He opened it and took out what looked like contracts. "These are ready to sign."

Trevor sat at the table and took the pen Brad handed him. "Where the flags are?"

"Yeah." Brad turned to Haven. "So how long have you been in sports broadcasting?"

Haven had her attention on Trevor, but pulled it away briefly to give a quick glance to Brad. "Oh, not long."

Trevor signed the contracts, then handed the papers back to Brad. "Here you go."

"Great. I'll have these countersigned and an executed copy should be ready for you within a week."

"Okay."

Brad closed his briefcase, then turned to Haven. "It was great meeting you, Haven."

"You, too, Brad."

Trevor walked him to the door, then came back. Haven leaned against the table and crossed her arms.

"What?" he asked.

"You didn't even read whatever it was he asked you to sign."

Trevor waited a few beats before answering her. "Oh. I'd already gone over those contracts in Brad's office. I knew what they were."

"Still. Don't you think you should have read them over to make sure no changes were made?"

"Nah. I trust Brad. We've been together since I started my career. If there'd been changes, he would have told me."

"I know it's not my business, Trevor, but really, that's not a good idea. You should always read anything before you sign it."

He came over and swept his hand down her arm, then clasped his fingers with hers. "Thanks for looking out for me, Haven, but really, the contract was fine. And so is Brad."

She shrugged. "If you say so." She untangled her hand from his and picked up her phone. "I need to go change for dinner."

"Yeah, me too."

She went upstairs and took a shower, did her hair and makeup and put on a pair of capris and a tank, then chose a sheer long-sleeved button-down blouse to put over it. She slipped into her shoes and went downstairs.

Trevor was already there, wearing cargo pants and a short-sleeved shirt that hugged his well-muscled chest.

She sighed in appreciation. "You look good."

He smiled and came over to her, picked up her hand, and kissed the back of it. "And you look gorgeous."

He tugged her close and kissed her, wrapping an arm around her waist to pull her against him, making her wish they were staying in tonight instead of going out. Just the feeling of his body pressed tight to hers, and the taste of his lips and tongue as he moved his mouth expertly over hers, ignited a fire inside her that demanded to be extinguished.

But she knew they had somewhere else to be, so she laid her palms on his chest and broke the kiss. "If you keep that up, we're not going to make it to dinner at your coach's house tonight."

His eyes gleamed hot with desire, the evidence of that in his erection that brushed against her. "Is that a bad thing?"

She shuddered against him. "For me? No. For you? Probably."

He sighed. "Okay. I'll just drive with a hard-on."

"You're not the only one turned on here, you know."

He fished a condom out of one of the many pockets in his pants. "We could have a quickie. I could make you come in a hurry."

She cocked a brow. "You think you're that good?"

He lifted her onto the kitchen counter. "I know I am."

In seconds, her shoes were on the floor and he'd tugged off her capris and her underwear. She'd thought about objecting, but she'd ignited in a hurry with the way he'd kissed her and held her, and she wanted this as much as he did.

She'd missed him last night, and it was ridiculous to deny herself such great sex. As long as she was clear about where this was headed between them—which was nowhere—she could put that lock firmly back on her heart and at least enjoy the chemistry between them.

So when he spread her legs and put his mouth on her sex, she was more than ready. She leaned back on her elbows and draped her legs over his shoulders, giving him access and letting herself fall under his spell.

He was right to be so confident. His lips and tongue performed magic, and she was there in seconds, delightful pleasure building to a fast crescendo. Her orgasm was a fast rush of intensity, a welcome release that made her quiver and moan, her body shaking as it felt like every part of her body had lit up as she climaxed.

Trevor pulled her off the counter, then turned her around and bent her over it. He unzipped his pants and put on the condom, then entered her with a quick thrust. She was wet, throbbing, waiting for him, welcoming him with a whimper as he drove into her.

He grasped her hips and pushed into her, then retreated, doing it again and again until all she could feel was him—every inch of him—thick and swelling inside her as he rushed to his own release.

She reached down to rub her clit, wanting to go again, knowing she could because the way he pumped into her drove her into a frenzy of need.

"You going to come for me, Haven?"

"Yes. I need this."

She was there—right there, and he eased out, slowing his pace, giving her the few minutes she needed to reach her orgasm. She thrust back against him and cried out when she released, this time so much better because he was inside her. She felt him, squeezed him, her body pulsing around him as she came.

And when he came, he groaned and laid his body over hers, his body shuddering against hers. He held tight to her and kissed her back as he rode out his orgasm.

Shaky and grasping for breath, she held on to the counter, Trevor holding tight to her.

He released her and he turned her around, cupping her face as he gave her a lingering kiss.

"That might have been a little bit more than a quickie."

She brushed her fingers over his bottom lip. "You're not going to get a complaint from me."

He grinned, then they grasped at clothes as they raced upstairs. Haven did a quick cleanup and repair of her hair and makeup, then got dressed and met Trevor back downstairs. She once again found him leaning against the kitchen counter, only this time with a smug smile on his face.

"This is like déjà vu," he said.

"Isn't it, though?"

When she came to him, he pulled her into his arms and once again gave her a devastating kiss. Sparks of desire reignited.

"You start this again, we really won't get there," she said, rubbing her lips against his.

He skimmed his fingers up her arm, inciting delicious tingles.

"I can't help it. You tempt me."

Before they did end up spending the night in the house, she grabbed his keys and walked to the garage. "Come on, let's go."

His coach's house was in Tampa, so it took about a half hour to get there. There was a full contingent of cars in the driveway and on the street.

"We're late," she said as they parked.

"That's okay. I'll tell Larry we were having sex. He'll understand."

She shot him a horrified look. "You will not."

He laughed. "Come on."

They rang the bell, and a woman opened the door. She was curvy and had gorgeous green eyes, with brown hair cut in a bob. She looked to be in her midforties and was absolutely beautiful. She smiled at Trevor.

"Hi, Trevor."

"Hey, Sally. This is Haven. She's working on an interview about me."

"I've heard about the interview. Larry told me about it. Nice to meet you, Haven. Come on in, you two. Everyone else is already here."

"Yeah, sorry about that. We were . . . delayed," Trevor said.

Haven felt herself blush.

"It's no problem. We haven't started dinner yet. Go make yourself at home. Larry's in the living room with the guys. Haven, you can come in the kitchen with me if you'd like. All the women are in there. Or if you'd feel more comfortable hanging out with Trevor . . ."

"No, I'd love to come with you, Sally."

With a lingering smile at Trevor, Haven followed Sally down the long hallway into a beautiful kitchen that was all turquoise and creams. It had a huge peninsula where several women were sitting, and a table off to the side where several more sat.

"Everyone, this is Haven. She's here with Trevor."

"Well, lucky you," one of them said, then stood. "I'm Felicia, Brady McCall's girlfriend."

She recognized a few of the other women from the scavenger hunt, as well. She spotted Allison, Elvin's girlfriend, and met Tania Ford, Rodney's wife. Rodney was one of the offensive linesmen, and she'd interviewed him already.

She was introduced to the rest of them, and just hoped she'd remember all the names.

"What would you like to drink?" Sally asked. "We have wine, margaritas, iced tea, and water."

"I'd love some wine."

"Come choose which one," Sally said, and Haven chose a sauvignon blanc.

Sally poured her a glass.

The kitchen also smelled great. She didn't know what Sally was cooking, but she couldn't imagine having to fix dinner for all these people.

"Is there something I can do to help with dinner?"

"No, thank you, Haven. We've got that under control. Steaks and chicken are already fixed and are warming, and the ladies here all brought sides. It's an easy meal tonight."

"Oh, Trevor didn't tell me to bring a side. I'm so sorry."

Sally laid her hand on Haven's arm. "You weren't required to bring anything. Just sit back and enjoy your wine."

Haven took a seat at the table.

For a while, she sat and listened to the women chat. Being an outsider, she wanted to get a feel for the group. Many of these women had been together for a lot of years. It showed, too, as they talked kids and husbands and boyfriends and team wins and losses. They talked about the games and the guys traveling and what team they'd be playing next.

These women knew their football—and their players—an angle Haven hadn't considered before. But it was in her head now, and it was something she wanted to explore.

"You haven't said much, Haven," Felicia said. "I hope we're not boring you."

"Quite the contrary, actually. I was listening to all of you talk about football. I don't know how many of you know this about me, but I'm actually a sports reporter for a network. I'm working with Trevor doing an extensive interview about his life and career."

Tania raised a brow. "Really? That should be interesting. And informative. And a ton of fun."

Haven laughed. "It has been—all of those things. Anyway, as I've been listening to all of you, it occurred to me that there's so much about the wives and girlfriends of the players that's unknown—or possibly misrepresented. You really know your football. All the teams and all the players. I'd love to do a story about all of you."

Sally frowned. "A story about us? Why?"

"I think you're all fascinating. Kind of a behind-the-player—or the-woman-behind-the-player type of feature. Even the coaches' wives as well. I don't really have it all figured out yet, but you all know so much about football. Not just what your guy does, but you have an in-depth knowledge about the other players on the team, and the other teams Tampa plays. It's impressive."

Amanda laughed. "If you're going to date or marry a football player—or in my case, a coach—you'd better know football. We don't just go to the mall when our guys are playing football. I love football. I loved the sport before I met George. Having someone involved in football was just icing."

"That's true," Tania said. "I love that Rodney plays football, but I was a sports nut before he and I ever met. My dad played college football, too. It was ingrained in me from childhood."

And it was those types of human interest stories that would make for a great piece. "If you all are interested, when I'm done with Trevor's story, I'll take down your numbers and get back to you."

They all looked to each other, and she got an immediate positive response.

She thought about the Rivers team as well. Liz, who was a sports agent. Alicia, who also worked for the Rivers. Tara, who owned her own company. So many women rich with experience on their own, but who also knew their players and the team so well.

This could be a great interview.

TREVOR WAS DEEP IN CONVERSATION WITH LARRY, George, and the other receivers, talking strategy and potential plans of attack, when Sally came in with the women.

"Okay, gentlemen. Dinner is ready, so it's time to take a break. We want to eat before the Thursday night game starts, don't we?"

Larry raised his head. "Yeah, we sure do, honey. Come on, guys."

Trevor found Haven in the kitchen. She handed him a plate.

"How's it going?" he asked.

Her lips tilted. "Very well, actually. How about you?"

"Great. We don't get a chance during practice to have intense meetings like this. It's helpful to get away from the field and just talk about how we're going to approach it."

"Good to know."

They found a seat at the dining room table. Trevor ate steak, potatoes, and broccoli. And then went back for more.

"Hungry?" Haven asked.

"A little. Worked up an appetite at practice today."

"And it's a good thing you burn it all off at practice, too."

"It's how I keep my figure."

She laughed.

"This is all so delicious," Haven said to Sally, who was sitting on the other side of her.

"Thank you. We try to do this a couple times a season. It's good for George to have a sit-down with his receivers. And of course, for all of us women to get together somewhere besides the stadium."

"I told Sally I wanted to do a piece on the women of football," Haven said to Trevor.

"The women of football? You mean there aren't enough guys?" Rodney asked her.

"Oh, there are plenty of you. But your women have interesting stories to tell."

"Indeed we do," Tania said with a smile.

"That could be a great angle," Trevor said.

"I think so," Haven said. "And speaking of interesting stories, when I was reviewing your bio I noticed you have the Greater Tampa literacy project as one of your charities."

"I do."

"I made arrangements for you to do a reading with some of their kids next week as part of the interview. You'll go in and read to a few of the kids. I think it'll make for a great human interest piece."

Trevor's fork stilled on its way to his mouth. "What?"

"Oh, that's a wonderful idea, Haven," Allison said. "Several of our guys are invested in this project."

"Is that right? Maybe some of them could come along and read as well. If you could tell me who they are, I'll make contact with them and see if they're interested."

"I'm sure they will be. All the guys involved with the charity would love to have some focus turned on it. Isn't that right, Trevor?"

Trevor could barely focus on what Allison and Haven were saying. All he heard was Haven saying they'd film him reading to the kids.

He couldn't do it.

"Uh, yeah. Sure."

His throat had gone dry, his dinner now a brick sitting in his stomach.

He had to find a way to get out of this.

The rest of the night passed in a blur until it was time to say their good-byes. They climbed into the car and Trevor was dead silent on the drive back.

"It was fun tonight, wasn't it?" Haven finally asked.

"Yeah."

"I really liked all the women. And I have such a fantastic idea for a new story to present to my producer."

"That's good." He gripped the steering wheel, focusing on the road, the cars ahead of him, trying to keep his attention on driving, while at the same time his mind whirled with ways to get out of what Haven had planned for him.

Fortunately, she'd been busy making notes on her phone, so she stopped talking to him.

He needed time alone. He had to think, to figure a way to back out of this. But how was he going to do that without coming across as a dick?

Damn Haven for putting him in this position. Why couldn't she have asked him first?

By the time he pulled into the parking garage of the house, he was angry and on edge. He tossed his keys on the counter and went to the fridge to grab a beer.

Haven fixed herself a glass of ice water, then took a seat on the sofa in the living room.

"You were really quiet on the drive back here."

He took several swallows of beer, not saying anything to her. He needed a minute or two to calm down, hoping the beer would help.

He stopped at the door to the back deck and stared into the darkness, taking another drink of beer.

"Trevor. Is something wrong?"

Anger boiled inside him, looking for a way out. He tried to contain it, but he turned to face her. "You made a decision without consulting me."

She blinked. "Excuse me? What decision?"

"The literacy event."

"What about it? I thought you'd be happy."

He took a deep breath. "You shouldn't have booked that without consulting me."

"Why not? Is there some problem with the organization?"

"No. They're a great organization. That's why they're one of the charities I support."

"Then I don't understand the problem."

He saw her frown, and he knew he wasn't getting his point across.

And he knew why. Because there was something he wasn't telling her, something he couldn't tell her without divulging his secret.

He dragged his fingers through his hair. "I can't do it."

"Okay. Care to explain why?"

"No. Just cancel it."

He finished his beer and tossed the bottle in the recycling bin. It hadn't helped, so he grabbed another out of the refrigerator.

Haven got up and came over to him. "Trevor, I can tell you're upset about this. Talk to me."

He pushed past her and opened the door to the back deck, needing the cool night air to clear his head. He walked all the way out to the boat dock and sat.

Haven followed, pulling up a spot next to him.

"I've never seen you this upset. Please tell me what's wrong."

Instead, he downed half the contents of his bottle of beer, looking for a solution in oblivion. Maybe if he got drunk, his problem would go away.

"I don't want to talk about this."

"I think you should. Tell me why you don't want to do this story. If it's something about the facility . . ."

"It's not the facility. They're great."

"Then what is it?"

The last thing he wanted right now was to listen to her calm, concerned voice. He pushed off the dock, needing to get away from Haven. He went into the house, but he heard her right on his heels, quietly shutting the door behind her.

"Not now, Haven," he said, not even looking at her.

"I'm not going away, Trevor."

His blood boiling, he whipped around to face her. "Maybe you should."

The hurt and confusion on her face was evident. "What?"

"I think we're done here."

She paused for a second, then shook her head. "Oh, no. You don't get to push me away that easily. Something's bothering you, and it has nothing to do with you and me. So tell me what's up."

He shook his head. "I'm going to bed."

He tossed the empty beer bottle in the bin and headed up the stairs, intending to lock himself in his room, cowardly avoiding a confrontation with Haven. But she hurried in front of him on the stairs, blocking him.

"I'm not going to let you do this, Trevor. Talk to me."

"I don't have anything to say."

"Don't avoid me. Don't avoid this."

"There's nothing to avoid. I'm pissed you went behind my back and scheduled something you shouldn't have. It's as simple as that."

"No, it's not that simple. You're afraid. I can see it in your face. Now tell me what's going on, because I'm not going to let this drop."

They stood on the landing, right in front of her bedroom. He could push her out of the way and he sure as hell could outrun her. And yeah, he could hide in his room, but she'd still be there in the morning, asking the same goddamn questions.

"Leave it alone, Haven."

She grasped his hand. "I'm worried about you, Trevor. I've never seen you so upset. Please talk to me. Come to my room and talk to me."

She tugged on his hand, but he refused to yield.

If he told her, it would change everything.

No one knew. Brad knew, but he had to know. His agent knew as well.

They were the only ones.

Besides his parents, of course. And Zane.

But he'd never told anyone. Deliberately, he'd never told anyone.

His throat felt like it was closing up. It was hard to swallow. His heart pounded against his rib cage. He couldn't do this.

"Trevor. Why can't you do the literacy event?"

He could barely feel her squeezing his hand as he finally blurted out the words he'd sworn he'd never say to anyone else.

"Because I can't goddamn read."

THIRTY-ONE

HAVEN'S BREATH CAUGHT. IT WAS AS IF TIME HAD stood still for those few seconds after Trevor had told her he couldn't read.

"What?"

His shoulders slumped, the words barely audible. "Don't make me say it again."

She saw the pain etched into his features, the agony it must have cost him to admit that. "You can't read? That's impossible. I tutored you in college."

He finally sat on the stairs. Slumped in defeat was more like it, as if a balloon had burst. He had no fight left in him.

And she'd made him admit it. She felt awful.

She kneeled in front of him and said it again. "I tutored you. In English. History. Math."

"Easy enough to fake it. You did all the work. And I can read some. Just not good. I get confused. So I just . . . don't."

Oh, God. Tears pricked her eyes. She hadn't even noticed. She'd been so focused on her crush on him, on her irritation with him being the hotshot athlete who'd wanted to bargain with her to help him pass his classes, she hadn't paid attention to why he'd been struggling so much.

She'd thought he was lazy. Her stomach tightened as the guilt poured over her.

She laid her hands on his knees. "How bad is it?"

"Bad."

Then it hit her. The ridiculous organization in his refrigerator, the fact he hadn't read the contract his lawyer had brought him. She'd never actually seen him read anything. He played some games on his phone, but that day he'd made her punch in a phone number on hers.

It was starting to click.

"What about your playbook? I know football players have to learn a playbook."

"My agent and my lawyer know. They helped me through it, taught it to me play by play. Besides, there are pictures in the playbook. Fewer words. It's easier to understand."

For a brief moment, she closed her eyes, then reopened them. "That's why you chose the literacy group as one of your charities."

"Yeah. But I can't read to those kids. I can't let people find out about this."

"You can be taught to read, Trevor. I can help you."

He stood and started backing up the stairs. "No. Oh, fuck no. It's too late for me."

She stood, too, looked up at him. "It's not too late for you. It's never too late. You can't give up on yourself."

"Look. It's bad enough that you know. I don't want anyone else to know, and I hope you know this is off the record. If you try to put this in your interview, I'll sue both you personally and the network."

She gasped, horrified he'd think that of her. "Do you really think I'd use something as personal as this to get ahead in my job?"

He shrugged. "I don't know, Haven. Would you?"

She wanted to slap him, but she knew it was hurt and defensiveness causing him to lash out like this. "I wouldn't, and you know me. I would never hurt you that way. I'm trying to help you."

"You can help me by canceling the event at the literacy center. Tell them there was a scheduling conflict."

She shook her head. "I think it would only help you to—"

"You've helped enough. We're done here."

He turned around and started up the stairs.

Haven read the finality in his statement. She dashed up and got in front of him, laying her hand on his chest, forcing him to stop and face her. "Done here? What do you mean?"

The severity in his expression cut her deeply. There was no warmth, no caring there. She saw . . . nothing.

"I mean we're done. I have to concentrate on football, and you have enough footage to finish up your interview. Why don't you pack it up and leave."

And just like that, he was pushing her out of his life. She knew why, but it still hurt to hear him say the words.

"Trevor. Don't do this."

"You can stay tonight, but tomorrow I want you out of here."

"Don't. Please, don't. We can fix this together. I'll help you."

He didn't budge. She saw no emotion. It was like he'd completely closed off from her, from feeling anything. "Haven. You need to go."

She'd never seen that look on his face, the way he'd just completely shut down. Part of her wanted to push through, to refuse to leave until he saw reason. The other part of her hurt so badly because he didn't trust her, didn't care enough about her—about the both of them—to even try.

She wanted to beg him to let her stay so she could help him through this.

But why? It was clear he wanted nothing more to do with her. He'd made it nearly thirty years without her, and he intended to go without her. He didn't need or want her help.

He didn't want her. And she sure as hell wasn't going to beg him to let her stay.

"Fine. I'll be gone in the morning."

He gave a short nod. "I think that's best."

"Me, too." She turned and went to her room and shut the door, then entered the bathroom and turned on the water in the sink.

She looked into the mirror, seeing the unshed tears shimmer in her eyes.

Screw Trevor. She was not going to cry over him.

She leaned over the sink to wash her face as big, fat tears slid down her cheeks.

Oh, damn. Maybe she was going to cry over him after all.

THIRTY-TWO

HAVEN STAYED UP LATE TO FILE HER LATEST PRODUC-
tion notes and photos and to make plane reservations.

It wasn't like she was going to get any sleep anyway.

She'd cried for an hour, miserable and unhappy and wishing like
crazy that Trevor would knock on her door and tell her he was an
asshole and beg her forgiveness.

Ha. That hadn't happened.

She'd made plane reservations, but not back to New York.

She took a flight to Oklahoma, and arrived at her mother's
house the next evening.

Her mother was surprised to see her, and as soon as she saw her
mom, the tears came again.

She hadn't wanted to cry in front of her mom. Her intent was to
spend a couple of days there, regroup emotionally, then be on
her way.

"Oh, honey, what happened?" her mom asked after she'd let

loose a barrage of sobs and her mom sat with her on the sofa and comforted her with hugs and tissues.

When she had finished crying, she told her mom about Trevor, about letting her guard down and falling in love with him, about how he held himself away from her emotionally, and then, because she trusted her mother implicitly, she told her Trevor's secret.

"Wow," her mom said. "That's some painful secret to hold tight to for all these years. And how that poor boy must be hurtin' inside."

Haven shook her head. "How could I not have seen it? I tutored him, Mom."

"Honey, you didn't see it because he was clever in hiding it. From you, and obviously, from everyone."

"How did he get through school unable to read? Through college?"

"He said he reads some, right?"

"Yes."

"And you've worked with kids with literacy issues before. You know how easily they can slide through the system. Trevor's not dumb. He's very smart."

Haven nodded. "Smart enough to game me, and probably his teachers through the years."

"Yes."

She was still trying to take it all in. Not just Trevor's literacy issues, but him summarily throwing her out of his house—out of his life.

She took her things upstairs to her room and spent the first day sulking and feeling utterly drained. She slept late, then got up and had breakfast in town, went for a walk to clear her head, and did some work at the house during the day. When her mom came home from work that day, Haven helped her slice carrots and potatoes for dinner.

She had no more answers today than she had yesterday when she'd arrived. She was still smarting from Trevor asking her to leave and didn't know what to do about it. Her heart hurt, and it was an awful feeling she simply didn't want to have. She wanted it all to go away.

She had to get back to work. She'd already spent way too much time mourning her father. She wasn't going to let herself live in this state of hurt again. Burying herself in work was the solution to all her problems.

"So now that you know Trevor's secret, what are you going to do about it?" her mom asked as they stood side by side at the kitchen counter.

Haven paused, knife in her hand. "What am I going to do about it? Nothing."

Her mother slid her a look.

"What? He threw me out of his house. I begged him over and over again to talk to me. I offered to help over and over again, too. And still, he told me to leave. He threw me out."

"Haven. He's hurt. And obviously scared."

She wasn't buying it. She was hurt, too. "He had ample opportunity to talk to me, Mom. The bottom line is, he doesn't trust me."

Her mother laid down the paring knife she'd been using and leaned her hip against the counter. "I know you're hurt. You care about him, so you're lettin' your emotions cloud your judgment. You worked with people like Trevor when you were in school. You know how defensive they got when forced to face what they felt were inadequacies. Don't you think that's exactly what Trevor did when you backed him up against the wall and forced him to face the truth about himself?"

"I didn't—" But she had. She'd pushed him and pushed him until she'd made him admit a secret he'd held on to for his entire life. He'd been angry and upset and he'd lashed out at her. She'd seen it time and time again during her undergraduate studies, when she'd worked with people who had literacy issues. They got angry and defensive, a lot of times with the people they cared about the most who were only trying to help them.

Haven sighed. "This is hard. I care about him. But I can't help him if he won't let me in his life."

"Do you want to help him?"

"Of course I do."

Her mom picked up the knife and resumed chopping carrots. "Then you'll figure out a way. If anyone can, Haven, it's you. I've never known anyone more tenacious."

She thought about it as they prepped and then ate dinner, and long after her mom had gone to bed.

She'd let her own hurt and her own needs get in the way. She loved him, and she hadn't told him that. Would it have made a difference? She didn't know, but she should have tried. She'd walked away when she should have stood her ground and stayed. She should have been a support system to him, not a hindrance.

But maybe this break was good for both of them. Not for long, though.

She had to go back, had to make him understand that she would be there for him if and when he decided he wanted help. Because she could help him.

If anyone could, she could.

She wasn't going to give up on him.

And this time, she wasn't going to let him push her away.

THIRTY-THREE

THE GAME AT DALLAS HAD GONE OKAY. THEY'D WON, but only by a field goal. And they hadn't won because of anything Trevor had done. In fact, he'd downright sucked balls in this game. He'd dropped two passes, caught one for short yardage, and otherwise would have done better acting as the water boy on the sidelines for all the contributions he'd made to the team.

Fortunately, his teammates had more than made up for his deficiencies, allowing them to at least stay in the game.

He felt like shit. He'd felt like shit before the game started, and the two days before, when he'd come out of his room to find that Haven had left.

Not that it should have surprised him to find her gone. He was the one who'd asked her to leave. No. He hadn't even asked. He'd told her to leave. Hell, he'd tossed her out, so what had he expected her to do? And then, like a little boy, he'd run up to his room and locked himself inside, scared and afraid that the world was going to find out his secret.

He was such an asshole. For someone who always claimed to be big and bad and fearless, he hadn't shown any of that when he'd told Haven his secret. Instead, he'd hurled accusations at her and hurt her.

He'd blamed her, as if his problem had been her fault. And then he'd hidden away like a goddamned child.

Some big and bad he was.

He missed her. Just like it had been since she'd first shown up in his life to do the interview, whenever she was gone, he missed her absence. It was like there was a part of himself missing whenever she wasn't around.

He'd never let anything affect his game play. But losing Haven had an effect on his concentration. All he'd thought about during the game was her. It had shown in his performance today, too. Even now, after the game, he wondered where she was—how she was feeling.

He wanted to call her, to talk to her, but he couldn't. Not after all the things he'd said. Not after he'd kicked her out of his life.

And he had his friends here today. Garrett and Alicia had come down to Dallas to see the game, and his friend Gray Preston was here, since he'd had an auto race in Dallas yesterday. Drew Hogan was here as well, since he'd flown in to see Gray's race. They were meeting up for dinner tonight.

Right now he didn't want to see anyone, but these were his college roommates, his best friends. He had to honor his commitments. Besides, they would help take his mind off Haven.

Garrett and Alicia were waiting for him outside the stadium. He grinned when he saw them.

"That was a decent game," Garrett said.

Trevor laughed. "That's a nice way of saying we sucked."

"At least you won." Alicia gave him a hug.

"We did win. Barely, but we won."

"One in the W column. That's all that counts," Garrett said.

"Considering how badly I played, I'll take the W."

"You can't always be the superstar, stud."

Trevor stopped and stared at Garrett. "Of course I can. It's my trademark."

Garrett shook his head, then led them to his rental car.

"So where's dinner tonight?"

"Del Frisco's. For steak."

"Sounds good to me."

"Gray and Drew are meeting us there."

The steak house looked fantastic from the outside, and smelled even better inside. Trevor was hungry, and he smiled as he saw Drew and his fiancée, Carolina, and Gray and his wife, Evelyn, waiting for them. He shook the guys' hands and hugged the women.

"It's good to see you. Thanks for coming to the game."

"It was a good game," Evelyn said after they took their seats. The hostess put them in a private room. Obviously Gray had connections. Gray always had connections. Everywhere.

"It was a shit game, but thanks for being nice about it, Evelyn. And I'm surprised you traveled without Lucas."

She sighed. "It's hard to leave a new baby, but he has a great nanny, and I wanted to see the race. Believe me, I'm on the Preston jet tonight back home to him."

"It's been a whirlwind year for you, two, hasn't it?"

Gray put his arm around Evelyn. "It's been like that ever since I met this woman. As if I wasn't crazy busy all the time as it was with racing in a different city every weekend during the season. Then I met Evelyn, and we fell in love, got married, and now we have a son together. She keeps me on my toes."

Evelyn swiped her fingers over Gray's chin and smiled up at

him. "As it should be. And don't forget that small thing about your dad becoming the vice president of the United States. That kind of busy, too."

Gray grinned. "Right. That, too."

"But enough about us. Let's talk about your game. Thanks for the tickets," Evelyn said.

"You're welcome. I'm sorry I couldn't put on a better show for you."

"Oh, come on, Trevor. You played good. You only dropped two passes," Carolina said with a wink. "I've seen you play worse."

Trevor laughed. "Thanks."

"You did seem distracted. And you have played better," Gray said. "Something on your mind?"

"Nah. Just not on my game today."

"Where's Haven?" Evelyn asked. "I heard she was doing a big interview and feature story about you. I thought she'd be here."

"She . . . left."

"Oh. So the interview's finished?"

He stared at his water glass before lifting his gaze to Evelyn. "Yeah."

"I'm so disappointed. I was really hoping to see her again."

"Me, too," Alicia said. "Besides, I kind of thought you two would end up together."

He looked at Alicia, then noticed they were all staring at him. "Why would you think that?"

Alicia gave him a gentle smile. "Isn't it obvious? You were perfect together. I saw it. Liz saw it. You had to feel it."

His stomach tightened and he felt a pang of regret. "Yeah, well, I guess we weren't."

"Uh-oh. What happened?"

"Alicia," Garrett said, laying his hand over hers.

"Sorry. Not my business. But I really liked her, Trevor."

Trevor nodded. "I did, too."

"Okay, so what happened between you and Haven?" Evelyn asked. "Did you have a thing?"

Trevor shook his head. Leave it to the women to blurt it out. "Yeah. We had a thing."

"Interesting," Drew said, cocking a grin. "Now I want to hear about it. And why she isn't here."

Might as well get it out in the open. "I asked her to leave when we were still in Tampa."

"Why?" Carolina asked. "Did you two have a fight?"

"Sort of. I mean, not really, but sort of."

Alicia rolled her eyes. "That's man-speak for you acted like an ass and did something wrong."

"Hey," Garrett said, looking at Alicia.

Alicia puckered up her lips and blew a kiss at Garrett. "I wasn't talking about you. This time."

"So is it true?" Gray asked. "Did you screw this up?"

"Probably. Yes. Definitely."

"Then I guess the bigger question is, how are you going to fix it?" Evelyn asked. "Do you want to fix it?"

That was the big question. He already knew the answer. "Yes. I want to fix it. But I hurt her."

"Guys do that. Because we're thoughtless assholes," Drew said.

Carolina nodded. "This is true."

Drew laughed. "We think with the wrong head all the time, and we hurt the people we love the most." He picked up Carolina's hand and pressed a kiss to it. "Fortunately, the women we love tend to be the most forgiving."

Carolina smiled at Drew, then turned to Trevor. "What Drew's trying to tell you, Trevor, is that whatever you've done, ask for forgiveness. That's the first step. And be honest and open about your feelings."

Something he'd never done before. He hadn't been honest about anything. "You're right. I have a lot to talk to her about. And she has a lot to forgive. I don't know if she will."

"If she loves you, she will," Garrett said. "And if she's worth it, she's worth getting down on your knees and begging."

"Awww, begging?" Alicia asked.

"Yeah." Garrett looked at him. "Love's worth it, man. I never thought it was, until I met the right woman. But trust me, it really is worth it."

Trevor looked at Garrett. At Drew. At Gray. His friends, who not so long ago had sworn to him that being single and carefree was the most important thing in their lives. Now, they sat with the loves of their lives at their sides.

And they were happy.

Could he hope to have that kind of happiness?

He loved Haven. He was almost afraid to hope. He didn't deserve it, not after what he'd done.

He had a lot of work ahead of him.

THIRTY-FOUR

HAVEN KNEW SHE WAS TAKING A RISK SITTING INSIDE Trevor's house in Tampa. But she'd forgotten to leave her key, and she knew he was due home today.

So here she was, with all her books and notes and the research she'd done spread out on his table.

He could try to throw her out, but this time, she was going to put up a fight.

And even if he insisted she leave—which he certainly could, because this was his house—she was going to leave the material for him to look over. It could help him, and that was the only thing she wanted.

No, that wasn't true. She wanted him, missed him, loved him. But if he rejected her, then she wanted him to be happy.

She heard the garage door open and her chest squeezed tight. He'd know someone was at the house, because her rental car was parked in the driveway.

"Hello?" he said as he opened the door from the garage.

She stood. "It's me, Trevor."

He came in and laid his practice bag down. "Haven."

She was practically shaking, her nerves getting the best of her as she made her way toward him. "I still have a key." She held it out for him.

He ignored her outstretched hand. "What are you doing here?"

"I'd like to talk to you."

He cocked his head to the side. "I wanted to talk to you, too. I actually sent you a text message today asking where you were."

"You did?" She'd been busy all day making notes and writing out plans and hadn't checked her phone.

"Yeah. I was going to ask if you'd come out here and meet me."

Encouraged, she curved her lips into a half smile. "Well, it's fortunate that I'm here."

"You didn't tell me why you came."

"Oh, that." She scratched the side of her nose, nervous now that the ball was in her court. "I brought some things with me. I don't want you to get mad."

"I'm not mad, Haven. Show me what you brought."

She led him over to the dining room table. "As you know, I have dual degrees. One is in journalism, the other in special education. I spent some time working with students with learning disabilities."

He stared down at the table. "So what is all this . . . stuff?"

She lifted her gaze to his. "It's an assessment. And with your permission, I'd like to do an assessment on you. I'm not a professional, Trevor. Not even close to it. But I did plenty of these during my internship, and I know how to assess learning disabilities like dyslexia. I know you can read."

Trevor sucked in a breath. "I can read, Haven. Sort of. I can't read well. I get mixed up. It frustrates me."

"Okay. So let me do this assessment and let's see where you

stand. I really think I can help you, or at least guide you to the right resources and people who can help you."

He sat down at the table. She sat in the chair next to him and waited for him to gather his thoughts. The one thing she'd learned was patience. This had to come when he was ready.

Finally, he started. "My dad was illiterate. He couldn't read at all. He worked as a laborer. My mom tried to help him, but she didn't know about it until much later in their marriage, because he hid it from her. When she tried to help him, or encourage him to finish school, he got angry." He looked out the door toward the deck. "He was always angry. At her, and at me. He'd lash out at us all the time."

"Did he hit you?"

"No. It was always verbal. But it was loud and all the damn time."

"You had no escape."

Trevor shook his head. "I hung out there in the living room watching TV with my mom, listening to the old man rant and rave. And with every beer, he'd get louder and louder. He was just an unhappy son of a bitch, and took it out on us.

"She finally couldn't take his outbursts and she left. It was rough for a while. She had to work two jobs to make ends meet until she met my stepdad. Then things got better."

"Did you ever see him after that?"

"No. He didn't want to be around me, I guess. Or whatever. I have no idea what happened to him. I can't say I missed him all that much, and when my mom remarried, my stepdad was a much nicer guy. But then I realized I couldn't read, and I felt like I was going to turn out just like my dad."

Haven felt such sympathy for what Trevor had gone through. "Because you got frustrated and angry, too."

"Yeah. So I hid it from everyone. I was determined not to turn out like my old man. I never wanted anyone to know. I could fake it pretty easy. And I had the charm thing going, you know? I was nice enough and I could read just enough to get by."

"It must have been so frightening for you to try to hide this secret all these years. No one knew?"

"My brother did. He helped me out with homework. God, he's so fucking smart. I'd have never made it without him. And my mom would try to help, but she didn't know the extent of what was wrong with me. She'd already gone through so much with my dad. I didn't want her to have to deal with my shit, too."

She laid her hand over his. "Trevor. Nothing is wrong with you. If my guess is correct, your brain is just wired differently and you have to learn to use that difference in how you read and comprehend. There's nothing *wrong* with you. Understand?"

He shrugged. "So what are these tests?"

"There are several evaluations of comprehension, along with family history, that'll help me determine what might possibly be hindering your ability to read at an appropriate level."

He got up, went into the kitchen, and grabbed a bottle of water from the refrigerator. "Do you want one?"

"Sure."

He handed one to her, then opened his and took a long swallow. "Okay, then. Let's get started."

TREVOR COULDN'T RECALL EVER TAKING MORE TESTS than the ones Haven had given him. First they'd gone over his history, including familial history, health history, and school history. He'd been honest with her—hell, more honest with her than he'd ever been with anyone before.

Then there'd been the testing. Reading comprehension, vocabulary, verbal reasoning and spelling, math, and several other tests.

He was sure he'd failed them all, because that was what tests brought to mind. Sweat. Fear. Failure.

Tests had always equaled failure. But this time, he wasn't going to be able to charm or bullshit his way out of them. He was as honest as he could be with his answers. And there were a lot of things he just couldn't get through. But Haven was patient with him, and didn't once look at him like he was stupid.

After they were finished, he'd gone out and gotten them something to eat while Haven worked on evaluating the tests. She'd taken a break to eat with him, then gone back to the evaluation, while he'd watched some TV, but he wasn't really concentrating. He probably wouldn't until he'd gotten the verdict.

Though he already knew the verdict, didn't he? He was a failure. He was stupid.

Nothing he didn't already know, right?

And the two of them still hadn't reconnected on a personal level, so there was a wall between them that needed to be scaled. He hadn't figured out how he was going to start that conversation.

One thing at a time, right?

"Trevor."

He turned off the TV and came over to the dining room. "Yeah."

"Sit down."

He swallowed, hard, and took a seat, feeling as nervous as he always had every time he'd taken a test.

"I've gone over your tests, and I'm going to tell you again I don't do this for a living, so it's not a professional evaluation."

"Okay. Just tell me."

"This is going to be somewhat detailed, so bear with me. It's important to give you a comprehensive overview, so you understand what you're dealing with."

"Okay."

She went over every test with him, showing him where he'd done well and where he hadn't. She was thorough and took her time, making sure he understood what she was talking about. She didn't speed through it, and he made sure he stopped her if something didn't make sense. She was also honest—brutally so—and he appreciated it. This was what he'd dreaded for so many years, but also what he'd desperately needed.

Someone to help him.

"You have very good verbal abilities and a good grasp of vocabulary. Which is why you're so well-spoken, and likely why you've managed to fly under the radar so well all these years." She gave him an encouraging smile.

"Where you struggle is with reading comprehension and spelling. Though honestly, Trevor, it's not as dire as you might think. You have good memory skills, and I think with some professional assistance, you could work through the reading comprehension issues."

He waited, and when she didn't say anything else, he asked, "That's it?"

"It's a lot more complex than that. It sounds to me like your father was dyslexic, a trait that's been known to be inherited."

"I have dyslexia." Just saying the word made his stomach clench.

"It would appear so. Again, I'm not a professional, but I did train for this and did some diagnostic work with learning-disabled adults. But yes, based on these test results, you're dyslexic. It's not a severe form, but because you've hidden it all these years and haven't sought help, it just seems worse to you. It's something you can learn to work with. The problem is, you've been so frustrated with your inability to read and write well that you just stopped, didn't you?"

"Yes."

"And other people have been doing it for you all these years."

"Yeah. My agent and my lawyer."

"You need to stop that. And do you realize what a beacon of hope you could be for struggling youth, especially those who look up to you? If you come out publicly and say you have dyslexia, that it's something you've struggled with your entire life, and that you're working on getting help, you could help so many others."

He shook his head. "It's not something I want to discuss publicly."

"Why not? It's not something to be ashamed of, Trevor. This isn't your father's generation any longer. Hell, it hasn't been for some time. Do you know how many brilliant people are dyslexic? Albert Einstein had dyslexia. And he was by no means stupid. So did Alexander Graham Bell. Thomas Edison. Nolan Ryan, famous baseball player. George Washington, for God's sake. And Steven freaking Spielberg."

He leaned back in the chair. "No shit."

"Yes. And scores of others. Dyslexia challenges you, but it won't defeat you. Not if you don't let it." She grasped his hand. "You're smart, Trevor. You were never stupid. Ever."

He suddenly felt ashamed for hiding it all these years. "And I can help people—I can help kids—by talking about it."

She reached for his hand. "Yes. Definitely yes. Any time someone of your caliber talks about it, you help someone who—like you—is ashamed and not seeking help."

"Shit. I should have done something about this a long time ago."

She squeezed his hand. "I understand your fear. Your shame. Your father didn't help the situation. And you thought you were like him."

"Trying to read—to comprehend—every time I tried it made me mad. And getting angry and frustrated scared me, because it made me remember my dad. So I just backed away from it. I ran away from it. I've been in denial all these years, pretending it didn't exist. I hired people I trusted who would keep my secret, refusing to talk about. If I didn't talk about it, I didn't have to acknowledge it existed."

"It does exist. What you do about it now is up to you. I will never tell anyone about this. You can trust me."

It was time to push the fear and shame into the past. He was tired of hiding. "How do I get help? Will you help me?"

"I will help you, but I know scores of professionals who would do a much better job. Let me recommend some people to you, both here and in St. Louis. They're very trustworthy, and will take it slow and work at your own pace."

He had to trust Haven. He did trust Haven. He needed her. "Yeah. Recommend some people to me."

"Thanks."

"No. Thank you. For coming back here. I didn't deserve it after the way I treated you. I'm sorry, Haven. I acted like an asshole and I'm asking you to forgive me for that."

She came over and sat on his lap, and he'd never felt such warmth, such love. Such forgiveness and acceptance. "There's nothing to forgive, Trevor. Now I understand what you were going through. I backed you into a corner and for that, I'm sorry."

"You made me face something I should have faced a long time ago. I'm grateful. And I should never have asked you to leave. You don't ask someone you love to walk out of your life."

Haven lifted her head and stared into Trevor's eyes, not sure she'd heard what he said correctly.

"What did you say?"

His lips curved. "I said I love you. Want me to say it again?"

"Yes, please."

"I love you, Haven."

She smiled, and her heart swelled with so much emotion she felt like she might burst. "I love you, too, Trevor."

He swept his hand up and down her back. "I like the sound of that. Now you say it again."

"I love you, Trevor."

"We should probably seal this with some kind of kiss."

She nodded. "Followed by some equally hot lovemaking, I hope."

"Definitely."

Trevor stood and pulled her against him, cupping the back of her neck and dragging her lips to his for a kiss that definitely left his intentions clear. From the very first time their lips met, she'd known he was it for her. Maybe she hadn't realized it at first, because that initial spark of chemistry had distracted her, but now she realized it was more than simply biology that had drawn her to Trevor.

It was love—two people who were supposed to be together. They just . . . fit.

Especially when they kissed, when his mouth explored hers and exploded her brain cells left and right, making her sag against him until all she wanted was to tear every inch of clothing off to feel his skin against hers. There was something about this man that demanded she be close to him, touching him. She'd never been a big believer in that whole destiny thing, but he was it for her.

So when he broke the kiss and took her hand to lead her upstairs to his room, she followed along, taking in the sight of his very fine ass moving up the stairs.

And when they got there, it was her who pushed him onto the bed. She climbed on top of him and continued where they left off. She couldn't get enough of his mouth, the sexy fullness of his bottom lip, the slight scratchiness of his jaw when it was peppered with a day's growth of stubble. She straightened only long enough to pull off her top and undo her bra, then bent down to slide one of her nipples in between his waiting lips. And when he sucked, she was in heaven, a delight of sensation to feel him pull and tug on the bud until she wanted more.

Apparently, so did Trevor, because he rolled her off him and drew her pants and underwear off, then spread her legs and buried his face in her sex, his tongue and mouth doing decadent, delicious things to her pussy. She grabbed hold of the cover and held on while he took her right to the edge.

And over. She cried out with her orgasm, but barely had time to draw in a ragged breath before Trevor got undressed and put a condom on.

She was still pulsing, still reeling from her climax when he slid inside her, his face looming over hers.

"We're supposed to be together. I missed you when you were gone. I'm sorry I sent you away."

He said this as he pulled out, then eased back inside her.

She wrapped her legs around him. "You're forgiven." She swept her fingers over his brow, his temple, then his lips. "I love you."

"I love you, too. Feel free to say those words as many times as you want."

His lips curved. "Yeah, you, too."

Then he kissed her, and nothing else was said as he made love to her with a depth of passion that was filled with a new emotion. It was as if both of them had shed the walls they'd erected to protect their hearts. And as he moved within her, she knew without a doubt this was the man she was meant to be with, that he'd protect her, and she'd protect him.

He swept his hand under her buttocks and lifted her hips, grinding against her as he buried himself deep.

"Trevor." She whispered his name, and her pussy quivered around him, tightening as she came close to orgasm.

"I want to feel your pussy squeeze my cock. Make me come, Haven."

She loved the gritty sound of his voice when he was deep in the throes of passion. And the way he slid against her, rubbing her clit as he thrust in and out, was her undoing. She shattered, dragging her nails along his shoulders as she came. Trevor took her mouth in a hard, passionate kiss, taking in her cries and mixing his own groans in there as he released with a shudder.

They were glued together by perspiration and clasped arms and legs. Haven was in no hurry to move. Trevor rolled to his side, taking Haven with him. They stayed like that, stroking each other's bodies for a while until he disengaged and left for only a few seconds. When he came back, he pulled her against him and tangled his fingers in her hair, kissed her deeply, and tucked her close.

"Are you staying for a while?" he asked.

"Yes."

"When do you have to be back in New York?"

"After I finish my interview with you."

He looked into her eyes. "I'd like to include the dyslexia thing in your interview."

She drew back. "You want me to break it?"

"Yes."

"Trevor. Are you sure?"

"I'm sure. I trust you'll do it right."

She laid her palm over his heart. "I will do it right. And I'll get those recommendations for you starting tomorrow."

"I'll get started on it tomorrow. And I'll go to the literacy center and talk to them as well."

She laid her head on his chest. "I believe in you, Trevor. I always have."

"That's what'll get me through this."

She closed her eyes, listening to the sound of his heartbeat.

Together. They'd get through anything together.

THIRTY-FIVE

TREVOR WALKED OFF THE FIELD, A MUDDY, VICTORI-
ous mess. It had rained almost nonstop through the entire game
against Green Bay. He didn't know when he'd had more fun. He'd
caught two passes for touchdowns, and had over a hundred yards in
the game.

More importantly, they'd won, and that's what counted the
most, especially since the Hawks were on top of their division. He
wanted them to stay there, which meant playing well every week.
Right now they were firing on all cylinders.

Professionally, things were going well.

Personally, things were going even better. In the past two
months, he'd been working with a specialist in learning disabilities
who'd been patient in diagnosing his dyslexia and teaching him to
read, plus work on his frustration issues when things didn't go his
way. Denise Lancaster was formidable and no bullshit, and she

didn't fall for his charm. She made him work and work hard. For someone nearly sixty and barely five feet tall, she was one scary woman.

But she was his savior, and for the first time in his life, he was starting to enjoy reading. And even better, he was learning to comprehend what he was reading. It was like the lightbulb had finally gone off in his head, and a whole new world was opening up for him. He could already imagine diving into books he'd waited his whole life to read. Sure, he'd enjoyed audiobooks, but he'd waited a lifetime to read books—really read books.

Denise told him she'd set him up with someone just as scary as she was once he moved back to St. Louis.

He couldn't wait.

He'd flown home to Springfield and had a long talk with his mother, telling her everything he should have told her years ago. She'd cried. Hell, he'd cried, too, and they'd talked out a lot of shit about his dad. His mother apologized for not being there to help him, and he shouldered the blame for hiding everything, explaining about how he was afraid he was going to end up like Dad.

She'd understood, and she told him she was so grateful he'd had Haven in his life.

Yeah, so was he. He promised to bring Haven there so his mom could meet her and his stepdad soon.

Tonight, Haven's network was broadcasting his interview. His life story. Which meant the revelation about his dyslexia was going to be front-page news. He'd already told both his coaches and all his teammates. No one had thought it was a big deal, and many had asked why he'd waited so long to talk about it.

But he was talking about it, and he was going to keep talking about it. After the special, the network agreed to do a public service announcement about dyslexia and other learning disabilities, including an 800 number for people to call to find out more about assistance programs. Trevor had insisted, and Haven's producer had agreed that it would be a great public service.

Trevor and Haven had invited the team over tonight to watch. Trevor was having the event catered, which made Haven roll her eyes.

"I can cook, you know," she said in between showering and tidying the place up. She'd wrapped up her interview months ago, then promptly quit her job with the network, which had shocked the shit out of Trevor.

They'd argued about it, too. Trevor had told her she had all these ideas for interviews. And she'd told him she was trying to find her place, and while she'd enjoyed the interview, she'd found something she loved more.

"You don't need to cook for that many people. And are you sure when you watch this tonight you aren't going to regret giving up your job as a sports reporter?"

"Absolutely not. Working with you has reminded me of my first love—education. I'm doing exactly what I want to do—going back to school to get my master's in special education, so I can work with kids and adults with learning disabilities."

"You enjoyed sports reporting, but I've seen a real fire lit under you since you decided to reignite your career in education."

She finished setting the dining room table, then turned to him and grinned. "I know, right? Before my dad died, he told me to follow my dream. To do what I love. At the time, I thought that was journalism. And I did enjoy it a lot. But when I started working with you, I realized that this is what I was meant to do. This is what really makes me happy, Trevor."

He came over to her and put his arms around her. "You're what makes me happy."

"What? Not a dual career of baseball and football?"

"Surprisingly, no. You come first."

She wrapped her arms around his neck. "So do you. I've never been happier. And I think this—you and me—would have made my dad very happy."

He brushed his lips across hers. "I hope so."

"It's making my mom extremely happy."

He grinned. "I know. I've always been her favorite."

Haven rolled her eyes. "Whatever."

She started to pull away, but he held her tight. "It's true. When you were sad and depressed over your dad, she called me and asked me to help."

Haven frowned. "What? She did? When was that?"

"Right before you got assigned the interview."

Haven couldn't believe he'd done that for her. "You orchestrated that interview for me."

"Partly. And partly to be the focus of a feature story ."

"You weren't at all interested in that. You did it for me."

"Yes."

Haven took in a deep breath. Even back then, he cared about her. "That makes me love you even more."

"Wait till you see the interview. I'm handsome, I'm charming, I have charisma."

"Don't go overboard."

"I have a nice ass . . ."

She laughed as he walked away.

She was . . . happy. Content with her life, and looking forward to an amazing future. And for a lot of that, she had Trevor to thank.

If not for being assigned to interview Trevor, she might not have come to terms with her father's passing. And without Trevor's admission of his learning disability, she might not have rediscovered her love for teaching. She'd been honest with Trevor when she'd told him that while she'd thoroughly enjoyed her time in sports reporting, when she'd dug in and started working with him again on his dyslexia, she'd discovered a newfound passion. And it had taken this journey for her to realize this was where she was meant to be.

Funny how life had such twists and turns sometimes. And how one person could intervene and change your entire life.

She smiled, thinking about her dad. For some reason, she wondered if he had something to do with the matchmaking, if somehow, he'd maybe put a heavenly whisper in her mom's ear to send Trevor in her direction.

Knowing her dad, he would have found a way. Because Trevor had come into her life when she'd needed him most. He'd turned it upside down and inside out, but she'd ended up happier than she ever thought possible.

She smiled up at the heavens.

Thanks, Dad.

Dear Readers,

I hope you enjoyed *Straddling the Line*. Over the past four Play-by-Play books I've had a blast writing about college roommates Garrett, Gray, Trevor, and Drew, and you'll definitely see more of them in the upcoming books. The next Play-by-Play book, *Quarterback Draw*, coming in February 2015, introduces a family dynasty similar to the Rileys. Grant Cassidy, the quarterback first seen in *Playing to Win*, is the hero. I think you'll enjoy reading about Grant and his tight-knit but competitive family. He and his brothers don't always get along, and they always compete with each other, but they share a blood bond and are always there for each other. And yes, each brother will get his own book!

My next release is *Hope Burns*, coming in October 2014. It's the third book in my Hope series, contemporary romances that take place in the small town of Hope, Oklahoma. Carter Richards and Molly Burnett share a past, one Molly doesn't care to revisit. However, she's returned to Hope for her sister Emma's wedding, so she has to face her high-school sweetheart Carter and the town she's avoided for many years.

I fell madly in love with this couple, and I hope you will, too. Read on for a first-chapter excerpt of *Hope Burns*.

Happy reading!
Jaci

KEEP READING FOR A PREVIEW OF
THE NEXT HOPE NOVEL

HOPE BURNS

COMING FROM JOVE BOOKS IN OCTOBER 2014

THIS WEDDING WAS GOING TO BE A DISASTER.

Molly Burnett didn't know what had possessed her to agree to come back to Hope for her sister Emma's wedding. Love for her sister, of course. But she knew what was at stake. She never came home, hadn't been home since she'd left when she was eighteen.

That had been twelve years ago. She'd moved around from town to town, state to state, never setting down roots. Permanence just wasn't Molly's thing. And she sure as hell had never once come back to her hometown.

Until now. Even as she drove past the city limits sign her throat had started to close up, her breathing becoming labored. If she hyperventilated, crashed the car, and died a week before Emma's wedding, her sister would never forgive her.

Then again, with all the sputtering and coughing her ancient Ford Taurus was doing, it might just do itself in before she had a chance to crash it into anything.

"Come on, George," she said, smooth-talking the car. "Hang in there." She didn't have a new—or a newer used—car in her budget. Old George, currently age fifteen and she hoped heading toward sixteen, was just going to have to suck it up and keep working.

At the next stop sign, George shuddered and belched rather loudly, making the two little kids sitting in the backseat of the car next to her point and laugh. She gave them a smile, then gently pressed the gas. Obviously having cleared his throat, George lumbered on and Molly sighed in grateful relief. Gripping the steering wheel and forcing deep, calming breaths, Molly drove past the First Baptist Church, her favorite doughnut shop, the florist, and Edith's Hair Salon. So many places still stood, all too familiar.

So much had changed in twelve years. So much progress, so many new businesses had cropped up. New restaurants, the hospital was bigger than she remembered, and they'd widened the highway. When she'd lived here before, there'd been only one shop to stop at for gas and sodas along the main road. Now there was one at every corner.

She purposely turned off the main road, determined to avoid the high school. Too many memories she wasn't ready to face yet. She headed toward the main strip of town. There was a new bakery, and on impulse, Molly decided to stop and buy some goodies for the family.

She headed inside, the smell of sugar and baked goods making her smile.

After buying a box full of croissants and cream puffs, she made her way outside, stopping short at a very fine ass bent over, inspecting her car.

"Can I help you?"

He straightened and turned, and Molly almost dropped the box of baked goods.

The last person in Hope she wanted to see today stared back at her.

Carter Richards, her first and only love, and the main reason she'd left Hope all those years ago.

"Hey, Molly."

"What are you doing here, Carter?"

"My auto shop is just a few doors down. I saw you get out of the car."

Recovering, she walked over to the driver's side, placed the box on the hood, then opened the door. "And you thought this would be a good place for a reunion? Really, Carter?"

She hoped he wouldn't notice her hands shaking as she slid the box onto the passenger seat and climbed in, shutting the door.

He leaned his forearms inside the car. "That's all you have to say?"

"I think we said all we needed to say to each other twelve years ago."

She turned the key and winced at George's attempts to fire on all cylinders. She tried again, and this time, the car started. Sort of. It mostly wheezed. And then died.

Dammit. *Come on, George. I just need you to start this one time.*

"Let me help you with that."

She shot him a look. "I don't need help. I can do this."

She tried again. No go.

"Molly."

Carter's voice was deep and low, causing skitters of awareness to race down her spine. She wanted him to disappear. She wanted to pretend he didn't exist, just like she'd tried to erase him from her memories for the past twelve years. She wanted to be anywhere but here right now.

"Slide out and let me give it a try."

With a resigned sigh, she opened the door and got out. Carter slid in and fiddled with the ignition.

"George is a little touchy," she said.

He turned to face her. "George?"

Crossing her arms, she nodded. "Yes. George."

His lips curved, and her stomach tumbled. God, he was even more good looking now than he'd been in high school. Thick, dark hair, and those mesmerizing green eyes. He wore a polo shirt that stretched tight over his well-muscled biceps. Why couldn't he have turned out bald and fat and hideously ugly? Not that it would have made a difference anyway, because it still would have been Carter.

When George's engine finally turned over, tears pricked Molly's eyes.

Carter got out and held the door for her. "There you go."

"Thanks."

He shut the door, then leaned in the window again. "Molly . . ."

She looked up at him. "Please don't."

He nodded and backed up a step so she could back out of the parking spot, which she did with a little too much fervor. As she drove away, she saw him watching her out of her rearview mirror.

She forced a tight grip on the steering wheel and willed the pain in her heart to go away.

It was in the past. Carter was in the past, and that was where he was going to stay.

CARTER WATCHED MOLLY DRIVE AWAY, THAT OLD junker she drove belching out smoke and exhaust like it was on its last legs.

He shook his head and leaned against the wall of the bakery shop, needing a minute to clear his head before he went back to work.

He'd been thinking about Molly for a while now, knowing she was coming back to Hope. She had to, because she was in Luke and Emma's wedding. He hadn't expected to see her today, though, when he'd stepped out front of his auto body shop to take a breath from all the damn paperwork that was his least favorite part of being a business owner.

He'd always liked watching the cars go by on his breaks.

When he'd seen an unfamiliar one—an old, beat-up Taurus choking out a black trail of exhaust, then wheezing as it came to a stop in front of the bakery—he couldn't help but wonder who'd drive an old piece of shit like that. Surely the owner had to realize that poor junker should be shot and put out of its misery.

His heart slammed against his ribs as a gorgeous brunette stepped out of the car. She had on shorts, a tank top, and sandals, and she was hurrying into the bakery like she didn't want to be recognized. She even kept her sunglasses on, but there was no mistaking who it was.

Yeah, like he could ever forget the curve of her face, the fullness of her lips, or her long legs. It might have been twelve years, and she might have changed from girl to woman, but Molly Burnett was someone Carter would never forget. His pulse had been racing and he knew damn well he should turn around and go back to his office. But for some reason his body hadn't been paying attention to what his mind told it, and he pushed off the wall and started down the street toward the bakery.

He debated going inside, then thought better of it and decided to figure out what the hell it was she was driving. So he'd walked over and studied the car.

A '99 Taurus. Christ. He wondered where Molly was living, and how the hell that car had made the trip. It had dents all over, the muffler was nearly shot, and the tires badly needed replacement—like a year ago.

In retrospect, he should have let her be, should have kept his distance from her. But when he'd seen her, he'd closed his eyes for a fraction of a second, transported back in time to the last time he'd heard her voice. It had been in hurt and anger. The last words they'd said to each other hadn't been kind ones.

And maybe he'd wanted to change all that.

But it hadn't gone at all like he'd planned. She was still hurt, still angry with him, even after all these years.

Carter dragged his fingers through his hair, pushed off the wall, and made his way down the street toward the garage, then back to his office. He shut the door and stared at his laptop, but all he could see was Molly's long dark hair pulled up in a high ponytail, and her full lips painted some shimmering pink color. She was tan, and her body had changed over the years. She was curvier now, had more of a woman's body.

But she was still the drop-dead gorgeous woman he'd fallen in love with all those years ago.

He'd thought he was over her, that what he'd once felt for her in high school was long gone. But they'd had a deeper connection than just being first loves.

And seeing her again had hurt a lot harder than he'd thought it would.